KIDZ

Mark Barrass

Diadem Books

KIDZ

Diadem Books
Newcastle-upon-Tyne
www.diadembooks.org.uk

ISBN: 978-0-244-27486-3

I wish to dedicate this, my first novel,
to the memory of my Mam and Dad
who made me who I am,
both literally and literary.

Friday 12 April
0730hrs

The two boys whispered as more pupils arrived for the early morning breakfast club. As the latest group passed, the two ducked out from behind the PE shed and got the spray can out again. They finished off their work W-A-N-K-A in 3-foot high white letters, each one on a separate windowpane – cool. They ran across the yard giving one last glance to admire their work from a distance and then they were off into the corridors and away. Only ten minutes later the head teacher closed her car door and set off across the yard towards her office. She stopped dead in her tracks. It seemed to take a few seconds to comprehend what faced her. Tears formed in the corners of her eyes as two other members of staff arrived behind her.

"Miss Tindall, who has done this?" asked Sally Cowan, one of the young English teachers.

"We'll soon find them Miss Tindall," said Ian Taylor. "Don't worry, we'll find them."

Joanne Tindall shook her head; the tears disappeared. She had to be strong so she turned to face the two teachers. "At least I can see some improvement in their spelling." And with that she strode off purposefully towards her office. She passed one of the caretakers also 'admiring' the artwork. "Mr Peel can we make that go away? As quickly as you can please."

"Of course Miss Tindall, should I get someone from the ICT department to get pictures of it like we normally do?" he replied as he turned to face her.

"Yes Mr Peel, if you would please."

"No problem."

"Thank you Andy," she said in a hushed tone as she continued to her office.

The caretaker only nodded in response, quickly heading towards his storeroom.

0805hrs

In another school hundreds of miles away there was more trouble. Arthur Richards, one of the older members of staff at the secondary school was half-walking, half-jogging along the main corridor. He turned into the administration corridor and up to the head teacher's door. He knocked loudly and entered "Mr Tennent, they've all gone. Every single one of them!"

"Arthur calm down," replied the other calmly. "What are you on about?"

"The books, they've all gone."

"Which books?" the head asked.

Arthur Richards, slightly overweight, caught his breath after his efforts, "I've just been to the library to prepare for my first lesson and there are no books on the shelves."

"Are you sure?"

"Come and see." Richards led the head back out through the administrative corridor along the main corridor and out across the main yard. Approaching the building containing the library Richards started to look around as if searching for something.

"What is it Arthur?" Tennent asked.

"I'm just wondering what happened to the books." He waved his arms around. "I mean there was thousands of them, they couldn't have just disappeared."

The pair of confused men walked in through the library door to be greeted by an empty room except for sparsely scattered furniture. The head walked round in a big circle before returning to Richards. "I was in here yesterday talking to Isobel. There were books everywhere, all the shelves were full."

"I know. It's a mystery." Richards shrugged at the head teacher. They both look at each other bemused.

Their silence was interrupted by the school caretaker, Billy Haig. "Mr Tennent, I've spotted the remnants of a huge fire around the back of the sports block." He started back up the corridor. "Come on, follow me."

The head quickly followed leaving Richards fumbling around the main desk in the library. As the two men exited the main school building a young lady waved at them as she locked her car door.

"Morning gents, you look busy!"

The caretaker continued walking, head down. John Tennent stopped and waved over Isobel Harding, the Librarian.

"What is it John?" She asked as she quickly walked towards him.

"Come on. Walk with me." He guided her gently with his hand as they continued on after the now distant caretaker.

"Can't you tell me what it is?" she asked, now with worry in her voice.

"Arthur Richards discovered that someone has taken all the books from the library."

Isobel let out a short laugh but as they reached the front of the sports building, she grabbed the head's arm. "Are you joking with me?"

The head slowed as they reached the back corner of the building. "I'm afraid not Izzy," he stopped her. "There's more bad news around the corner I'm afraid."

Isobel took a step back. "What bad news?"

"Billy Haig has found the remains of a large fire," he pointed around the corner.

The young librarian took another step back, tears welling up in her eyes. She put her hand up to her mouth to stifle a cry then set off to see what was around the corner. The head followed. The site that met them both was quite overpowering to those who had given so much to education. There was a large pile of smouldering, burning books. With a diameter of about 20 metres it was clear the extent of the fire. The caretaker sat over a half-burnt pile of books pecking at them like a chicken at a mound of seeds. He carefully picked them up one at a time, reading what was visible from the covers: "Sallinger, Hardy, Illiad, Tolstoy."

"Okay Billy that's enough," the head interrupted. He moved and stood next to Isobel. "Don't worry, we'll sort this out."

"Are there any books left at all?"

"Arthur said the shelves were empty," he said in a hushed tone. "Nothing left."

"My God, who could do this?" She was now in floods of tears.

"I'll go straight over to check the CCTV."

"I want to come with you."

"Okay, come on." They began to walk away from the site. "I've heard reports of similar vandalism at other schools, not to this degree though."

"What will we do when we catch them John?"

"As much as we can Izzy, as much as we can."

1801hrs

People all over the country tuned in to the evening news. An African famine and renewed conflict in the Gaza Strip played second fiddle to the main story.

"And now to the main news story. Today there were calls for the government to act on the increasing problems developing in our schools. As outraged parents and other members of the public marched on 10 Downing Street to hand in a petition there were more calls for the government to debate the issues immediately. The planned debate on reforms in schools is due to take place next month after MPs return from their Easter break."

The newsreader, Natasha Dunning, turned to face camera three, "Here is an item recorded for BBC North East news yesterday afternoon." She turned in her seat and viewed the screen behind her and the camera zoomed in as the footage commenced.

"Hi, my name is Josh Thorpe for the BBC and this afternoon I am visiting St Thomas' Secondary School in North Tyneside. I have been to speak to the local Education Council and have been told this is one of the schools they have earmarked to close if the current trend in misbehaviour continues." It was close to three thirty and the end of the school day. "We have been waiting in the news van for over thirty minutes to see if anything would happen. We witnessed a group of school-age children pass our vehicle parked here opposite the school entrance but they were chased away by the adults waiting there. Let's find out what it was about." He and his crew got out of the van, approached the group and asked one of the women closest to the school gates. "Hello, I'm a reporter for BBC North East. Could you tell me what the problem is with the gang of youths that you have just chased away?"

A large surly looking man in his thirties spoke for the group, "Those kids were here to cause trouble. They come by the school every morning and every afternoon at going home time."

The woman he spoke to first had her say, "They are trying to scare away the kids who still want to come to school."

"Is that why you are all here today?" the reporter enquired.

"Yes," said the man. "We come every day to make sure they leave our kids alone."

The reporter sought more information, "Has there been any conflict?"

"Not yet but the gangs are getting bigger and the police won't come here even though we've asked them loads of times."

"How long can you keep coming here to protect your children?"

The lady spoke up again, "My husband works shifts so he can't always be here and some of us have to take time off work especially to be here. It's not right."

The reporter finished off the piece as he turned to camera, "So there you have it. Parents having to protect their own children from other children while the police are nowhere to be seen. I am Josh Thorpe reporting for BBC North East from North Tyneside."

Natasha Dunning faced the camera; "We will now see a report from another school in the region."

Josh Thorpe was standing at the entrance of a School. He began, "I have been standing here at the gates of Embledon High School in the picturesque county of Northumberland since seven thirty." The camera zoomed out to reveal the main school building in the background. "As you can see children are starting to arrive for their school day but also gathering here are parents; angry parents." The cameraman focused in on a small group of adults, some of them holding up small placards.

The commentary continued, "What they are angry with is the lack of response from the local council and the local police force to their requests for an investigation." The camera returned to Thorpe. "In the past three months, five teenagers from this school have been hospitalised. The shocking part of this story is that not one single person has been charged with any wrongdoing, not one. Let's see if we can speak to some of them."

The reporter and the cameraman moved toward the group of women. Now standing out of camera shot the reporter asked a question, "Good morning ladies, I'm a reporter for the BBC, can I ask you why you are protesting today?" He held the microphone up to the nearest women.

"We want the school to close down," a short, plumpish woman responded loudly into the microphone.

"Don't you think that's a little on the extreme side?"

"Extreme!" shouted another member of the group. "My son was in hospital for over a week after being attacked by a group of other lads."

A third woman grabbed the microphone, "The police are doing nothing."

The first woman pulled the microphone back to herself. The reporter becomes anxious remembering that this was a live feed. He regained control of the microphone and asked a direct question to the first woman, "Do you know who the attackers are?"

A little calmer the first woman responded, "Two teachers saw the attack but have refused to identify them."

Another woman leaned between the first two and commented, "They are too scared and that's a fact." The remaining nodded in agreement.

The camera turned and focused back onto the beleaguered Josh Thorpe. "So there you have it. Here in the North East gangs of teenagers are roaming the schools, inflicting violence and nobody is able to stop them." He took a breath as the camera tightened in, "This is Josh Thorpe for BBC news at Embledon High School in Northumberland.

Back in the studio Natasha Dunning spun in her chair turning her back on the shot of Josh Thorpe and faced a second screen. "Thank you Josh and now we head to the Welsh capital to speak to our Cardiff reporter, Gethyn Edwards." She paused, unsure of what was happening with the feed from Cardiff. The picture flitting in and out was unclear. "Gethyn, are you there? This is Natasha in the studio."

The screen behind her was blank but there was an audio feed, "Hello Natasha, I apologise if you are having some problems with the video feed but we have had to take temporary cover."

"Can you explain what is happening Gethyn while we are trying to get video back?"

"Of course, we have had to take cover inside the Bishop of Llandaff High School here in Cardiff. I was interviewing the head teacher Mr. David Thomas when we came under attack from a hail of stones and other missiles. The police have been called."

Back in the studio the producer was trying to control the story and prompting Natasha who asked, "Gethyn can we hear if the head teacher knows who the stone-throwing assailants are?"

"Yes. Mr. Thomas do you recognise any of the young people who are out there?"

The unseen school principal answered, "I don't know their names but I know by the uniforms some are wearing that they are from neighbouring schools."

The picture suddenly kicked in. "Okay Gethyn, we have you on screen now."

"Thanks Natasha." He turned to a smartly dressed middle-aged man who looked a little flustered, "Mr. Thomas has this type of incident happened before?" Edwards extended the microphone to the head teacher.

"Yes on a number of occasions. I mean the two schools have always had a friendly rivalry on exam results, enterprise challenges and of course sports events, but recently it has turned nasty."

"Is it from both sides?"

The head was quick to respond, "I'm afraid to say it is although my staff and I have been trying our utmost to prevent any further instances of trouble."

Gethyn Edwards under prompting through his earpiece asked another question, "What started the problems?"

"It started from trivial things until we had our annual rugby match two months ago."

"What happened then?" he pushed.

"A dangerous tackle resulted in a mass brawl on the pitch, staff from both sides got involved and the situation has just deteriorated from there," his shoulders visibly dropped. "Just over a month ago we cancelled all sporting fixtures between the schools and a couple of weeks after that all ties had to be cut!"

Edwards tried to keep the thread of the story going, "You must be very disappointed Mr. Thomas, it's like admitting defeat."

"Yes it is," he looked out of the window. "The police have arrived. Look, two cars at the end of the road."

"Great, now maybe we can finish off outside?" The camera continued rolling.

"They won't disperse the crowd," the head responded.

"What do you mean?"

"The local police have had cars burned and destroyed by gangs of kids, they won't come any closer."

Under instruction Josh Thorpe had the cameraman turn and film the police at the end of the road. "As you can see the police are parked up blocking the road and are now just watching proceedings."

The large gang now turned their attention to the police. "I hope you can see the gestures and abuse the group of young people are directing towards the police." The cameraman returned the picture to the reporter, "This is Gethyn Edwards for BBC news in Cardiff."

"Thank you for that report Gethyn and let's hope that situation finishes safely." Again Natasha spun in her chair facing the opposite side of the studio, "Now we can hear from our schools correspondent, Lizzy McDonald." The camera briefly showed the correspondent stood against a screen with a slide entitled 'Problems in Today's Schools.' "Lizzy what are the major problems we have in our schools?"

The young correspondent stepped to the side allowing the camera to view the full slide. "Thanks Natasha," she began. "Over the past few years the problems that exist in schools have dramatically increased." A list appeared on the screen to her left and she continued, "What we would call normal problems such as truancy, petty vandalism and graffiti have increased and although they are unwanted problems many schools can continue educating whilst handling them." She moved across to the other side of the screen as the slide changed. "Here we can now see the items highlighted at the last head teachers' conference as being more difficult to control and which could lead to the partial or full closure of an individual school. Vandalism has increased threefold but now this is mainly composed of destruction of private and public property." She continued, "Instances have occurred of cars being set on fire, extensive damage to classrooms and equipment, some of it very expensive. The last reports show an alarming rise in the trend of burning schoolbooks. This in turn has caused more superficial damage to schools and other teaching institutions."

The camera switched back to the newsreader. "Lizzy have you any more information on a similar theme to what we have witnessed from our two live reports this morning?"

The reply was swift and to the point, "Actually this is one of the new developments schools are experiencing. Disturbing effects as the truancy rates increase to over ten per cent as a national average."

"Ten per cent," Natasha interruped. "That's one in ten children not attending school!"

"Yes Natasha, it's a shocking statistic."

"I'm sorry Lizzy, you were telling us about the effect of the truancy rate increase."

"Well as the rate increases the youths out of school have started gathering at their own and neighbouring schools and begun harassing those trying to attend." She half turned to allow the screen to show a new slide she could directly refer to. "This slide shows some of the reports we have received. Bullying, preventing smaller, younger children from getting to school and assaulting those who don't turn away. Theft of money, electronic equipment and again instances of school books being taken, destroyed and left at school entrances."

"This is outrageous behaviour."

"Yes Natasha and it is only compounding the problems further."

"What are local police forces doing to try and deal with these problems?" asked Natasha.

"In many cases the police are unable to act as witnesses won't speak out through fear and intimidation."

"But what about the teachers and staff at the schools, can't they identify the culprits?"

The young correspondent stepped towards the camera, "It appears that staff are, in some cases, the ones being intimidated. There are reports that some staff, and I only mean a small percentage here, have stopped attending school altogether."

The camera finished on the newsreader as she turned back to face the front of the studio "Thank you Lizzy McDonald for that update on the problems being faced in today's schools. If there are any parents or guardians who would like any information or support then they can ring the number at the bottom of the screen which is 0870 7070707 or visit our website shown."

She picked up some sheets of paper from her desk and continued with the next item.

Wednesday 17 April
0822hrs

London, capital of England, once the centre of a vast empire. It was a bright spring morning. Tourists and commuters filed up and down St. Margaret Street, some oblivious to the comings and goings at the Palace of Westminster.

The press, alert as ever were patrolling the pavements waiting for their headlines. This was the first time parliament had been recalled from recess since September 2002 when they came together to discuss Iraq and WMD. Most MPs were inside the halls of Westminster Palace, disgruntled at losing part of their break but also aware of the significance of their return. Groups of MPs like a swarm of honey-wielding bees were clustered together chatting quietly.

As the debate time approached the Prime Minister and his closest education advisors were having a quiet chat in the Members' Tea Room. Ronald Halford, the Minister for Education and his deputy, Sarah Greig, had been gathering information for a few days and were quickly briefing the PM and the Minister for Schools and Education, Jonathon Topp. As they huddled around a quiet corner table Halford, having already explained some facts and figures, was now outlining their options for dealing with the situation.

"You see PM, these figures show a steady escalation of problems," he paused. "We have to affect change now or the situation will only worsen!"

Richard Smalling, the Prime Minister sighed, "What is your suggestion then, Ronnie?"

"Well PM, we prepared that legislation last year about barring students who breach certain rules." Halford replied.

"Do you mean permanent exclusions from mainstream education?" the PM asked leafing through the notes. "And possible use of secure facilities for these young people?"

"Wouldn't that just put the problems on to the streets though?" said a worried Sarah.

A few seconds elapsed before the Minister of Education broke the silence "We have to protect the schools first PM, the children and staff!"

"You don't want Tim nice but dim to have a panic attack?" Jonathon Topp chuckled to himself.

"I wish you wouldn't call the leader of the opposition that," Sarah said bemused.

The others sat around the table giving each other a knowing smile.

"Sarah is right," the PM interjected "We should show Tim Cleaves some respect especially if we want him on our side."

Ron Halford slid a file across the table manoeuvring through the coffee cups.

"Is this the proposal Ronnie?"

"Yes PM, I prepared it last night," he gave a faint smile trying to show the hours he worked had somehow made him age considerably. "It gives the head teachers authority to exclude students without going through the normal process of paperwork, governors and parents."

Topp interjected, "Should we brief the Police Authority first, to give them a heads up?"

"Would be wise," Sarah offered. "We will need a hell of a lot of support from them if this proposal goes through."

The PM scanned through the information he had been given. He had only recently turned 40 but this last year he had been in the hot seat of the country and it had taken its toll: hair receding, turning grey, a few more wrinkles and a pale complexion. The doctor, during a recent check-up, had told him to 'take it easy.' Not possible in his current job!

Topp glanced at his watch, "Time to go PM."

"Okay Jonathon, let's see if we can get a result today otherwise this situation is going to get a lot worse judging by some of these figures and reports."

0844hrs

The four arrived in the corridor just outside the main chamber and there they waited with the remainder of the House. Most of the House had made it back from their breaks; some would be abroad, unable or unwilling to pay huge amounts for early return flights. Others would have an excuse not to be present but their absence would be noted.

Heads turned as the Black Rod walked up the long approach corridor, his shoes click-clacking on the freshly polished tiled floor. Eyes followed him as he passed. He stopped at the main doors and paused before banging his mace three times on the door. After waiting a few moments he repeated the process and the door opened. He walked forward and placed his mace on its pedestal before giving a slight bow to the speaker and leaving through the side door.

The House members filed in and started to take their seats. Richard Smalling looked across at his immediate opponent The Right Honourable Timothy Cleaves, MP and nodded. The gesture was returned. With the rows of seats now full the Speaker, Daffyd Thomas, rose from his chair.

"The House is called to order on this day the fifteenth of April, 2025," he paused and purposefully looked around all areas of the room. "Members of the House, you may be seated."

Thomas remained standing as the MPs on all sides started to sit. He was a large built man, balding but he held such an air of authority that he dominated the House. He was overwhelmingly voted in over four years previously and the members got exactly what they wanted. A man who could hold centre stage amidst some of the most powerful individuals in the country. He squinted as he checked that everyone was seated, "I will hand the chair over to the Right Honourable Richard Smalling MP," and with a nod he sat back in his seat.

Richard Smalling rose from his chair. Still feeling tired from his long trip back to London from his holiday, he picked up his spectacles, placing them on the bridge of his nose. He gathered up his paperwork before putting them onto the reading dais.

"Thank you Mr Speaker," he nodded towards Thomas before continuing. "Firstly, I would like to apologise to the members for having to cut short their Easter break."

There were groans and mutterings from various parts of the floor. He held up his hand to continue, "You will have seen the latest news reports showing the rapid decline in both behaviour and discipline in our country's schools. We feel this needs to be addressed now so we have until the end of this week to come up with a viable solution."

There were more murmurings from those seated opposite. This was countered by some approving nods from the members sat on Smalling's side of the room.

"Ladies and gentlemen we are facing a very real problem here, one which needs to be dealt with sooner rather than later." He looked around the other members "Most of the people sat in this House have children and it must be a worry to think that your child, just like any other, could be put in a dangerous situation similar to some of those I have read reports about. The escalation in the number of these incidents and the increasing veracity has led my senior cabinet ministers and I to seek your approval on the legislation we are going to put before you now. I will hand you over to the Minister of Education, Ronald Halford." He sat down folding up his notes and putting them into the inside pocket of his jacket.

Halford waited until he received a nod of approval from the speaker before rising to his feet. The murmurings from the floor quietened to a hush as the House waited for the next MP to address them. Ron Halford seemed a little reluctant as he stood; knowing that if this bill was passed people for years to come would remember it was he who initiated its reading.

"Prime Minister, fellow MPs, the bill I am about to put forward has been aired in the past but that was when the situation was a little less severe." He took a breath, glancing around the room. Sweat was forming on his brow and he felt it trickle down his back, making him flinch a little. He steadied himself and spoke in a clear tone "Our proposal is that students in public schools who breach certain rules are excluded instantly and further to this," he paused, taking another deep breath, his discomfort obvious for those close by to see, "a short period of detention in the more extreme cases can be issued in the newly available secure facilities."

Halford stopped as the noise level increased with a crescendo of boos and as he looked around the House he saw members start to get to their feet. Before the disruption could get any louder the Speaker rose and swiftly called for order. The room fell into an eerie silence.

The opposition leader stood and turned around to ensure his side of the House returned to their seats. When they had, he remained standing and gestured to the Speaker.

Daffyd Thomas rose again from his seat in its lofty position "The floor recognises the right honourable Tim Cleaves, leader of Her Majesty's loyal opposition." He sat, aware that he may be called upon again. "Fellow MPs, what has the government brought before us today?" he paused for dramatic effect, holding up the rough draft copy of the bill prepared by Sarah Greig. "You want us to lock up our own children?"

There followed a cacophony of jeers from his followers and others directed towards the government benches. Richard Smalling rose to his feet, the jeering continued for a short time even after he raised his hand for it to stop. "Ladies and gentlemen, we have brought this bill before you not out of want but out of necessity."

More jeering, mainly from the opposite side of the chamber.

The Speaker rose again to his feet. This was enough for the noise to die down. He remained standing for a few more seconds to ensure the noise had ceased and then he slowly sat back down.

The PM straightened his back, coming up to his full height after leaning on the dais. He took a deep breath and started speaking, slowly. "I know this sounds a little extreme but we have worked tirelessly on this bill and we didn't go into it lightly." He immediately raised his right hand to snuff out any protests before they began. "All I ask is that you please listen to the proposal we are putting forward. Do not think negatively but think of all the amazing young people in schools, up and down this fine country of ours who we are trying to help with this bill, thank you!"

With that he abruptly sat down in his seat. Ronald Halford looked at the sea of faces sitting on the opposite side of the room. Where before there had been jeering now he noticed some members deep in thought, others nodding their approval. He glanced around to his side and behind him. His look was met with a wink or a nod from some. One of his colleagues gestured for him to stand and seize the moment.

He turned to look at the Speaker who nodded and stood to re-introduce him. "The floor recognises the right honourable Ronald Halford, Minister for Education and pray silence for the duration."

Halford rose confidently. After the interjection from the PM and the Speaker requesting that he was not to be interrupted he felt buoyed. "Ladies and gentlemen of the House, we are not trying to put forward a bill to criminalise a generation. We are not seeking to destroy a perfectly good education system, in fact quite the opposite; we are striving to preserve it. To secure a better future for our young ones." He paused reaching for his bottle of water. He took the lid off slowly as he glanced around the vast room. Over 500 members of Parliament were now looking directly at him. Funnily enough, he didn't feel nervous at all. He took a cool drink, screwed down the lid and put the bottle at his feet.

He picked up his factsheet and commenced the most important speech of his tenure. "Serious incidents in schools have steadily risen over the past year. From the last four months the number of incidents reads 58, 65, 68, 75! This is an unacceptable upward trend that we must stop. We have spoken to various schools and they assure us that if they could 'release' two per cent of their more unruly population then those figures I quoted would more than half!"

He looked around the room; everyone now hung on his every word. "More than half!" he repeated with more emphasis. He put the sheet on the stand. "Now obviously we won't have to go that far in the vast majority of schools but in the ones that produce the most incidents, how far will we have to go?"

His voice quietened a little as he continued "We do have some secure facilities set aside for the more extreme cases, but we are hoping that won't be used very often." He looked across at the opposition. The sea of faces looked back "We have three days to try and sort this out because we have special dispensation to pass the reading of this bill on three consecutive days. All I am asking is for us all to work together to solve this matter. Okay, does anyone have any questions?"

There followed some furious glances and whispering before a member of the opposition raised their hand. The Speaker got up uttering "The floor recognises the right honourable Miss Lisa Reynolds, opposition Minister for Education, and then the floor is open thereafter."

Lisa Reynolds stood, clearing her throat. "Thank you Mr Speaker, I think I echo the thoughts of most of my colleagues when we first heard of your ideas." She quickly glanced up and down her own side of the house before continuing, "We are worried that you may have over-reacted to the situation?"

An immediate response from the government benches and Jonathon Topp, the Secretary of State for Children, Schools and Families stood to reply. "My thanks to Miss Reynolds for hitting the nail on the head, so to speak." He gestured to everyone present with a sweep of his arm, "We have thought long and hard about how far to take these proposals. Do we err on the side of caution or, as some of you may think, do we go too far?" He paused to ensure complete attention "We implement the bill and see where it leads, ensuring we keep firm control over it!"

Several members of the opposition raised their arms to speak. As they glanced round, the others noticed their leader slowly rise to his feet. They all lowered their arms. Jonathon Topp nodded across to Tim Cleaves and returned to his seat.

"We would like to thank the government for their candid response." He responded to the various nods and ayes of approval before continuing, "As long as we can be promised frequent updates in the house and a steady hand at the rudder we would be quite happy to vote the bill through to the House of Lords, as it stands." There followed more clapping and ayes from both sides of the House.

Before he could sit, Lisa Reynolds rose from the neighbouring seat and whispered into his ear. The general hubbub subsided and Tim Cleaves raised his arm to hold the attention. Lisa Reynolds returned to her seat as her party leader continued, "We would ask however that a working group be put together to monitor the situation closely and that all parties should be represented in this group." He gestured across to his opposite number.

Richard Smalling let out a sigh of relief as he stood and smiled "The most honourable gentleman has come up with a very good idea," he also nodded at Lisa Reynolds in recognition. "If all parties would pass the name of their nominee to Mr Halford we will organise the working group immediately."

And so the bill passed three votes in the House of Commons over the next three days before heading up to the House of Lords to become law.

Monday 22 April
0720hrs

On a cold, crisp morning the sun was trying to break through some ominous looking clouds. Not the type of morning people arrive at work looking forward to what that day would bring. Joanne Tindell did, she loved her job as Headteacher of a high school in the small town of Ashton in Northumberland.

Her first job as a head had not been easy thus far, funding cuts, job losses and a poor Ofsted report had all hit her in the first year. One year on and she had put a vast amount of time and effort into her work. Results would start to show soon, she was confident.

She walked in through the recently decorated entrance, smiling at the vastly improved appearance - her idea. As she turned left up the corridor beyond the main hall her footsteps echoed off the walls up to the high ceiling. She enjoyed the quiet at this early hour. No disruptions so she could get some decent work done. As she continued up the stairs towards her office she started running through the tasks she had lined up for the day. As she climbed the second flight she realised the events she had seen unfurl on the Parliament channel the previous day would start filtering into the school staff as the day progressed. With her key in the door Joanne knew she would spend most of her day talking to staff and parents about how her school would be approaching the possible outcomes of the parliamentary debate.

She put her bag on the meeting table and took off her coat, hanging it on the elaborately ornate coat stand in the corner. She walked past her desk tapping the space bar on the keyboard to initialise her PC. She clicked on her percolator and then returned to empty her bag of the items she would need.

A few minutes later with her desk in order, coffee steaming on the coaster designed by her year nine students. She looked at her monitor. Over 40 emails were waiting in her inbox. As she paged down she realised that apart from the normal half dozen she would have accrued overnight the majority were from individual staff members.

It was going to be a difficult day.

0733hrs

The phone rang, startling her. She took a deep breath to compose herself before answering, “Good morning, Ashton High. Miss Tindale speaking.”

The voice at the other end sounded a little over-excited, “Hi Joanne, it’s Adam O’Brien here.”

“Hi Adam, it’s a bit early for you to be in work?” she responded jovially.

“What do you expect Joanne, with everything that’s going on in the news. What have you got planned?”

“I’ve got the SLT in soon and then all the staff in the main hall before registration.”

Adam O’Brien thought for a few seconds before continuing, “Sounds like a good plan you have there, I might follow your lead?”

Joanne responded quickly “It’s all I could come up with overnight.” She scrolled her mouse over some of her emails, quickly scanning the texts. “I’m just looking through some of the multitude of emails I have received this morning.” She leaned forward a little reading a particular text, “Even Ian Taylor, one of our dinosaurs is worried about where it will all lead.”

“I thought old-man Taylor would love the opportunity to be able to use greater sanctions against some of the more unruly kids you have?”

“He says in his email that he is worried about the knock-on effect with some of the lesser well-behaved pupils,” she continued reading. “He thinks that if we start giving out more severe exclusions that it will cause more anger and violence from them?”

Adam let out a slow breath “What are we going to do to keep the peace?” he paused “What do we do when parents and guardians start getting involved?”

"We'll just have to deal with things as they arise, let's keep each other up to date."

"Okay Joanne, good idea. Let's make sure we are both singing from the same hymn sheet." Adam O'Brien paused checking his watch, "I had better let you go, you've got lots to do. Speak again soon?"

"Thanks Adam, we must keep in regular contact. Love to Michelle and talk to you soon, Bye."

0742hrs

She hung up the phone, clicked her earring back on and checked her watch; nearly quarter to eight. She heard distant mutterings as her SLT approached her office. She stood up, picked up her diary then headed to her seat on the conference table, stopping to collect her coffee on the way.

"Morning Joanne!" Will McCormack, her deputy head was first through the door. Hot on his heels came the three head of years: Year nine – Pete Thornton, year ten – Sheryl Townsend and head of year eleven – Tom Cawthorne.

"Morning guys, get yourselves a coffee if you want one and let's make a start." The three men gathered around the small table, making their coffees. Sheryl, a long-time friend and confidante of Joanne had a look of anguish on her face and walked over to her side. "How are you coping Jo?" she gently put her hand on her friend's shoulder.

"I could scream sometimes!" She forced a smile as she looked at her friend, "But I have to stay strong to set an example to everyone else."

"If you need to talk you know where to find me?" Sheryl sat at her place at the table just as the others sat down.

0750hrs

Joanne Tindell took a deep breath then began, "Good Morning everyone, thank you for coming in early," she paused, looking around the table at each of her senior management team in turn. "I wanted to speak to you all before the school day began just to let you know my thoughts about the recent events and how they might affect our school." The others glanced nervously at each other before their head teacher continued.

"You will all know that the government has decided to allow schools to bring in stronger measures to counter the growing trend of violence and disruption that is threatening the education system." She stopped and picked up her pen, ready to write.

A pause developed as each of her co-workers thought on what she had said.

It was the longest serving member of the group, Tom Cawthorne, who spoke up first, "Well Joanne, I've been keeping up to date with the deliberations in Parliament and firstly, I would have to say I agree with them," he paused, waiting for a response. None was forthcoming so he continued. "Secondly, I have to say I'm not sure how far we should go?"

Pete Thornton intervened "I know what you mean Tom, once we have set a president, so to speak, we can't go back."

Joanne Tindell listened intently as her most trusted members of staff continued discussing the pros and cons of the government's new legislation. She had gained her headship two years earlier after a large turnover of staff due to policy changes and funding cuts. As part of her acceptance of the role in a declining school she had insisted on having the staff she wanted in key positions. This was the outcome she had wanted, Tom Cawthorne an 'old-school' disciplinarian, Sheryl, a friend of many years and Pete Thornton, a young, up and coming go-getter. Her team was balanced out by her pragmatic and unambitious deputy-head, Will McCormack, his organisational skills and tact were second to none. Between them they had dedicated themselves to get Ashton High School back up to 'Satisfactory' and within five years to a 'good' school, in the eyes of their biggest critics Ofsted. Joanne was confident that the variety of ideals and characters she had put together would come up with the perfect approach to the new guidelines.

She continued to make notes as she listened. Sometimes with a frown, sometimes with a smile as they explored both extremes of the predicament they found themselves in.

A natural pause developed in the discussion and she decided to interject, "Okay everyone, some great ideas, and some not so great," she smiled to show everyone she was pleased before continuing. "I think we need to draw up a list of those students we need to release now and maybe those who are on thin ice."

She turned towards Will, "Can you draft up a letter for those we are releasing today and also a final warning letter for the rest."

Will nodded before responding, "How shall we dispose of the unwanted?"

A chorus of sniggers followed his choice of words.

Joanne frowned at Will. "Let's hope the parents share your sense of humour when they suddenly find out they now have full-time care of their children!" She looked at each of her colleagues in turn. The worried expression on her face finally gave away her true feelings. "This isn't going to be as easy as some people think," she sat down and her head fell forward into her hands.

The others were now ashen-faced. They had not really thought beyond getting rid of the worst behaved pupils.

They continued their discussion for another twenty minutes managing not to confront the main issue; what would happen outside of school? When the meeting concluded the participants left the room deep in thought. The light-hearted mood of earlier had quickly evaporated after the head's comments. The future now seemed less clear, more foreboding.

0830hrs

In the main hall the rest of the staff were gathering. The atmosphere was subdued as the SLT arrived and dispersed just in front of the main stage. Normally staff meetings involved jovial introductions or statistic-laden power points, but this time once silence had descended on the staff, the steely silence was prolonged.

Joanne Tindell was not into dramatics but her inner turmoil inadvertently delayed her announcement. Will stepped forward, prepared to open proceedings, but Joanne stopped him with a gentle wave of her hand. He stepped back with a slight nod; she gave him a weak smile. The gathered staff seemed bemused.

"Good morning everyone, sorry to keep you from your lesson prep time but there are some changes happening that I wanted you all to be aware of." She glanced around at some of the perplexed expressions trying to sound reassuring "As of today we are releasing a number of pupils, 28 to be exact...permanently."

A murmur spread among the assembled staff. Will raised his hand, "Quiet please." He looked at Joanne who seemed to gain some energy from his support.

"The list of names has been displayed on the main notice board in the staff room, make sure you all check to see if any of your tutees are there." She paused to let the news sink in. "We are also drawing up a list of students who have been placed on a final warning prior to expulsion. Letters are being prepared for all parents and guardians concerned."

She looked around the members of staff who were now wide-eyed, some in disbelief, others in shock.

She faced Will and gave him a quick nod. He stepped forward to speak, "You have all been watching events unfurl in Parliament over the past few days so this shouldn't come as too much of a shock." He walked slowly up the centre aisle of the hall glancing from side to side to try and catch as many faces as possible. "It goes without saying that life inside the school should become a little easier as is the governments want but we should think of the long term effect?" He had now turned and walked back to the front of the hall and he spun on the spot to face everyone. "We should also be aware of the effect these measures may have outside of our school."

Joanne Tindell stepped forward, in front of Will, "I must emphasise that I am thinking of your own personal interests here...your safety."

0840hrs

As the staff left the hall the atmosphere was very subdued. Small groups of teachers broke off from the main crowd and began furiously whispering to each other.

How would parents react to having their kids kicked out of school? The government had sat in chambers and come up with what they thought was a perfect solution to the increasing problems of vandalism, delinquency and mass truancy. Had they stopped to think of the repercussions of their decisions? As usual they would not see at close hand the results of their over-indulgent procrastinations.

Tuesday 23 April
1215hrs

The corridors of the school were quiet. It was five minutes before lunch break. Inside classrooms students were donning their coats and packing up their books in readiness for the bell; the bell that would release them from lessons for a short period of time. Mobiles would be switching on, a surge on the local networks as the majority of students and some staff checked texts, accessed Facebook or tweeted.

1220hrs

In the staffroom a small group of teachers were deep in conversation. Yesterday's announcement was at the forefront of their minds. Various teaching unions were voicing their opinions and some members of staff were already contemplating their futures.

Ian Taylor had spent nearly 20 years at Ashton High School as a history teacher. Head of Humanities now he had taken on the responsibility of being the NUT representative for the majority of teachers in the school. Sat in the staffroom, he was looking through a collection of emails he had been sent from various departments and the main teaching union, the NUT.As he sat, manoeuvring pieces of paper into different piles, he grew more and more frustrated. Some teachers came and went as they checked mail and collected lunch and drinks.

Sally Cowan entered the staffroom, packed lunch in her hand. A recent arrival at the school, she had not had the opportunity to make any friends yet but had known Ian Taylor who was involved in her induction.

"Hi Ian, are you busy?" she asked.

"I am, yes. Got to get this union stuff sorted before a meeting tonight." He looked up and saw Sally hovering, glancing around at the other tables. "Come on Sal, sit down. I need some lunch anyway and a breather from all this." He gestured to an empty chair next to him.

Just as Sally sat down, Ian's department LSA came up. "Can I join you?"

"Of course you can Jackie, pull up a pew, the more the merrier," he smiled.

The three of them settled down and the furious opening and closing of plastic containers and the rustle of paper and tin foil ended as Ian looked at the other two. "We could talk about the weather or the upcoming summer holidays?" He paused, a sly smile crossing his face. "Or, we could talk about what's happening in school?"

Sally who had caught on to his thinking entered the conversation, "Any particular topic Ian?" she said, tilting her head slightly to one side.

"We might as well talk about the students who have been thrown out!" Jackie interjected. The other two smiled. "I know I'm glad to see the back of some of them."

"I know Jackie, but the question is who is going to be seeing them now?" He took a bite of his sandwich and chewed it a little "You know they are going to be annoying someone, somewhere."

Sally covered her mouth as she let out a little snigger. "Sorry Ian but you have to admit that lessons are a lot easier now that group have been expelled."

"Not the point Sally, I have been snowed under with information from the unions about our legal position. No-one seems to know how we stand, legally."

Jackie turned to Ian "But the government said we had to do it?" She glanced at Sally and back to Ian. "I saw it on the news!"

"That's right, we are only doing what the Prime Minister has told us to do?" Sally added.

Ian scrunched up the wrapping for his sandwich and threw it at the bin. It bounced off the wall and into the waiting bin. "He shoots, he scores."

The other two laughed at his mock celebrations.

"Glad you can take this so lightly," Jackie smiled.

"No Jackie, I'm not taking this lightly, far from it. But you must let me enjoy my lunchtimes because all I can see is a future of doom and gloom, for all of us."

"It won't be that bad, it's not as if they are going to come back into school?"

"They are going to get bored sooner or later." Ian said as he took a nice, shiny apple out of his sandwich box. "Let's hope they don't turn their attention towards us!"

A few moments later Will McCormack strode purposefully into the room and after a quick search of the staff present he made a beeline for Ian Taylor.

Stopping just behind Sally he said, "Hi Ian, was hoping we could get together straight after school to talk about the unions?"

"I was hoping to get away early tonight. It's my wedding anniversary?"

"It won't take long Ian," Will turned and made for the door. Looking back over his shoulder, "I'll be in my office." And with that he was gone.

Ian shrugged.

Sally smiled "So what have you got planned for tonight?"

Ian looked puzzled.

"Your anniversary?"

"Oh yes," he sat back in his chair and put his hands behind his head. "I have booked a chef to come round the house and cook us a fantastic three-course meal."

"You're joking," Jackie cut in.

"No, I have it all planned. She is due home at six thirty and the dining room will be transformed, the chef will be cooking in the kitchen, the kids will be at my Mams and I will be in my tux."

Sally let out a little squeal of delight "That is so romantic, Helen will be blown away."

Ian just nodded, a grin spreading across his face.

"Which chef have you got?" Jackie asked.

"You know that new Italian restaurant just over the bridge?" The other two nodded. "I am friends with Antonio, the owner, he said I could borrow one of his chefs for the night."

"That must have cost you a bomb?"

"Not really, do you remember his daughter, Isabella, who came to this school a few years ago?"

Jackie nodded, "Yes I remember her, she didn't speak much English when she first started."

"That's right, she had been brought up in Italy by her mother. Well, I helped her with some extra tuition and a little home schooling." He smiled with pride. "She got an A in her GCSE's. Anotonio was over the moon and he always said he owed me a big favour. We play 5-a-side together on Thursday nights and we got chatting in the sports centre bar after a game a few weeks ago. I said that it was coming up to my 25th anniversary and I was looking for something special and he suggested the chef – no cost!"

"Wow, that sounds like a good friend to have, do you use the restaurant a lot?" Sally asked.

"Maybe…once a month, oh and special occasions like birthdays."

"I might take a look in there one night."

"It's worth it Sally, the food has a really genuine Italian taste."

Silence returned with each of them deep in thought.

After a few moments Ian's thoughts inevitably returned to his current problems. He had had some difficulty in sleeping the previous night. Knowing his workload was growing and the thought of unruly children wandering the streets of Ashton looking for mischief troubled him. Although he lived five miles away the thought still worried him. The future looked so uncertain.

1240hrs

He was brought back to the present by a gentle shaking of his shoulder.

"Ian. Ian are you in there?"

Ian looked up and saw his long-time friend, John Reynolds, looking down at him with that smile of his that put you in a good mood just to see it. "Hi John," he tapped him on his hand. "Sorry mate, I was miles away."

"I can see you have the weight of the world on your shoulders, again!"

"Oh it's just this union stuff," he picked up a pile of papers. "They want to know what our reaction is to the…changes."

“Thought so.” John squatted next to Ian’s chair, “Give me a shout if you need a hand mate, I used to do some of the union rep duties a few years ago and it can be a pain in the arse!” He quickly glanced at the other two, “Excuse me ladies.”

They both nodded back at him and Sally smiled.

“It’s all happened so fast and everybody wants everything done by yesterday.” He cast the papers down onto the small table they were sitting around.

John Reynolds recognised the frustration in his friend’s voice. He stood up and had a quick glance at his watch, nearly quarter to one, he had a few minutes to spare.

“Is this seat free?” he said as he grabbed the chair next to Ian and dragged it back. He looked at the papers on top of Ian’s pile. “County – ignore that one, the Trust – ignore that too.” He discarded a few more then paused. He scooped up one of the printed emails, “Ah, David Nelson, Member of Parliament – this is the only one you need to worry about. The rest pale into insignificance.”

Ian took the email from him and quickly glanced over the contents. His friend watched as his face contorted through the various lines and paragraphs.

John grabbed the email, “Do you want me to give my understanding of the whole palaver?”

Ian nodded, “Please.”

Sally leaned forward and snapped the lid of her Tupperware container closed. “I could do with a decent explanation too?”

“Okay then, in stages,” John sat back and exaggerated a full stretch of his body. Suddenly he sat forward and stuck out the index finger of his left hand before continuing, “We all know that the general behaviour of young people in this country has been steadily worsening?”

Ian responded, “True, over the last couple of years.”

“Okay then,” John continued. “A few events of an unsavoury type happened over a short period of time. Secondly,” as his middle finger extended, “this caused a knee-jerk reaction from the government. If they had been in normal session we wouldn’t be in this predicament but, alas, they were on Easter break. The PM over-reacted by bringing everyone in from their break which only fed the flames of an already expectant press, hence, they had to be seen to be doing something as dramatic as they have." His third finger shot out joining the first two, "Finally, they try to enforce some critical changes on every school in the country regardless of status; trusts, academies or individual schools. All have to bow to these improvements."

His emphasis on the last word was not missed by anyone sat at the table or those nearby who had suddenly paid an acute interest to John's account of events.

"And that in a nutshell is why we are where we are and you Ian, my dear friend, have a pile of crap sat on this table." He patted the pile of papers, with a smile.

Sally looked up, bemused. "Is it as simple as that?"

"In my opinion, yes." John sat back, as if suddenly drained of energy. "Does that help you at all, my friend?" he spoke, looking at Ian.

Ian leaned forward and started gathering in all the papers he had spread across the table in front of him. He had a resigned look on his face but as he straightened up all the sheets, tapping them on the desk lengthways, then widthways, he smiled. "Do you know something John, you're right."

"But of course I am," he paused looking at his friend. "What are you thinking?"

"I am not going to get stressed out by this. What will happen will happen and it is no fault of anyone here."

"Well said."

Jackie chose this point to speak up, slightly worried, "Surely you can't just do nothing?"

"You are right Jackie, but I can't do much about what happens outside of my remit."

"You just need to keep track of anything that happens that affects us," John said.

"Yes," Ian thought for a few seconds. The others waited. "I am going to keep some sort of diary…of events."

John slapped him on the shoulder, "Good idea, cover your back."

"It's not just for that reason. Sometime in the future, if this goes pear-shaped, we need a record of events: dates, times, occurrences, that sort of thing."

Sally spoke up, keen with interest, "Yes, you're right. A diary of everything that happens, I can help you, if you like?"

"Thanks Sally that would be great. It will be good to get a different perspective and not just my opinion because I feel we are going to have a lot to write about." He shrugged, "Anyway, you can take over the writing if anything happens to me," he gave her a wink.

"Don't say something like that Ian," Jackie reached forward and put her fingertips on the table. "Quickly, touch wood."

"Come on Jackie, you know me, I'm not into all that mumbo jumbo."

They all laughed at Ian's last comment.

1255hrs

John stood up and with a little wave, he departed. Lunchtime was nearly over and he had to prepare for his next lesson.

A quick glance up at the staffroom clock and Ian Taylor stood up, tucked his sandwich box under his arm and headed for the door. "I will see you ladies later, have a nice afternoon."

"You too Ian," Jackie said as she quickly headed over to the other side of the staffroom to check her pigeon hole.

1300hrs

That afternoon, school life continued as normal. The general atmosphere seemed a little quieter and more relaxed. Had the government made the right decision? Only time would tell.

Wednesday 24 April
1120hrs

The door slammed. The young man stood there, gazed at his reflection in the hall mirror and smiled. Nearly six feet tall, blond hair, stocky build, not bad for a 16 year old.

He started up the stairs and as he moved upwards he heard the living room door open below him and waited for the inevitable onslaught.

"And where have you been all night Brad?" the boy's mother asked, voice slightly raised.

"Out Mam, where do you think?" came Brad's response.

"Out where?"

"With my mates!" came the angry reply. He continued walking up the stairs.

His mother growing ever frustrated slapped the bannister in anger. "You won't be out tonight then," she snarled up the stairs.

The response "Whatever," echoed down the staircase just adding to the angst his mother already felt.

Pam Jones had been in this situation quite a few times. More frequently now that Brad had no school to get up for in the mornings. He was one of those selected to be excluded from Ashton High School. Pam tried to think of another approach to try and reach out to her wayward son but nothing came. She went back into the living room and spoke to her husband, Phil. He was slighter in stature than his oldest son and for a few years now had not exuded any authority over him.

"Phil, did you hear him out there?"

"Yes, I heard," Phil responded from the comfort of his corner leather chair.

"What are you going to do about it?"

"Nowt!" He frustratingly pressed the mute key for the TV. "I've tried everything and he won't listen to me."

"Well, we have to do something," she sat on the couch and looked at him. Tiredness etched on her face. She was only 35 years old but bringing up Brad and younger brother Tom had taken its toll.

Phil Jones sat forward. "You won't let me raise a hand to him Pam! He would probably fight back anyway and I don't fancy taking him on!"

Her voice quietened, "I'm at my wits end love, the school don't want him anymore, and we can't trust him around here."

Phil stood up instantly. "Has he been stealing money from you again?"

He was angry and his wife had to stretch out and grab his arm as he was set to march up the stairs and confront Brad. This had happened before and a final warning had been given to him.

"We told him that the next time he stole from us we would throw him out!" Phil was irate.

Pam had to stand up now to prevent her husband from getting through the door of the living room. "It was only a fiver Phil."

"That's not the point love, he stole, from us."

She looked into his eyes and saw the rage there. She felt a lot of his angst but tried to remain calm for all their sakes.

"Listen Phil, we can't put up with his attitude, I know that but if we throw him out, won't that make things worse?" she said in a pleading tone.

Phil Jones slumped his shoulders, the initial rage subsiding as he looked at his wife. "Listen pet, we have to draw the line somewhere. He's gone too far, we have to think about Tom, the example Brad is setting him."

"Tom is a good lad, he doesn't take after his brother."

"Not yet he doesn't," Phil gently took hold of his wife's face in his huge hands. "If Brad stays here then Tom is bound to copy some of the things he does. It's too late for Brad but we can still keep our Tom on the straight and narrow."

1135hrs

The couple continued talking quietly for a few more minutes working out how best to approach the situation. They eventually realised that to give Tom the best chance of making a success of his life Brad had to be moved. Phil Jones came up with the idea of getting his brother to take Brad for a while. Marty Jones lived in Doncaster where he worked for his friends building firm. He was a bit of a lad but would see no harm came to Brad. The decision made, they decided to tell him together.

As they went up the stairs Pat grabbed hold of her husband's hand. He gave her hand a quick squeeze, for reassurance.

The first knock was met with silence so Phil knocked a little louder not wanting to enflame what was sure to be a volatile meeting anyway.

This time a response, "Yeah."

Pat spoke up, "Can we come in son, we want to chat?" She tilted her head towards the door so she could hear the response. None was forthcoming.

Phil opened the door and popped his head through the gap. "We need a chat Brad, it's important."

There was no response from Brad who was sat on his bed playing a game on his PlayStation. "Brad can you just stop the game a minute while we talk?" his father asked, his voice remaining calm.

Again, Brad made no response as his parents slowly shuffled into his room.

The tension seemed unbearable to both Pat and Phil as they gave their son as much leeway as possible, but Brad continued to ignore them and play the game.

Phil finally had had enough; he reached across and switched off the TV screen.

As the screen darkened Brad flew into a rage. "What do you think you're doing," he threw down the game controller onto his bed as he stood up to face his parents. "I was in the middle of a game!"

Phil was on a short fuse too. "You were ignoring us boy, that's what you were doing!"

"Maybe I think that what I was doing was more important than talking to you two." He took a step towards his Dad, "All you do is moan and complain anyway."

Phil closed the gap to his son. "That's because you're always in trouble; bringing the police to our door or getting kicked out of school!"

"I suppose that's my fault is it?"

"Well who else is to blame?" his father responded.

"You're my parents, you brought me up." He jabbed a finger at both his parents.

Just as Phil was going to grab his son's hand Pat stepped between them, forcing them both to take a step back. She had thought this would be the way the situation would go.

Brad took a deep breath, focusing on his Dad. He had always thought over the past couple of years that he would end up in a physical confrontation with him. Maybe it was a male thing, working out who was 'Alpha male'.

Despite what others thought about him or the reputation he had gained at school he was at heart a Mammy's boy. He would never physically harm her so as she stood between him and his Dad his threat slowly declined. He quickly looked round his room, he was thinking fast now.

Pat turned to face her husband. "Just give us a minute Phil," she gave him a faint smile. "Please."

But before Phil could respond and head towards the door, Brad was already moving. He bent down and dragged his Adidas bag from under the bed, tugging open the zip and dropping it onto his bed.

Phil and Pat shared a quick glance as Brad opened one of his drawers and dragged out some tracksuit bottoms, some t-shirts from another drawer and a handful of underwear before stuffing them into his bag. He started grabbing other items and putting them into his bag.

Phil turned and walked out of the room.

Pat was torn between relief that Brad was leaving and fear of where he would go. "Brad where will you go?"

Brad put the belongings he was carrying into his bag and slowly pulled the zip closed. "I'll be okay Mam," he looked up at her and half-smiled. "I'll stay with one of my mates until I get sorted."

He hooked the bag over his shoulder and leaned forward to give her a kiss on the cheek.

Pat reached into her pocket and quickly pulled out a tattered ten pound note. "Here you go son," she said as she stuffed it into his hand.

"Thanks Mam," he smiled at her. "I'll come back in a day or two to collect some more of my stuff." With that he was through the door and heading down the stairs, leaving his Mam to sit on his bed with her head in her hands.

Just as Brad reached the bottom of the stairs his father came out of the sitting room to his side.

"Take care of yourself son." He grabbed his hand to shake it and Brad realised he was putting something into his hand. Phil Jones patted his son on the arm and quickly turned to go back into the sitting room.

Brad watched him go, torn between feelings of love and hatred.

He looked down as he opened his right hand. The scrunched up piece of paper had a strange purple tinge to it. He swallowed hard to hold his emotions in check as he put the twenty pound note into his pocket. He took a step towards the sitting room door, then checked, paused, lifted his head up, turned and walked out of the front door, closing it behind him.

1200hrs

The One Stop shop had only been open a couple of months. The previous occupant had been a shoe shop but its location, away from the main town shopping area and competition from cheaper mainstream shops had seen it quickly make losses.

When Ali Bhendazi had bought the lease on the premises he had looked around the local area to see what was missing and what the local residents wanted. He also looked into the history of the shop, it had been a newsagent in the past but he didn't know why it had closed down. It has also been a sewing shop and a physiotherapist for a couple of years until the owner passed away. He knew it would be tough for him and his family in this area and so far it had been. He was just about finished restocking the refrigeration unit with lunchtime snacks when he noticed the group of youngsters hanging around outside and his heart sank.

He quickly put the basket away he had been using and crossed over to where his young wife, Venisha, was stood, behind the counter. “Veny darling, did you want to go upstairs and check on your mother, maybe have a little lunch?”

Venisha gave her husband of 6 years a strange look before glancing at the time displayed on the till “But Ali, it is coming up to our busy lunchtime period?”

“I know darling,” he looked over his shoulder towards the front window before continuing. “But you have been up for the early papers, wouldn’t it be nice to have a rest?”

His wife moved around the counter and saw who was outside, she sighed. “Ali, I’m not going to hide away from those evil children and leave you on your own.”

Outside the group of teenagers, partially clothed in the uniform of the local high school were chatting and laughing. Some of them were smoking and then their attention was drawn up the road as they caught sight of their ‘leader’ walking towards them, bag slung over his shoulder.

Brad smiled as he walked up to meet his friends, he had known them for most of his life and they had grown up very close. Jack Mills was Brad’s best friend; they had lived next door to each other for a few years and become ‘blood brothers’ one summer. Jonjo Tait although small was a tenacious little character who anyone would like stood next to them in a fight. Tasha, although a girl was both scary and alluring, sometimes it confused Brad in his feelings for her. Finally Louis Carr, he was the brains of the operation - if that wasn’t too much to say - but he was as equally adept at getting them into trouble as out of it.

“Alright guys, how’s school?” Brad said through a beaming smile.

Jonjo punched him lightly on the arm. “Same shit as always mate.”

“No one has burnt the place down yet.” Tasha added.

Brad and the others laughed.

“Maybe one day Tasha,” Brad lowered his voice, “we’ll give it a proper burning!”

Louis slapped the bag Brad was carrying. "You off on your hols then Brad?"

Jack put his arm across Brad's back and pulled him closer. "Magaluf man!" he shouted.

The others all laughed at Jack, he was always hyperactive and a fair mix of AHD and Dyslexia only added to his fiery personality.

Brad set the bag down on the floor in the middle of the group. "Well folks, this is my life in a bag." He pointed down to the blue and white Adidas holdall.

"What you on about?" Louis interjected.

"I've left home."

The group fell silent.

People walking along the street veered around the group, their reputation preceded them.

Tasha was the first to speak, "Has something happened?"

"Were you kicked out?" Jonjo chipped in.

Brad thought for a couple of seconds and remembered the money sitting in his pocket. "Let's just say it was mutual consent mate," he smiled sarcastically. "They didn't want me there anymore and I didn't want to stay anymore."

Jack gently put his hand on Brad's shoulder. "Is it because you stayed at mine last night?"

"You mean spliff city?" Tasha joked.

"No mate, but as old man Williams likes to say 'it was the straw that broke the camel's back'."

Everyone started laughing at Brad's comment. He wasn't bothered about his knew predicament.

"You remember shit like that but you can't do your five times table?" Jonjo said, taking another drag of his cigarette. A quick slap across the back of his head startled him as Tasha gave him a nasty look.

"You're right Jonjo, I haven't got a clue what my five times table is," he looked around the group. "But now I don't need to know, do I?"

Again he burst out laughing. Leaning over he ruffled Jonjo's hair.

The laughter subsided and then Brad reached into his pocket, pulling out a twenty pound note. "Come on guys, dinner is on me."

A great cheer went up from the group.

"Yeah, let's go and see how the Muslims are getting on," Jack squealed.

They all turned and looked through the shop front window at the owners and headed for the door.

1210hrs

Inside the shop, Ali gave one last pleading look towards his wife, with no response. He shrugged and then headed towards the front of the shop just as the gang of youths entered.

As Jonjo reached the door, cigarette in mouth, Ali Bhendazi held up his hand. "No smoking in the shop please."

Jonjo flicked his cigarette on the ground outside before turning and blowing his final mouthful of smoke at Mr Bhendazi, then ducked under his arm and heading up the first aisle.

As Ali Bhendazi finished coughing he turned and glanced around the shop. He could put up with verbal abuse; he had grown used to it. It was his wife he worried about, she was quite young and being recently arrived from Bangladesh she was naïve to the ways of some English people. He quickly circled around the back of the aisles heading for the toiletries and medicines section.

The stacks of shelving stood about five feet tall but with various household items sat on top they hid most of what was happening in the furthest aisle.

He quickly stopped and turned looking to where three lads were closely gathered around the condoms, a usual occurrence. He often wondered if these spotty, unsociable boys would actually have the need for these items. Happy that they were not trying to steal anything he backtracked slightly and noticed the other two up the neighbouring aisle. A girl and the boy he thought was the leader whispering and nudging each other looking towards the counter where his wife was standing.

As Ali moved up the aisle towards them the two youngsters made a sudden move away from him towards the counter. Just as they reached the end of the aisle they stopped dead in their tracks and Ali's momentum forced him to nudge into Brad's bag, still slung over his shoulder.

"Oi, watch it fella!" Brad exclaimed.

Tasha pulled Brad out of the way allowing Ali to get past. "You're not one of them extremists are you?" she smiled at Brad as she spoke.

"What are you talking about young lady?" Ali responded as he finally reached the counter and turned to face them. He was suddenly aware of how tall and broad the lad was. He also saw the look of distaste on the girl's face, something he had now grown accustomed to.

"You know, Muslim extremists," she gave a little chuckle as the other three walked up to the side of the counter.

Ali Bhendazi realised there was no-one else in the shop apart from himself, his wife and these five youngsters. He looked around and saw how grey and dreary the inside of the shop looked. He had chosen the décor hoping his wife would want to spruce it up when she arrived to live with him and help him with the shop. She wasn't interested. Now he thought it looked very pale as he glanced around before focussing again on the five smirking faces stood around him.

"And why do you think I am a Muslim?"

This produced more bemusement amongst the intimidating youths who now held him at bay.

It was Jack who spoke up next, "Aren't all you Pakis, Muslims then?" Followed by more laughing.

"I am not from Pakistan," he looked around as he spoke, "I am English."

The group gathered closer to him but didn't respond with laughter this time. It was more astonishment on their faces.

Again it was Jack Mills who spoke, "How can you be English then?"

"Because I was born here," he folded his arms with pride, "In Ashton."

Jonjo was now stood to the side of Ali Bhendazi and he peeled up the sleeve of his school jumper revealing his milk-bottle white arm underneath. He stuck out his arm next to Ali's, the others all looked, including Ali, at the difference in skin colour.

"Not exactly the same, is it?" Jonjo said.

The youngsters all laughed. Ali's wife spoke to him quickly in their native tongue, worry showing in her voice.

Ali answered quietly but assertively. She did not want them in the shop and thought she might call the police. She was very scared. Ali tried his best to calm her saying the police would only make things worse.

Tasha saw the look of fear in Venisha Bhendazi's eyes and picked up on the theme of their conversation, "What's up then, your old lady scared or something?"

"She was just wondering why you have all come in here today if you are not going to buy anything?" Ali replied.

Brad now stepped into the conversation as he rounded on the hapless shop owner. "We can go where we like, this is our country."

Ali was now on the back foot, he had tried to be polite but being faced with this racism and the brashness of these 'kids' he was getting worried. If only his wife had not been so close he would try to throw this lot out. He wished that his brother had been here but a quick glance at his watch showed him that was still hours away. He casually turned around to his young wife and asked her to go into the back storeroom and stay there. She made to protest but there was the determined look in her husband's eyes and she started to move from behind the counter.

At a nod from Brad, Jack quickly stepped back and blocked her escape route.

"Is you missus trying to do a runner there mate?" Brad quipped.

Anxiety suddenly showed in Ali Bhendazi's voice, "No, I have just asked her to do some work in the storeroom," he paused, gesturing to the shelves in front of him. "We need to restock."

The others looked around the shelves seeing them full. Like a pack of wolves circling their prey they could smell the fear.

"Shelves look pretty well stocked to me?" Jonjo laughed as he spoke.

The tension was mounting now. The gang had no idea what they were going to do, they were just responding to the situation. Ali could feel sweat trickling down his brow. He looked nervously at his wife who stood stock still, her eyes pleading with him.

He took half a step backwards feeling his back touch the counter. He felt as if he was suffocating. From somewhere deep inside, his desire for survival kicked in, adrenalin raced through his body, a cornered animal. "I would like you all to leave now, quickly!"

The sudden resilience in his voice caught the youngsters by surprise. They started sharing anxious glances.

Brad tried to regain control of the situation. "What if we want to buy something?"

Just then the doorbell above the door tinkled. Two hefty looking men walked in, dressed in builders gear; cement-stained trousers, builders boots and hi-vis vests.

"Morning Ali," one of the men waved as he cut left up the first aisle.

"Good morning Pete," Ali felt a surge of relief. "Got much on today?"

The two men were now at the fridges at the far end of the shop, searching for their lunch.

"Still working on those new houses up by the railway station," Pete replied.

Time seemed to slow for the seven people gathered around the counter.

The other man started walking up the aisle behind where Brad and Tasha stood, looking around nervously.

"Is this your fan club then Ali?" he asked.

The gang started moving towards the shop door now, all momentum lost.

"Not exactly," Ali replied.

The second man saw the fear in Venisha's eyes and realised this group of kids had something to do with that.

Even as large in build as Brad was, the man now standing opposite the counter filled the end of the aisle. His massive tattooed arms and shaven head gave him a menacing look.

The five young people continued moving towards the door and started to leave. Just as Brad passed the end of the counter he quickly slapped the lottery card carousel, making it spin round quickly and it teetered, without falling. He glanced around at Ali Bhendazi, "See you later Mr Muslim," and with that he was out the door and gone.

1230hrs

A few moments of silence followed as the situation subsided.

“You okay Missus B?” Pete asked as he joined his friend at the counter.

She was now shaking and Ali quickly went behind the counter to comfort her.

The carousel slowed to a stop.

The second builder, who was called Dave Murray, placed his items on the counter. “I know a couple of their Dads from the club, I can have a word if you like?”

Ali looked up from his wife and shook his head, “No thanks Dave, it will only cause more trouble in the future.”

Pete placed his milk and sandwiches next to his friends. “It would be a lot easier if they were all in bloody school,” he remarked, then corrected himself. “Apologies Missus B, for the language.”

Venisha let out a nervous laugh and tears started to roll down her cheeks.

Friday 26 April

It was another cold and frosty morning. Spring was an amazing time of year as winter disappeared, new life was born and plants emerged from the cold. Living in the more rural areas of England made this time more magical, especially in the villages and towns of Northumberland, England's most beautiful county.

Ashton was such a place, well in parts. Like most of the country it had its nice areas and its less delightful areas.

On the northern edge of the town a new housing estate was springing up. Next to it the older 1930's houses looked ancient, some had boarded up windows, others garden wildernesses. On the outskirts of this built-up area was Woodley Gardens and partway along this terraced row – the house of the Mills family. Father, who worked in a pharmaceutical plant, Mother, who was a nurse in the local general hospital. Their son Jack had been a difficult birth, the reason he was to become an only child. He was a good lad at heart but his parents worried about his future. While some of his friends had been part of the 'big exclusion', Jack was still attending school, quite intelligent but not expecting great grades. They weren't happy about his friendship with Brad Jones but they didn't want to block it as they feared losing him. They tried to keep a close eye on him but he had started staying out late and when he came in they could smell cigarette smoke on his clothes.

Now to further infuriate them he had turned up the previous night with Brad in tow. Apparently Brad had been kicked out of his own house by his parents.

Jack had promised it would only be for a night or two until Brad got sorted.

0735hrs

Early in the morning, Jack woke. He opened his eyes slowly, taking in his surroundings. He stretched and stifled a yawn then rolled onto his side.

Lying on the floor in an old sleeping bag lay his best friend Brad. Jack smiled and reached across to his bedside table, grabbing a bottle of water that sat there. He slowly and quietly undid the top and held it over Brad's head. He slowly tipped it, sprinkling water over his face.

Brad woke suddenly screaming. "Hoi, what's going on?"

Jack continued laughing as he twisted the lid back onto the bottle and flung it over the other side of the room, "Wakey wakey, mate," he scoffed from his perch on the bed.

That soon changed as Brad stretched up and pulled Jack's quilt with all his strength. Jack tumbled to the floor, falling in between Brad and the bed legs.

Brad quickly put his arm round his friend's neck and held it tight. "So who's the funny guy now then?"

"Okay Brad, you win," he tapped him on the arm, their sign of submission. Brad always won as he was a lot stronger than other lads his age.

"What was that anyway?"

"Pee," Jack laughed.

"You're joking?" came the response.

"Course I am," replied his friend. "It was just water."

Brad sat up and stretched.

Jack turned and sat with his back to the door. "Was it comfy enough last night on the floor?"

"Not bad," he stretched again, joints clicking, "Need to find something more permanent though."

Jack got up slowly and headed over to a chest of drawers and started fishing around for something to wear. "Any idea where you are going to live?"

"Not thought that far ahead yet mate."

As Jack pulled a t-shirt over his head he came up with an idea. He sat back on his bed and Brad flopped onto a bean bag pulling on a sock. He looked up at his friend and saw the puzzled expression on his face.

"What's up mate, you got an idea?"

"Hurry up and get dressed, I want to get out of here and show you something."

Brad put on his other sock and pulled a t-shirt out of his backpack.

0755hrs

The two lads now dressed headed down the stairs and into the kitchen.

Jack held the back of his hand against the teapot. The heat made him take his hand away. "Any chance of a brew Mam?" He looked across the room at his mother.

"The pot should have brewed by now son, help yourselves." She managed a smile as she glanced from her son to Brad. Jenny Mills was still troubled by her son's friendship with the notorious Brad Jones.

"Thanks Mrs Mills" Brad said as he grabbed two mugs from the overhead cupboard. "I promise I will be out of your hair soon."

Jenny grabbed the milk out of the fridge, gently closing the door. She walked over to where the lads were standing, Brad spooning two sugars into his cup and then one into Jack's.

"You know you're welcome here Brad," she paused, placing her hand on his shoulder. "As long as you need."

Brad smiled "Don't worry Mrs Mills, I know I need to get myself sorted and out of your hair."

She poured milk into the two cups and almost sighed out loud with relief. Returning the milk to the fridge she felt a little guilty. Glancing back towards the two lads she pressed again, "I mean it Brad, you will always be welcome here," she crossed back towards them taking the bread out of the bread bin. "You've been like a brother to Jack for as long as I can remember. I won't see you out on the streets!"

Brad smiled and quickly kissed her on the cheek, taking her by surprise. "You are a star Mrs Mills. Thanks."

An awkward silence followed before Jack broke the tension, "You better not let my Dad catch you doing that," he said laughing.

His mother's cheeks turned a rosy pink. "Don't be daft Jack, Brad is showing that under all that bravado he has a sensitive side."

They all laughed, Brad getting a slap on the arm from his friend.

Jenny Mills quickly changed the subject. "You lads want some toast?"

"Yes please Mam," Jack beamed.

"Got any marmite?" Brad chipped in.

The lads finished their tea and toast while watching the sports news. They were in good spirits and Brad could sense that Jack was holding out on him.

They took their cups and plates back through to the kitchen.

Jenny Mills was sorting out her weekly wash into different piles. "What you lads going to do now?"

As he picked up his school bag Jack turned to smile at his Mother. "Don't worry Mam, Brad is going to walk with me to school then he's got some things to sort out."

He straightened up and tucked his shirt in before leaning over the table to peck his mother on the cheek. "I'll see you at tea time Mam."

And with that he headed for the door dragging Brad with him.

0820hrs

As the two lads reached the end of the street Jack took a quick look backwards and then headed left, walking quickly, Brad behind him. It took a few seconds for Brad to catch up with his friend. They were now dodging through the early morning pedestrian traffic, mainly heading towards the school.

When Brad finally caught up with his friend he grabbed his arm. "Where are we going mate?"

"You'll see." Jack avoided a small group of young students, "Watch it, you lot!" He forced them to scatter with a swing of his bag.

After a few minutes the two lads turned up a narrow side street. The houses were older here, the gardens smaller.

It was quieter; nobody else was on the street. "Nice and quiet up here mate." Jack said in a whisper. "Lots of oldies live around here."

“I know that Jack, that’s why we call this place the graveyard!” he sounded annoyed now. “What have you brought me here for?”

They stopped in front of number fifteen. Jack turned to his friend, “I have to come here three or four times a week to feed the fish and on a weekend to clean them out,” he smiled. “Oh and water the plants too.”

Brad looked from Jack to the front of the house and back to Jack. “You do realise I’m going to thump you in a minute.”

Jack’s response was to dangle a key in front of him. “Let’s go in.” And with that he set off up the garden path.

Brad sighed, but eventually followed him more out of curiosity than anything else.

A quick twist of the key and the front door opened, crushing some letters and a copy of the local free newspaper under its trim. The two lads entered, Jack scooping to pick up the debris from the entrance way. Brad followed him into the first door on the right. It was dark inside, the curtains still closed. He clicked on the light just as Jack threw his bag onto the couch and collapsed into a big, black recliner. He leaned back, clicked a lever and the front raised up lifting his legs off the carpet.

Brad, still bewildered, sat on the small chair opposite looking around at the room’s contents. Apart from the couch and two chairs there was a cabinet, a glass-topped mahogany coffee table and a small bookcase in the corner. Photo frames adorned every available flat surface. Then he spotted a big, grinning face he recognised on one of the photos, Jack. “How come your ugly mug is in that picture?” He pointed across at the cabinet.

Jack looked across and smiled. “This is my Gran’s place.”

“So where is your Gran then?” Brad asked.

“She is still in hospital,” he paused as he clicked his reclining chair back into the upright position. “Remember I told you she had gone in for a heart operation?”

Brad leaned forward in his chair. “Of course, I remember you telling me. The op went okay though didn’t it?”

“Oh yeah, no problems but she has to stay in for a few weeks being monitored and stuff.”

“So?”

“You can crash here mate, no dramas!” Jack beamed.

"What if your Mam or Dad come round?"

"You're joking, my Mam and Dad come round this estate? No chance!"

He got up and grabbed his backpack. "My Mam hardly came round to visit my Gran when she was in, no way would she come round here when she sees her in the hospital."

Brad sat up, deep in thought.

"Don't worry mate, I am the only one who comes round here, only one with the key."

They both laughed.

The lads had a walk round the house and Brad got his bag put into the spare bedroom. The décor generally was old fashioned but he wasn't complaining. "This is great Jack."

"Spot on for you mate, all the bills are sorted through the old girl's pension and benefits."

In the kitchen they looked through the fridge freezer and cupboards. Their search produced some tins and packets still in date, enough to tide him over.

"Got some stuff here to keep me going too."

"How are you for cash?"

"I'll be okay. Parents gave me some when I left yesterday."

"Out of guilt?" Jack ventured.

"No, I think they want to see me okay, even Dad dug into his pocket."

Jack put his arm around his best friend's shoulder. "You know they both love you to bits Brad?"

"I know mate, they just don't want me being a bad influence over our Tom."

"He's a good kid, he'll be fine." Jack closed the final cupboard door.

"Especially with me not there," he said painfully.

"I'll keep an eye on him at school mate."

As they both walked back into the living room and crashed into the seats Jack had a thought, "I should text Jonjo and get him to cover for me in registration."

"Don't bother," Brad chipped in. "You go on in, so you don't get any grief off your Mam."

"You sure?"

"Yeah."

"I don't mind spending the day with you mate, got to be better than double English with Hedley!"

"Ha-ha, you love it." Brad threw one of the cushions across the room. Jack picked it up and tossed it back. It bounced off the arm of the chair and crashed into the cabinet, knocking one of the photo frames over. Brad caught it before it hit the floor and gently put it back where it had stood for a long time. Some dust rose in a cloud from the cabinet surface. Brad blew across the surface and huge plumes of dust flew into the air.

"I might give this place a quick clean over today."

"You, do some cleaning?" Jack said jokingly.

"Yeah, I help my Mam out with the cleaning on a Saturday," he paused, thinking. "Well, I used to anyway. I'll nip to the shop later and get some stuff," Brad said.

Jack picked up his bag ready to leave "You mean after you've done the cleaning?" And with a laugh Jack slapped his friend on the back "Once you've done the dishes you can watch Sky Sports on the box."

"Your Gran has Sky Sports?"

"Yep, she never got rid of it after Granda passed. I came over to watch the Toon games."

"Cool." Brad flopped into the comfy recliner, grabbing the sky remote control. "The cleaning might have to wait."

The friends parted.

1855hrs

Later that day Brad was standing on the corner of the street where Woodley Gardens met Second Avenue. Just as he was finishing his second cigarette he ducked back behind the wall as a door opened part of the way along the street. Out of the house came his Father.

Brad knew his routine, up the club for a few pints and a game of darts or bingo with the lads. He knew his routine off by heart and after giving him a few minutes to get away he walked towards the house.

At the door he stood for a few seconds, he closed the door loudly, to let it register. "It's just me, Brad!"

The living room door opened and his Mother stood there, head tilted to one side and a huge smile on her face.

"Hello son, what brings you back?"

"Just popped back for some clothes Mam."

"You just missed your Dad."

"Yeah, I know, I saw him head up to the club." Brad walked up and gave his Mother a quick hug. They looked at each other and smiled. The silence seemed to go on for a while until a couple of footsteps and a shout came from upstairs.

"Hi Brad," his brother stood at the top of the stairs, crouching slightly to see Brad. "Can I have your room?"

All three of them burst out laughing at the comment.

"Course you can Tom." He looked back at his Mother. "Keep an eye on him Mam, and don't let him turn out like me!"

Wednesday 1 May
0830hrs

Ian Taylor squinted as he opened the last of the blinds in his form room. The sunlight beamed in through the slats and filled the room. His form class, normally quite chatty, were very subdued this morning. He heard the odd murmur as he returned to his desk and tapped the space bar to switch his screen on.

He sat, looking around at the faces of his tutor group. He knew them all very well now; in the second year he had been their tutor he had nursed their injuries, listened to their thoughts and dreams, spoken to and met each of their parents and siblings. Today though his expression was downcast. He started to take the register on his laptop. By the end he had nine missing and he had only received one sick call from a mother. He had noticed this trend over the last week or so. More and more students not turning up, no reason, no excuse.

He looked up. "Jenny, do you know where Olivia is today?" He smiled. "She was in yesterday."

Jenny Thomson was caught a little unawares, "I don't know Sir."

"Don't you normally revise with her on Tuesday nights?"

"Yes Sir, I went over last night but I didn't stay long," she looked down to her desk.

"Why not, was she ill?" He got up from behind his desk and moved towards a now worried looking young girl. She shifted uncomfortably as though guarding some long-lost secret.

She lowered her voice in reply. "Her Mam and Dad were arguing, about school I think."

Ian Taylor slid into the seat opposite Jenny. "Did you hear exactly what they were saying?"

Jenny took a deep breath. "I think her Dad wanted her to come in but her Mam was scared."

"Scared?"

“Yeah, she wanted her to stay at home and get work from school.”

He slumped a little in his seat. Was this what he had feared when the government had put its new strategies in place? Getting rid of all the disruptive students just moved the disruption onto the streets. The ‘Good’ kids were now going to suffer and they would be outside the protection of the school environment.

“Can I ask you why her mother thinks like that?” He knew the answer but just wanted confirmation.

“I’m not exactly sure,” she paused unsure as to whether to explain or not. “I did go to collect her one morning last week to come to school but I couldn’t reach her house.”

Taylor looked puzzled, “Why not?”

“There was a gang of kids at the end of her street and I couldn’t get through, they wouldn’t let me.” Jenny shrugged her shoulders and Ian Taylor noticed that her lip was trembling slightly.

“I had to text Olivia to explain that I would meet her outside school.”

“What did she do?”

“She texted back a few minutes later saying her Mam said she would stop her coming in. Her Mam drove her in that day though.”

Ian Taylor slowly raised himself out of the chair and made his way back to his desk. As he sat down he tapped his space bar to open his screen again and then typed in his password. He quickly clicked onto his school email account and entered the email address of the Head Teacher. He paused as he gathered his thoughts before typing ‘Absent Students’ as the title and moved to the text section. ‘Morning Joanne, I am growing worried about the amount of absences in my tutor group. I have 9 out today with only one absence call. These are kids who are regular attenders; in fact four of them had 100% attendance so far this term. I have just heard a disturbing account as to why one of my top students has not come in today. There was a gang of youths at the bottom of her street last week stopping other young people getting past.

Have we made a rod for our own backs?’

He finished and quickly read back through the contents. He slowly shook his head as he hit the ‘Enter’ key, slowly closing the lid of his laptop.

0845hrs

It was a bright, chilly morning. Joanne Tindell wrapped her jacket tightly around her as she stood in the car park, looking at the front of 'her' school. A shiver ran down her spine. Was it the cold or the numerous emails and phone calls she had received over the last few days? Some of her colleagues were worried; others were starting to panic. Attendance figures were declining, rapidly.

She stamped her feet and wrapped her arms around herself a little tighter. As she looked up she smiled as she saw her friend and head of year ten, Sheryl Townsend, coming through the main entrance.

"Hi Jo, are you okay?" Sheryl asked.

"Yes, just taking a moment to think."

Sheryl walked up and gave her friend a little nudge, "And what brings you outside to think in weather like this?"

Joanne turned to face her friend. "Oh, I just wanted to get out of the office for a bit." She felt herself slump a little.

Her friend noticed and put out a consoling arm. "I have been bombarded with phone calls and emails for the past few days."

"Worried teachers?"

"Yes, very worried. School numbers are down."

"I had noticed the slightly smaller classes."

Joanne looked her friend straight in the eye, "I checked the average figures earlier, and it is over 28 per cent!"

"You're joking, 28 per cent? More than a quarter of the students aren't coming in!" The shock was evident in Sheryl Townsend's voice.

Joanne nodded towards the door and the two of them turned and started to slowly walk towards it. She linked her friend's arm and continued in a quieter tone, "Even if we take into account the normal absences like sickness, appointments or even the skivers that normally only accounts for two or three per cent."

She pulled open the door allowing her colleague in. "It still shows a quarter of the kids are being kept away."

"Or being forced to stay away?"

"I know," replied Joanne. "I have heard about that too. I have a meeting with the governors tonight to discuss what we can do."

They walked up the corridor acknowledging people with a nod, a smile or a 'good morning' as they passed.

As they turned left onto the main corridor Sheryl spoke quietly. "What can the police do?"

"I spoke to them last night," another sigh. "They say there is very little they can do. They can break up some of the groups that are blocking routes to the school but they don't have the manpower to keep that up constantly, only the mornings."

"What do you think the governors will say?"

They turned and walked up the stairs to the first floor. A1 sized pictures adorned the walls. Mainly of students in lessons, smiling, being happy. Would those days ever return again?

As they reached the top of the stairs Sheryl stopped and turned to face her friend. "Let me know how you get on later with the governors meeting, I'll be in all night."

Joanne gave Sheryl a quick hug before she responded. "Thanks Sheryl, I will give you a quick call when I get home."

She turned and stepped into her office, "See you later."

Sheryl headed up the corridor towards the school's inclusion zone.

1230hrs

The lunch bell was just ten minutes away but to John Reynolds it seemed like a lifetime. He was with his year eleven engineer class and it was not the easiest of groups. Even though the recent exclusions had removed two or three of the worst behaviour cases, the smaller group had become more resilient to any school punishments. They mobbed together and refused to follow any instructions their teacher gave them.

John Reynolds had restricted them to the bottom end of the classroom but they were starting to meander through the machines towards the other end of the room. John was tired of having to raise his voice and fleetingly thought of just letting them continue their progress, but he had a built-in safety valve, as he liked to think.

"Okay guys, far enough!" he walked straight up the middle of the room, blocking the narrow passage at the end. "Back to your seats please. Now!" Two of the lads circled around and slowly twisted and turned their way back to the seated area of the classroom. The other two had different ideas though. Corey Taylor jumped up and sat on a workbench clearly aiming to wind up his teacher whilst the other lad, Kyle Wanless started moving the pillar drill up and down, jamming into the steel plate at its base.

John turned his attention to Corey. Walking up to him he asked, "Come on Corey, fun's over, back to your seat mate."

"I'm not your mate!" He responded. Jumping down from the bench he turned and headed back in the general direction of his seat.

John Reynolds turned quickly as he heard one of the machines powered up. It was the pillar drill with Kyle Wanless at the controls. As he quickly covered the ground to the machine and hit the power off switch, Kyle had already moved on to the centre lathe and just as the pillar drill powered down, the centre lathe whirred into life.

John Reynolds' patience was now being stretched to the limit. As he made a move to reach the power switch, Kyle Wanless dodged in the opposite direction heading for two other machines. John knew he wasn't quick enough to stop him so he stopped, looking around at the other students. All eyes were on the two of them but at least they were all still seated.

He came up with a plan. He moved slowly around the lathe, hitting the off switch. As Kyle circled the other way, John quickly backtracked towards the opposite wall. Every student was now watching John Reynolds. He turned quickly and hit the large, red, main cut off switch. This switch killed all the power to the room effectively cutting off any plans Kyle had for further misbehaviour.

John walked back over towards Kyle holding out his hands in front of him, hoping to calm him down. "Fun's over Kyle, come and join the rest of the lads and wait for the bell?"

Kyle was cornered, he wasn't happy that Mr Reynolds had stopped his fun. He quickly looked at his classmates and back to his teacher. He would not be shown up by this old git. Kyle made a final move towards the tools cupboard but Reynolds was one move ahead and quickly dodged sideways to block him.

The rest of the class started to stand for a better view as it was blocked by some of the machines.

The two protagonists collided as they reached the cupboard. Reynolds held out his arms to prevent Kyle from being able to reach any of the myriad of tools held there.

"No you don't Kyle," Reynolds gave a worried cry. "Back to your seat, now!"

He moved forward with his arms held out to the side forcing Kyle back but Kyle tripped and stumbled into the Router machine.

As Kyle tried to right himself John Reynolds leaned forward intent on helping him, he grabbed Kyle's arm. Kyle saw red and just as he grabbed the edge of the bench with his left hand he forced his weight back up and threw himself into Mr Reynolds. The resulting collision knocked the teacher over and he flipped back, striking his head off the edge of the cabinet. A collected groan came from the rest of the class as John Reynolds hit the floor.

As he lay still for a few seconds different emotions fired through Kyle: fear, panic, sorrow.

Suddenly John Reynolds started to stir.

Kyle stepped back, still looking down at the prone teacher. "It was an accident, I swear down!"

He turned to look at his mates, seated to his left.

All he got in return was a few despairing looks and a shake of the head from Ronnie, one of his best friends.

John Reynolds sat up and tried to clear his head. He put his left hand up to the side of his head then took it away and looked at it. Red. Covered in blood!

Suddenly a deep-set survival instinct kicked in with Kyle. He looked down at his teacher and saw the blood. He hurdled the gap between teacher and bench. He had reached the door and was through before Reynolds could bring himself to speak, "Kyle, wait. It's okay!"

Kyle was now heading past the main hall, pausing only as he bumped into two students carrying piles of brightly yellow-coloured textbooks between classrooms. One pile of textbooks was knocked flying producing a mumbled curse from the young year nine student who had been carrying them.

Kyle now turned right towards the main entrance. The adrenaline was pumping. He kept getting an image in his mind of Mr Reynolds lying on the floor – blood oozing from a head wound. He suddenly looked down at his own hands, expecting to see blood.

What did Miss Lesley in English call it? The blood on his hands was metaphorical. He passed the main office, through the door and arrived at the main entrance. A postman pressed the buzzer to get into the building: Kyle pushed the blue, plunger-like button to release the electric locking mechanism. As the postman, carrying two large parcels opened the door Kyle barged past and was running again. As he cleared the steps which led to the main door he took one final glance over his shoulder, expecting to see members of the school staff chasing him. There was no one. He was free.

Not until he was two streets away up Highland Close did he come to a stop, gasping for air.

1802hrs

Joanne Tindell stood up as the final member of her Senior Leadership Team walked in. She surveyed the faces sat around her large meeting table. She could see the angst on some faces, the tiredness showed through on others and not a single soul was smiling?

A quick glance down at her planning folder showed the notes she had prepared for this emergency meeting but she hesitated, thinking.

She jumped, lurching back into reality as Will McCormack spoke up. "Joanne?" a short pause followed, giving her the time to quickly catch her breath. "What have we got on the agenda for tonight then?"

She smiled. "Thanks Will, sorry ladies and gents but I have a lot on my mind. Some of which I want to transfer to you."

Joanne sat down and ruffled various sheets of paper she had stacked in front of her. The others' eyes were on her now, she was glad that today she had decided to wear her formal dress suit. She straightened up the smart black collar and gathered her thoughts. A quick glance up showed the time fast approaching 6:10PM. She heard the click, click, and click as the second hand circled the flat white surface.

"Thank you for coming tonight, I know this was going to be an SLT meeting but an event today has forced me to ask for a nominal appearance of our governors." She paused to look at the top sheet of the pile on her desk.

"I would like to thank Evelyn, Carrianne, John and Jimmy for coming in at such notice." She nodded towards each of them, "We have four out of seven governors present so any decision we make can be ratified tonight!"

She sat and flicked over the top sheet of paper maintaining her air of authority. "This meeting was originally called to discuss the dramatic fall in attendance the past few months."

Tom Cawthorne who was making notes on the meeting interjected, "Should I still enter 'Low Attendance' as the theme of the meeting?" He looked back towards the Head.

"Yes Tom." She thought for a moment, "We will use the incident as an addendum."

"Thanks Joanne, I have everyone's name and absences, ready to go."

"Okay, well I have had figures produced and you all have a copy in front of you showing the rapid decline." Joanne paused to allow the nine people present to have a quick look through the hand-outs.

The meeting continued for another fifteen minutes with various members of both the SLT and the governors having a say, putting forward recommendations but mostly listening intently. The mood in the room darkened as the end of debate approached and conclusions were reached. Reducing some classes and combining others were the main outcomes reached. All of the decisions made would be enforced either immediately or after half term at the end of the month.

An eerie period of silence followed as those present gathered their notes and hand-outs. There was the odd whispered comment but the atmosphere in the room was subdued. Joanne Tindell had had enough of this; she had seen it all afternoon since the incident. People whispering in corners, looks of disdain, no more!

"Okay now for the addendum to the meeting." Joanne stood up suddenly, catching some of the group off guard.

She wanted to meet this situation head on and not be seen as shying away from it. "Today during period three a student assaulted John Reynolds in DT3. He was taken to hospital where he received 13 sutures to a head wound."

She slowly set off on a slow lap of the table and its occupants whilst she continued to talk. "John is now at home where I am going to visit him either tonight or first thing in the morning. The student, Kyle Wanless, has still to be located. We have police and relatives out looking for him at this time and I am sure he will be found soon enough."

Tom spoke up, "He was never the brightest boy."

"Yes Tom, so hopefully he will soon be in custody."

This caused a sharp intake of breath from several of those sat around the large Victorian oak table, a gift to Joanne from her father. He had used it as a meeting table himself when he had been a Head Teacher.

Joanne was now back behind her seat. "Oh, don't worry young Mr Wanless will receive the full weight of the law."

Jimmy Duffy an ex-pupil and popular local business owner commented, "Damn right Joanne, the little bugger should be locked up."

Immediately to his right sat Evelyn Williams, the presiding member of the Local Women's Institute, "You can't want the young child locked up, surely?"

Jimmy responded immediately, "He attacked a teacher Evelyn, what do you expect us to do?" He leaned a little closer to his old friend gently tapping her on the back as he said, "Pat him on the back and say there, there?"

The room grew quiet, that last expression hung in the air.

Sheryl Townsend broke the silence, "The main thing is that we find Kyle and make sure he is safe before we start thinking of how we can punish him."

2005hrs

The trauma of the day had given way to exhaustion for John Reynolds as his taxi pulled up to the driveway of 16 Castle Terrace. He paid and thanked the taxi driver and then turned to face his house as the taxi slowly pulled away. He noticed that the lawn needed trimming and the rose bushes surrounding two sides of the lawn could do with some pruning.

As he set off up the path he saw the curtains twitch back into place. He slowed and took a deep breath as the door swung open. There stood his wife, Tracey and behind her he could see his son, Tom and his daughter, Kath. "I'm okay, don't worry," he said as he approached the door.

Tracey reached out to hug him. "Too late darling, lots of worrying has been done already."

They hugged, holding each other tightly. The light from the hall forced John to squint a little. He looked down and smiled at his young daughter, stood behind her mother, looking up at him.

He slowly pulled away from his wife and looked up the hall at his son who was standing in the doorway to the living room. "Are you okay Tom?" He asked.

"Fine Dad, what about you?"

"Bit of a headache that's all," John replied as he half turned and closed the door. Tracey let out a little gasp as she noticed the ugly line of staples running down the back of her husband's head. Together with the badly shaved hair surrounding it, it probably looked worse than it was.

"Your head looks a bit nasty there love?"

"It's not too bad, any news on the lad yet?" John asked.

"Why are you bothered about him Dad, after what he did to you?" Tom asked, approaching his Dad.

John moved further into the hall and spoke quietly to his son, "It was an accident really Tom, he just tried to barge past me!"

Tom sounded a little annoyed now, "Have you seen the mess he has made of your head Dad?"

"I'm okay," he tried to appease his son.

But his wife spoke up, "Tom's right John." She linked her husband's arm and led him into the kitchen. "It wasn't an accident, he caused your injury, and he should be punished!"

John sat at the kitchen table: his wife clicked the kettle on. His son Tom sat next to him but they all turned back towards the door when Kath commented, "Does it hurt Daddy?"

John held out his arms for his daughter as she approached him and then she climbed up onto his lap.

"It hurts a little bit darling, but Daddy is okay." He gave her a hug.

"Are you going in to work tomorrow John?" Tracey asked.

"I should think so."

"What if you're not feeling well?"

"Then I might just have to pop in to give a statement and see Joanne."

Tracey looked surprised. "Joanne, has she called you then?"

"No, she popped in for five minutes just before I left the hospital."

"Well that's good news; she will get the situation sorted."

John shrugged. "That's what she was saying. Anyway love, is there any chance of a cup of tea?"

Tracey smiled as she picked some cups off the mug tree, relief showing on her face.

Monday 13 May

The previous two weeks had shown a steady build-up of tension in Ashton High School. The fall-out from the attack on John Reynolds had seen a new strictness and lack of tolerance encompass the whole school. Teachers and staff who were in the past seen as friendly and a little lenient with the rules were now united in a wall of resistance.

The majority of young people now noticed that they could not get away with anything. The Senior Leadership Team seemed to be constantly roaming the corridors telling students to 'do their ties up', 'get to lessons' and generally being annoying, as many students viewed them.

0920hrs

The facility set aside to place the more unruly pupils was called the 'Inclusion Zone'. Students could spend a day, part of a day or in more serious cases longer periods of time in here. Today it was a little lively, 'a full house' as the Inclusion Officer, Tommy Johnson liked to say - eight students in all. He was a large amiable man but did not suffer fools easily and the students despatched to spend time in his domain knew where the line was drawn. The room consisted of eight bays with a desk and chair facing the wall. Each person seated could not see or interact with any other student. The centrally placed desk allowed the Inclusion Officer or the member of staff on duty to see every student.

Tom Cawthorne has come to check on his year eleven students currently being kept in inclusion.

"Morning, Mr Cawthorne. How are you?" asked Tommy Johnson.

"Hi Tommy, oh I am fine, just come to check on the two lads I have in here," he replied.

"You need to have a word with two of your girls too?" Tommy gestured to a pair of young girls sat at opposite sides of the room, Lauren Hayton and Megan Small.

Tom pulled up one of the spare chairs and sat next to one of the girls. "Lauren, what have you been up to?"

"It wasn't my fault Mr Cawthorne, it was Megan." She lowered her voice a little as she finished her sentence.

Megan had still heard her. "You lying bitch!" She got out of her chair to cross the room.

Tommy, used to the behaviour in his room was quickly out of his seat and blocked her path.

Megan grew more annoyed, "She's lying Sir; don't believe a word she says!"

Tom stood up now. "Megan, just sit down," he pointed to her chair, now lying on the floor. "I'll come and speak to you in a minute." He gestured again. Megan slowly turned and went back to her booth, picking up her chair and sitting down, with attitude.

Tom turned back to Lauren, "What started all this?"

"Well she fancies a guy who asked me out, so I went out with him. I didn't know she fancied him, honest."

"You two are as thick as thieves; you must have known how she felt?"

"She fancies loads of lads, we both do. I can't ignore all of them?"

"You probably should have said something before you went out with the boy?"

"It happened suddenly at a party, I didn't have time, she wasn't there."

Tom Cawthorne left them to think and returned to speak to Tommy, "How is Louis doing today?"

"He was well out of order yesterday, as you know and he has just turned up late today."

"Where is he now?" Tom asked as he looked around the room.

"I have just sent him to the toilet to sort himself out. Wrong shoes, no tie, looks like he has just crawled out of his bed." Tommy nodded towards the door as Louis Carr entered.

Tom span round in his chair just in time to see Louis slide into a seat in the corner. "Good morning Louis," he announced.

"Don't start on me today; I can't be fucking bothered with you!" Louis responded.

Tommy Johnson was quickly out of his seat and moving towards the hapless student when Tom Cawthorne grabbed him by the arm and gestured for him to return to his seat. Just as Tommy sat down his colleague leaned over the desk and in a lowered tone spoke, "Just leave it Tommy, I'll go down and chat to Big Will to see about getting him out of here."

"Cheers Tom, he makes this job really difficult."

"I know Tommy, give me an hour."

Tom took a last glance around the room giving the two girls a stern look followed by a smile.

Those two were excellent students and he was so bemused to see them in the Inclusion Zone. He walked out of the room, hopeful of a resolution.

0940hrs

The school corridors were quiet for the early part of the day. The Deputy Head, Will McCormack, popped his head into the main office as soon as he arrived at the school.

"Morning Ladies," his beaming smile lit up the darkened office. "That's me back from my meeting with the middle schools."

Mary Summers, the main school receptionist, looked up from here paperwork. "Hi Will," she smiled back. "I'll book you in. I think Tom is looking for you!"

"Thanks Mary, I'll pop straight in and see him." Will turned into the corridor, stopping outside the second door, the office for the Heads of Year Nine, Ten and Eleven.

Tom Cawthorne was at his desk, scribbling furiously. Across the room sat Pete Thornton, new to the team having just taken on the role of Head of Year Nine.

"Morning guys, has the day started quietly?" he asked cheerfully.

"Not really," replied Pete, spinning around on his chair with a grimace on his face. "We had a near riot in assembly; extra staff had to come into calm everything down." With that he spun back to face his PC. "There will be repercussions though!" He continued rattling away at the keys on his computer keyboard, still muttering under his breath.

"Tom?" He looked toward this friend.

Tom Cawthorne rose slowly from his seat and turned to look at him. "We need to talk," he leaned across and clicked on the kettle, "about Louis Carr?"

"Ah, I wondered when he would raise his horrible head again."

"He needs to be excluded Will." Tom said.

"This will be his third strike you know?"

"I know," Tom looked a little dejected at this.

"I doubt he will go quietly."

"I've left a message with Mam and Dad," Tom shrugged. "They say just to do what we think is best!"

Will slumped in the empty chair at Sheryl Townsend's desk, "Parents have never really been supportive have they?"

"Nope. They will have him full-time now though. Might finally open their eyes."

Will McCormack shuffled uneasily in his chair, "A little late though." He let out a sigh. "Okay then, can we have a coffee first though, I'm parched?"

At that moment the kettle clicked off.

1010hrs

Tom Cawthorne and Will McCormack made their way up the stairs, heading towards the Exclusion Zone. Tom sighed, "I hope he doesn't kick off." He reached in to his pocket to pull out his key card. "I am not in the mood today!"

Will chuckled. "You're never in a good mood."

They reached the top of the stairs and passed the empty Deputy Head's office and then they glanced into the Head Teacher's office as they passed. Joanne Tindell was sat at her desk on the phone, looking busy as normal.

As Tom reached the door to the Inclusion Zone he swiped the access panel and waited for the 'Beep' accompanied by the green light to enter. He turned again towards his friend and whispered, "I wouldn't like to be in her shoes?"

Will, still in a jovial mood responded, "You wouldn't look good in heels?"

"Ha, ha, very funny." Tom pushed open the door to a wall of noise coming from the main Inclusion Office.

Will McCormick entered first and saw that there were too many students in the room, especially with just one member of staff to handle them. Tommy Johnson was trying to calm the more raucous elements down but control was gone.

Now in the doorway Tom Cawthorne started slapping his hand against the metal cabinet just inside the door. It had the desired effect as the noise quelled rapidly.

Will spoke first "Okay everybody, quieten down!"

Silence prevailed.

He continued, "Those of you who were here yesterday sit in the same seats; any new arrivals just stand next to the desk and wait to be allocated a seat."

As the students started to move to their appointed locations Tom Cawthorne moved to the side of the room where Louis Carr was sitting.

"Louis, we need to have a quiet word."

He slowly backed away gesturing Louis to follow.

Looking confused at first Louis started to get out of his seat.

One of the group now stood beside the desk, chair-less, shouted up, "Hey Louis, do you need that chair?"

Louis shrugged his shoulders.

Tom replied, "He won't be needing his seat today."

The boy retorted, "Ha, Ha, they're kicking you out Louis!"

One of the others in the group chipped in, "No exams for you mate, you lucky bugger."

Louis didn't respond but he turned to look at Tom Cawthorne who was still trying to draw him towards the door. Then Louis snapped. "Fuck that, you're not taking me anywhere," he started backing off towards his chair.

Tom realised he had lost the initiative. "Come on Louis, we just want a chat down in the office."

Louis pushed his chair across the room, it glided to a stop against the wall, it's wheels jarring noisily. "I ain't going with you, if you've got something to tell me, do it here." With that he pointed downwards, showing that he wasn't going to move

An unnerving silence followed.

Tom Cawthorne looked across at Will McCormick before breaching the quiet atmosphere, “Louis, we need to talk to you in private, that’s all.”

Some of the other students started getting out of their seats.

An instant later and other chairs were wheeling back and forward across the room.

The two members of the Senior Leadership Team saw that they were losing the situation so moved in for a quick result. Tom Cawthorne put his arm around the young man and started to force him towards the door.

That turned out to be a bad move.

Louis Carr suddenly found he had some allies amongst the other students in the Inclusion Zone.

Chairs were being flipped now and the odd textbook and exercise book was flying through the air.

As Louis’ attention was drawn by a textbook landing loudly on the table next to him, Tom Cawthorne made a final effort to get him towards the door. Just as Will McCormick opened the door and he thought his colleague had made it out with this charge, the remaining students surged forward. As the mass of bodies pushed through the door Tom Cawthorne stumbled and Louis was away, up the corridor. They were past the offices before any members of staff could react.

The Head Teacher was coming up the staircase which caused the group of ‘escapees’ to divert further along the first floor corridor. They burst through the double doors and moved into the first open room they could see, MFL2.

1022hrs

Joanne Tindell stood at the top of the staircase. She stared along the corridor after the group who had just flown past her. Two of her SLT, hot in pursuit. “Tom, what the hell is going on?”

Tom Cawthorne stopped mid-stride and turned, immediately recognising the voice of the Head Teacher. As he did so Will McCormick slowed and looked back. It was just long enough for the group of escapees to close the classroom door and slip the latch. Will turned the handle and pushed but to no avail. He heard some screams from inside, a shout then silence. He turned, leaning back against the wall with a look of exasperation on his face.

Joanne and Tom walked casually up the corridor towards the Languages classroom.

Will sighed, "Sorry Joanne. We were just trying to get Louis Carr out of Inclusion when the whole lot kicked off."

"Not much we could do," Tom cut in. "They just surged towards the door."

"It's okay you two, pressure has been building up in the Inclusion Zone for weeks. Something like this was always going to happen."

"What do we do now then?" Tom looked quizzically from Joanne to Will.

She thought for a few seconds, "Okay Tom, I need to know exactly who is in there, which teacher and class, also a list of those from the Inclusion Zone. I will go down to the Main Office and try and sort out a spare key. Will, stay at the door and try to talk to them – calmly."

She set off back up the corridor towards the stairs. As she turned at the top of the stairs she spoke again, quite firmly, "I want this resolved quickly gentlemen!"

Tom gave Will a knowing glance then headed towards the Deputy Head's office.

Will turned back towards the door and pressed his ear against it for a few seconds trying to hear inside before gently tapping. There was no response. He heard some muffled voices.

"Hello guys, it's Mr McCormick here, we need you to come out. We can talk about this."

A few minutes later and there was still no response.

Tom came back up the corridor. "Okay Will, there are seven kids from Inclusion but we have a small revision group in there doing French with Sally Cowan."

"Okay Tom, go down and tell Joanne, I will keep trying to talk to them."

1024hrs

Joanne Tindell was sorting through the key press in the main office when Tom arrived.

"Joanne, there is a revision class in there with Sally.

Joanne Tindell turned with a set of keys in her hand, "Spare keys for the MFL department, let's go and let them out."

They both left the Main Office. "Here Tom," she handed him the keys. "I'm going round the back to have a look through the windows."

"Okay Joanne, what about the seven 'escapees'?"

"Don't worry about them for now, just get them back into the Inclusion Zone and we can sort them out later."

As Joanne headed out through the Main Hall, Tom ascended the stairs up to the first floor.

1030hrs

Will McCormack was standing with his head against the classroom door, frustrated. He had spoken briefly to Sally Cowan, the language teacher but had soon been shouted down. He turned as he heard Tom approaching and quickly stood up straight.

Tom stopped in front of him. The two old friends gave each other a half smile. "Negotiations failed?" Tom asked.

Will shrugged. "Sounds like the other kids are okay but Sally sounds a little scared."

Tom held the keys up, "These might help?"

Will grabbed the keys and turned towards the door, he paused. "Do we need any more support?"

"We'll be okay," he gave his friend a wink, "I could call in the SWAT team if you like?"

"Ha Ha, very funny." With that Will turned and put a key gently into the keyhole.

When the rowdy group of youngsters had barged into the room Sally Cowan had been working quietly with four students on their French coursework. She recognised some of the students from her more unsavoury year nine classes of previous years. Luckily none of them had decided to opt for languages in year ten. As the last of the youngsters had barged in and slammed the door closed, dropping the latch, Sally knew she was in trouble. She stood and spoke in the most controlled voice she could. "What are you all doing in here, you can't lock the door!"

"Don't worry Miss, it's just a game," said Louis.

Sally suddenly felt very uneasy. "Who's outside?"

Louis stepped forward into the middle of the classroom. "Just a couple of old farts!"

The others all laughed in response. Sally moved her students to the back of the room and had them sit around a small table.

She turned back to face the interlopers who were settling on desks around Louis, the ringleader. "I don't know what you lot are up to but I want to take my class out," Sally pleaded.

"Sorry but we are not opening that door for anyone," he pointed at the classroom door. "In fact, Les you and Jonathon stay next to it just in case they try to barge their way in."

As the lads moved towards the door an eerie silence fell over the room as the position became clear. No one was leaving.

1035hrs

Joanne Tindell was now stood outside the back of the school looking up to the first floor windows. She caught the odd glimpse of a student's head bobbing along but no one she could recognise. She counted the windows along and fixed her gaze on the ones belonging to the MFL classroom.

Meanwhile inside on the first floor Will McCormack was just about to slide the key into the lock when the faint sound of distant sirens grew louder. The Police.

Inside the classroom the boys standing next to the door heard the lock being opened and leaned against the door, one of them shouting to the others, "The bastards are trying to get in!"

The rest of the inclusion gang surged towards the door just as the two senior teachers pushed against the door from the outside. The door was open with a one-foot gap when suddenly the weight of five other youngsters powered it closed. Will stepped back just in time but Tom Cawthorne was sent flying back and crashed into the opposite wall. His head and shoulder taking the brunt of the fall.

As the sirens grew louder outside the school Joanne Tindell started moving back towards the door. Her plan was to greet the arriving police and take them straight to the source of the problem.

In the classroom, a triumphal cheer went up as the door slammed shut and a cry was heard from outside. Sally Cowan moved towards the group of reprobates as she thought of pleading with them again. The four youngsters sat in the corner now sat in fear. One of them got up to look out of the window seeing the head teacher walking away. Young David Milton glanced around and caught sight of the fire escape which exited the building from the office next door. After a quick glance over his shoulder, in his panic, he climbed onto the rear bench and opened the window.

The police car screeched to a stop and the two young officers jogged into the main entrance where they asked for the Head Teacher. They were quickly directed through the hall towards the door to the rear of the building.

Will McCormack helped his friend into a comfortable position but saw how much pain he was in. He got on his handheld radio, "Main Office, can you call for an ambulance please. Mr Cawthorne has been injured."

David Milton pushed the window fully open. The fire escape staircase was no more than three feet away, he sat on the window's ledge and leaned out. Hearing the window open and the shouting emanating from the classroom, Joanne Tindell turned, looking up. She saw the student, unrecognisable, perched precariously on the window ledge and drew in a sharp breath.

The two police officers burst through the fire door immediately making eye contact with the panic stricken Head Teacher. A cry echoed from above as David Milton lost his grip on the fire escape. All three of the people on the ground turned in time to see David spinning through the air.

The crunch as he hit the paved area was sickening.

Joanne's hand went to her mouth as she stifled a cry.

One of the officers moved quickly to check the youngster out while the other officer radioed for an ambulance.

Shock rooted Joanne to the spot.

Sally Cowan appeared at the window. Looking down, her face contorted into a scream.

The police officer kneeling looked up at his colleague and shook his head.

Tuesday 14 May
1758hrs

Even before the news had started, the mood in the studio had been hushed. After weeks of sporadic news stories on disruption and turmoil in education this was the first time a death had been in the headlines.

The evening news team waited patiently as the evening news theme music trundled along to its final few notes.

Natasha Dunning swung idly in her chair searching for a comfortable position. Her co-host, who was still quite new to the job on national news, was still fiddling through his cue sheets trying to memorise everything. Natasha reached over, gently placing her hand on his and gave him a motherly smile. Michael Maddison was 28 years old, just five years the junior of his vastly more experienced colleague. He looked across, saw her smile, quickly took another deep breath and turned to face camera two. "Thanks Tash."

The floor manager held up his hand complete with bright yellow clipboard, his sign for attention. He suddenly took it down, thrust his other hand up in the air with five extended digits and then started his countdown. "In five, four, Natasha, in two, one." As he finished his countdown he pointed at Natasha Dunning from the side of camera one. The theme music faded and Natasha looked directly in to camera one.

"Good evening, this is BBC news at six with me, Natasha Dunning."

In the control box the director changed to camera two.

"And Michael Maddison."

Back to camera one. "The headlines this evening: fuel prices are to rise for the fourth time this year; the EU is set to lurch into another monetary crisis as Spain withdraws from the latest round of talks on the Euro." She paused before continuing. "But first closer to home we have the sad news of the death of a pupil in a school in the north east of England, Michael."

To the viewers watching the broadcast, the link was seamless to Michael.

"The tragedy occurred in a high school in the town of Ashton in Northumberland." He glanced down before continuing, "The pupil concerned fell from a first floor fire escape, more detail from our North East correspondent Adele Hoy, Adele."

After a slight pause for the link to update Adele Hoy appeared, stood outside the main gates of the school. The school's sign just over her left shoulder showed the large badge, yellow and red stripes of the county and a big wheel, symbol of the mines around which the town was built.

"Thank you Michael, I am here outside the gates of Ashton High School where today a tragic incident occurred which resulted in the death of one of the students."

She glanced quickly down to her iPad, "News has just reached us of the name of the student who lost his life, David Milton of Dewsburn, a small village not far from this school." She paused as she dropped the iPad out of sight. "We will shortly be receiving a statement from a representative of the school so if you want to return to us then?"

The producer quickly cuts back to the studio where Natasha is sat with a shot of the outside unit behind her on the main screen. "Thanks Adele, we will get back with you soon."

As the main news continued in the studio the outside broadcast crew were feverishly preparing for their next live link. Two other TV companies had turned up to cover this breaking story: the ITN and Sky News. They jostled for the best shot, the school's main sign being an obvious backdrop.

1814hrs

As Natasha came to the end of a news piece about the latest elections for the former Ukraine the producer passed a message to both newsreaders telling them that the statement at Ashton High School was ready.

Michael picked up when Natasha finished, "Now we have an update from our studio in Newcastle on the tragic events of today. Margaret Steadman can tell us more."

Margaret Steadman sat emotionless at her news desk. Knowing that the studio would be the focus of national news this evening she had worn her best dress suit to work. She had even managed to get her hair done especially. Some of the crew had commented on how nice she looked for her national TV debut.

The red light on top of camera one lit up, they were live. She heard the live feed coming direct into her earpiece from the main studio in London.

"Margaret, can you give us an update on the situation?" Michael Maddison asked.

Margaret steadied her nerves and replied. "Hello Michael, yes we have an update from the school. Just to recap on today's events: a year nine student from Ashton High School fell to his death in what appeared to be a tragic accident."

She paused taking a breath. "This follows over two months of general unrest in many of the region's 200 plus schools." The director switched to camera two as Margaret half turned in her seat, this brought the live camera feed into view from the outside broadcast unit immediately behind her. "A statement has just been released by the school and we can now cross live to our reporter Adele Hoy who has been at the school for most of the day, Adele hello."

After a slight communications delay Adele smiled and then responded. "Good evening Margaret, yes it has been a long day today at Ashton High School. There have been many visitors today: staff and students from other schools, local business representatives and family and friends. We had a candlelit vigil at four thirty marking the death of young David Milton. As senior members of the school work into the night preparing for the school to open tomorrow, one of the deputy heads has just approached the media and passed us a copy of a statement.

She waves a sheet of A4 paper in the air before holding it at reading distance from her eyes and glancing through the information before looking up quickly to the camera. A mixture of apprehension, at the subject matter, and excitement crosses her face as she brings an unheard piece of news to the waiting world. "I quote 'The Governors and Staff of Ashton High School wish to pass on their heartfelt condolences to the family of David Milton. A very popular boy who we all think had a bright and meaningful future ahead of him'." Adele glanced up at the camera, taking a quick pause. Around her the twilight was settling in and what was a modern, colourful building in the background now took on a gloomy, monolithic demeanour, towering above the slightly built reporter preparing to deliver the remainder of the statement.

"David was well liked by students and teachers alike and will be sadly missed by everyone." She slowly folded over the top of the sheet of paper as she read the final paragraph at the bottom. "Everyone can be assured that together with the local authority we are working to ensure that a tragic accident like this can never happen again'." She lowered the sheet just as a small chorus of boos rang out from outside the camera shot.

The producer cut back to the London studio where the two newsreaders were sat facing the screen behind them. Michael Maddison was the first to react, "Adele, there was some booing there as you finished reading out the school's statement?"

"Yes Michael," the reporter gestured to a small crowd gathered just out of camera shot. "The local people here are not happy with the use of the term accident!"

She moved to her left a few steps, the camera following, bringing into shot some members of the crowd. "We have some parents and relatives of students who attend here and who are not happy with safety standards in the school. I have been talking to them during the day and the general consensus is that the school shouldn't re-open until a full external investigation has taken place."

1818hrs

Natasha was now facing the camera in the studio. "Strong feelings up in the north east after the tragic death of a high school student."

Camera two cut in; focused on her co-newsreader. "We will have a special report later from our education correspondent, Lizzy McDonagh."

As the producer cued camera one in the control room the screen behind the newsreaders changed as the words 'General unrest' appeared in large bold letters. The background showed some typical classroom items: a calculator, a ruler, a pair of compasses plus other equipment.

The viewers were drawn back to Natasha Dunning. "Elsewhere in the country the level of minor unrest has been slowly rising. Incidents of minor confrontations have more than trebled, vandalism is on the increase, and fires at schools have reached double figures in this month alone.

Michael continued, "This is the first death; let us hope it is not the start of a downward trend, Natasha."

"Thanks Michael and now news on the economy."

Wednesday 15 May
0730hrs

It was cold. The sun was trying its best to cut through the early morning clouds, but it was failing. It added to the already chilly atmosphere amongst the group of people standing outside the main entrance to Ashton High School. The grey sky reflected the mood of the families who chatted quietly. Some of them carried placards, hastily made: Protect our Children, Safety First, NO more DEATHS. They didn't shout or scream. They let cars pass but they ensured their messages were seen.

Billy Hayton was the main organiser. His daughter, Lauren, had been in the Inclusion Zone just prior to the tragedy and had seen the outcome. She had come home visibly shaken so her Dad had decided something needed to be done. In respect to the Milton family he decided to make a protest hoping the school would heed their advice and not open until it was declared safe to do so.

His Boss at work had been very supportive, "Do what you feel is necessary Billy." He had said knowing that his friend and colleague would make up any work-time he missed. He also knew how much he loved his kids and wouldn't see them in harm's way.

Billy and his wife Ellie stood next to the main entrance of the school holding up a placard each. Around them stood over a dozen other parents and family friends wrapped up against the chilly start to the day. The noisy click, clack of high heels made them turn to see two figures almost scurrying along the path towards them. Euan and Catherine Ramshaw.

"Sorry we're late guys," Catherine said as they reached the group. "Euan has been on Skype for a quick meeting." She smiled.

The Ramshaws were quite well off compared to most in the town as Euan worked as a barrister in Newcastle and was very well thought of. Any one-upmanship was purely accidental.

Ellie Hayton leaned over and gave Catherine a quick hug, "You haven't missed much. Two members of the SLT have already arrived."

Billy chipped in, "We think the Head has been in all night?"

"She must be taking this really hard," Catherine sympathised.

"So she should Cath, she runs the school and ultimately everything that happens there is her responsibility."

"That's not fair Billy, Joanne Tindell can't control everything!" Cath replied firmly.

Billy thought for a few seconds, "Truancy, gangs, bullying – it's been coming."

Euan put a friendly hand on Billy's shoulder. "I don't think any of us could have thought one of the youngsters would be killed?"

"Suppose not, still vexes me though."

Ellie interrupted, "I wonder how the Miltons are coping?"

Catherine looked at her best friend shaking her head, "It must be awful for them."

"Look here comes more cars." Billy was pointing up the road. "Do we stop them?"

His wife grabbed his arm, "No, we can't stop them but see if we can talk to them. " She looked at her husband pleadingly.

Billy was well known throughout the town and was well respected; he was also on the school council so most of the teachers knew him and his reputation. After failing to get a response from the first driver he pushed a little harder with the second driver asking if school would be open and he got a response. No decision had been made yet, but discussions are ongoing. He didn't believe them.

0740hrs

A police car crossed the nearby roundabout and approached the main school entrance. A window rolled down and words were exchanged. The car moved into the car park and pulled over to the side and stopped. Two police officers exited the vehicle and circled to the front of the high-powered BMW to have a quick chat.

"Okay Dan, I will go inside and see what the score is," she glanced towards the main gate. "You see what feelings are like with the families." With that Sergeant Dayna Thomas strode off towards the main entrance of the high school with authority in every step.

Many of her friends and some family had kids who came to this school and recent events had worried her. As she climbed the entrance steps the door swung open and she was greeted with the smiling face of Deputy Head, Will McCormack. "Good morning Sergeant Thomas, how are you?"

The door swung closed with a gentle squeak behind the police officer. "Hi, Mr McCormack, I am fine thanks."

"How can we help you today?" he smiled.

"Well, the Chief Constable sent me down to see what the school's plans were for today."

"I thought as much, follow me please." And with that off he walked into the main corridor.

As the police officer dutifully followed her ex-teacher and mentor, thoughts of her teenage years came flooding back. Happy memories. She half-recognised some of the old posters on the walls. Here and there a certain door brought a flashback of a memory.

They turned left at the main crossroads and headed past the hall. The building was spookily quiet and quite dimly lit adding to the gloomy atmosphere of the school as a whole.

They had started to climb the stairs to the first floor before Will McCormack spoke again, "I am glad it is you who has come to see us over this Dayna," he glanced to his side as she returned his smile. "A friendly face makes a big difference."

Dayna Thomas appreciated the sentiment.

Outside young Police Constable Dan Clemence was talking to the small crowd of families trying to gauge their emotions. Another Police Officer who was born in the local area, he had strong feelings on the way the current situation had deteriorated.

"So Mr Renshaw, how is your Joely getting on, she must be sitting her exams soon?"

"Yes Dan," Euan Renshaw replied. "She had some great results in her mocks but her revision has been a bit disrupted, in the past few months especially."

Ellie Hayton chipped in, "I thought you lot would have been a bit more helpful with the problems the school has been having?"

Her husband rounded on her, "Come on Ellie, don't have a go at the lad."

"Yeah, he's not in charge you know." Euan added.

"No fellas, your wife is right Billy, we should be getting more involved." He seemed to sag at the shoulders, a sign of his frustration. "We get briefings and they tell us about some of the incidents that have been reported but there's nothing we can do about it, our hands are tied."

"It must be annoying Dan?" Ellie said.

"Yes it is. We have asked if we can have a permanent officer based in each of the major schools."

"Great idea," Euan said with relish.

"How did it go down?" Ellie continued.

"In theory the top brass were happy with the idea but they rolled out the same excuses they always do. Lack of officers, lack of funds, not enough cause for involvement."

The group were silent for a few seconds, deep in thought.

Billy Hayton was dragging one of his feet back and forward through some gravel on the footpath then he spoke up, "The situation is only going to get worse you know."

"A child has died!" Catherine interjected. "How much worse can it get?"

"A lot worse," the young officer replied.

0745hrs

Sergeant Dayna Thomas tapped lightly on the office door. She had examined the doorplate as she had stood there moments earlier: School Principal – Miss Joanne Tindell.

She heard the strong feminine voice respond, "Come in."

Dayna tentatively opened the door and poked her head around the corner. "Good morning Miss Tindell," she moved past the door and into the brightly lit office. "How are you?"

Joanne Tindell stopped what she was doing and looked up. A smile lit up her face, "Hello Dayna or should I call you Sergeant Thomas?" She emphasised the Sergeant as she know Dayna had been recently promoted.

"Dayna is fine Miss Tindell."

"In response to your question, I have been better." The smile slipped away from her face and was replaced by a tired expression. "I am a bit overwhelmed by yesterday's events, the poor Milton family must be waking up to their worst nightmare."

The young officer sat down in one of the chairs on the opposite side of the desk. "You're not to blame in any way, it was an accident."

"Such an easy thing to say Dayna, I still feel responsible." She shrugged. "Anyway, why have you visited us today?"

Dayna sat up automatically as she broached the official business she been sent to the school for. "My boss wanted me to see what your plans are, for today especially, but the next few days too?"

"Sorry, I should have thought about contacting Mr Craig." She looked through some of the papers on her desk, "Here is a copy of the message I have sent out to all parents." She passed a sheet of paper to Dayna.

"I have also sent out a parent email alert informing all parents that school will be closed today and tomorrow."

"What about Friday?"

"We are hoping to open up because the year elevens are getting ready for exams and we have lots of important information to pass on to them."

"I suppose it is an important time of year for some pupils?"

"Extremely important." Joanne gave a half smile as she sat back in her luxurious leather chair, enjoying the comfort it provided. "I feel dreadful for the family of David Milton. I really do but I have over 200 students sitting life-changing exams over the next few weeks. I have to focus on them, I know it's going to be difficult but I'm hoping some good can come out of all this."

Dayna looked at the school principal for a few moments, trying to see if any cracks were appearing in her demeanour. She realised that whatever torment lay beneath the surface, Joanne Tindell was a woman of very strong character and that she should be able to cope with the upcoming pressures.

"I will get this letter to the Chief Constable and let him know about Friday."

Joanne leaned forward, seeming a little more relaxed. "Tell Mr Craig I will keep him in the loop from now on," she paused thinking.

"In fact I will invite him to join the weekly meetings we have been having recently, if he can make himself available?"

"I am sure he will do his best or at least send a subordinate. We are doing our best to keep a lid on this."

Joanne Tindell stood up, pre-empting the end of their conversation. A quick check of her watch showed she was a few minutes away from a scheduled meeting.

Dayna stood also. "Thank you for seeing me Miss Tindell; I appreciate how busy you must be."

"That's okay Dayna." Joanne Tindell was keeping an informal approach as she was just about to ask for a favour. "Do you think some officers will be available on Friday morning? I know those parents mean well," she gestured out of her window towards the main gate. "But we do want to have the school fully open."

As Dayna reached and opened the office door she replied, "I will speak to the Duty Sergeant for Friday and get a patrol car over here first thing."

As she walked into the corridor Will McCormack stood leaning against the opposite wall, he smiled as she caught sight of him.

Dayna turned to face Joanne Tindell. Two strong-willed women woven deep into the fabric of Ashton.

It was Joanne who spoke first, "Thank you Dayna, for your help. I have a feeling we will be seeing a lot more of you around here."

Dayna offered her hand. "You can rely on me Miss Tindell, I won't let you down."

With a brief shake of their hands they parted. Sergeant Dayna Thomas strode purposefully down the stairs with a renewed vigour.

Friday 17 May
0735hrs

It was very much a late spring morning. Over the past few days the temperature had dropped especially in the early mornings. This had been mirrored in the atmosphere at the high school. A parents meeting the evening before in the nearby church hall had certainly raised the temperature of a cool mid-May evening. The main discussion arose around two opposing sides. Those who wanted their children in school with exam season so close and those who wanted their children to be as safe as possible, away from the school. Although many of the attendees wanted their children in a safe environment those with children in year eleven and thirteen were adamant that the GCSE and GCE exams had to be sat when scheduled. Lots of ideas were thrown into the hat ranging from attendance for exams only to the extreme measure of bringing in private security. The meeting had broken up with no real decision being reached. A demonstration was planned for this morning as the school was due to re-open but it was not fully supported.

Joanne Tindell stood in the main entrance of her beloved school. Although the decision to re-open had been unanimous she still had some trepidations and knew that a couple of her closest allies had reservations too. The education of the child must always come first and exams season was in full flow. A smile crossed her face followed immediately by a shiver up her spine as the first car pulled into the school car park. Another smile as Sheryl Townsend stepped out of the driver's door and gave her a quick wave. Sheryl took her bag out of the back seat and set off towards the school's main entrance.

"Morning Sheryl, nice to see you in so early."

Sheryl reached the bottom of the steps and had a quick glance around, "Am I the first here?"

"Yes."

"How long have you been in?"

"Since early o'clock," Joanne beckoned her friend to follow her in through the entrance.

"Coffee is on the go if you want a cup?"

They walked to the main office and Joanne poured her friend a coffee from the percolator. The warm, strong aroma of freshly made Bolivian coffee filled the room and they both settled into the receptionists' chairs.

The noise of the main door closing was followed by the head of Ian Taylor appearing around the side of the doorframe. "Morning Ladies."

"Morning Ian," Joanne replied.

"How many do we think will show up today Joanne?" He asked.

"I'm hoping for a full house Ian," she thought for a moment. "Maybe about 75 per cent, definitely more than half anyway!"

"I hope you're right Boss, exams start on Monday." And with that he disappeared around the corner on his way to his office.

0745hrs

Joanne Tindell was still worried; only a few members of staff had turned up so far. She looked at her jewel encrusted watch, a present from her very proud parents when she had made school principal at the age of 35. Quarter to eight. Still early. She decided to head back up to her office to be near her phone.

Sheryl Townsend left her office and headed down the stairs towards the main office again. At the foot of the stairs she bumped into Joanne heading the opposite way.

"Hi Joanne, have you been waiting for staff to arrive?"

"Yes Sheryl," another quick glance at her watch. "Still a bit early yet," she said hopefully.

"Will has gone to check the assembly is getting set up."

"Oh yes, year elevens, exams brief."

"Do you need me there?" Sheryl half-smiled.

"No, I am ready for that. Thanks for asking though."

Sheryl placed a hand on her friend's arm. "We will be okay, I will pop through to the main office for ten minutes or so, until the kids start arriving."

Joanne put her hand on her friend's. "Thanks. I will be back down in a bit, just need to get my notes for the assembly."

They parted and headed their separate ways.

Back in reception Sheryl got to the main office just as two of the younger members of staff turned up at the doors. Andy Peel was an up and coming Maths teacher, destined for great things. His partner, Sally Cowan was a bright star in the PE department. They hadn't tried to keep their relationship secret; far from it they were very open about it.

"Hi guys, how are you both?" she asked as they came through the door giggling.

They stopped at the counter, composing themselves. Sally was quite tall with long blonde hair and dressed in her favourite school PE tracksuit. She put her hair up in lessons in a bun or a ponytail but still managed to look glamorous. Meanwhile her partner of two years, Andy was a favourite of the students, especially the young girls who swooned over him. His appearance was always smart and never dull; pin-striped suits, bright ties and a truly cool collection of shoes avoided any adverse pupil comments.

As Sheryl looked at them she could tell how much in love they were just by how they were together. She envied them a little. "Well?"

"Fine thanks Sheryl." Andy responded. "I got all marking up to date, at last!"

Sheryl glanced to her right, smiling at the young lady stood on the opposite side of the counter. She saw so much of her younger self in Sally. She too had been madly in love through her NQT training but the move to another school had quelled those feelings. Sheryl was glad that Sally had been kept on full time after her NQT year. "I'm guessing you haven't been helping Andy out?"

"No Sheryl, Maths not my strong point."

"You're a county hockey player aren't you?" Sheryl enquired.

"Yep, I had a game on Saturday, in the pouring rain."

“I doubt you would let them dampen your spirits?” Sheryl replied thinking that a monsoon season couldn’t dampen this girl’s spirits. She felt a little tang of envy, again.

“We won three-one and moved back to the top of the league.” Sally responded with a glowing smile.

Andy re-joined the conversation, “And tell Miss Townsend how many goals you scored?” He swung his arm around her shoulders as he spoke.

Sheryl’s view was moving from one to the other as Sally held up two fingers, reversed of course.

“Well done you.” Sheryl beamed.

“She should play professionally.” Andy said as he moved behind Sally and gently put his hands on her shoulders. “She is good enough.”

“I’m sure she is.”

“I love my teaching, I wouldn’t leave these kids,” Sally declared.

“Even in these times?” Joanne quietly enquired.

“Definitely not, we have to stick together.” She cocked her head as if the question was ridiculous.

Sheryl felt a little warm tingle run through her body and she gave them both a broad grin. “Well thank you, both of you. With people like you working here we should be fine.”

With that the young couple continued on their way to their respective work locations. More members of staff had been walking in as the conversation had continued and Sheryl realised they should be okay to stay open today.

0805hrs

Outside the front of the school quite a large group of parents and relatives had gathered, intent on keeping the school closed. Their feelings had been vented at the public meeting on the previous evening when news had reached them of the school’s intention to re-open. There were some parents who were already refusing to send their children in but thought that that was enough to change the school’s policy. Others added their voices to those who now stood in the group outside the school, intent on trying to stop any young people from entering the site.

Even though the posters around school showed 'Every Child Matters' and 'Education comes first', they thought the school was not safe to open; it should not open.

Over 30 people stood in the group covering both sides of the main entrance road. Mostly parents, a couple of older siblings and a granny. All concerned about their young ones.

Euan and Catherine Renshaw stood next to the gate in what seemed to be their usual spot. "Not a bad turnout love," Euan said, a smile growing on his face. "Hopefully a few more will turn up and we can make our presence felt?"

"We have to make our point today." Catherine quickly glanced around. "With work we can't keep this up indefinitely."

At that moment Jenny Mills came around the corner. She looked flustered. "Sorry, I couldn't get here any sooner," she put her hand on Catherine's shoulder. "Just come off nightshift."

"Were you busy?" Euan chipped in.

"Not bad for a Thursday night."

They all stepped across the road as another staff member's vehicle approached. They were not here to stop any staff from getting into the school, it was the students they were more interested in but they wanted to make their point.

Jenny looked along the path to where some of the film crews were standing. "How long have they been here?" she said gesturing, looking at Catherine for an answer.

"I think some of them have spent the night here in their vans." Euan looked around at the others. "My mate Carl works the bar in the Premier Inn over the river, he says bookings are up 50 per cent on normal for this time of year."

"I bet these lot like a drink too!" Jenny added.

They all laughed.

More cars approached from the roundabout, their left hand indicators flashing to show they wanted to turn into the main school entrance. What would the rest of the morning bring? No one knew.

0820hrs

Two members of staff were hurriedly sliding the huge curtains closed along the side of the main hall. The early morning sunlight beamed in across the rows of seats casting strange shadows. Near the entrance teachers milled around some tables covered in a variety of tasty breakfast snacks: croissants, choc au pains and cereal bars. The snacks were neatly arranged but the onslaught of teaching and support staff had decimated the display.

Two of the canteen staff were busily pouring cups of tea and coffee from two large Burco boilers on a table against the wall. Their smart white chef's jackets a stark contrast to the blood red colour of the wall behind them. Just as the last members of staff took their seats, Tom Cawthorne stood up from his seat at the front asking for quiet.

Sheryl Townsend and the remainder of the SLT entered through the main doors heading towards Will. In what seemed like a pre-planned exercise, the SLT, as they reached the front row, fanned out in a display akin to military precision. They all turned to face the expectant crowd, Joanne Tindell central, Pete Thornton and Sheryl Townsend to her left, Tom Cawthorne and Will McCormick to her right.

A few seconds of silence followed as Joanne waited for the room to hush. "Good morning everyone, sorry to drag you all away from your preparation but I have some important information to pass on to you all." She paused and took some steps forward trying to ease the tension that was evident in the gathering. She glanced across at the huge curtains seeing a shaft of bright light had cut across her legs and she continued, "We have been through some very traumatic events, as a school, over the past few days. I just wanted you all to know that we are here to support you." She gestured to the individuals stood either side of her. "If there is anything you need then please come and speak to one of us, our doors are always open to you."

A slight murmur developed in the room, maybe a sign that this was away from the norm.

Joanne and the others cast a nervous glance around the puzzled faces. Their leadership of the school had never been brought into question and now was not the time for doubts. Joanne continued, "We have decided to close the school on Tuesday in respect of the funeral of young David Milton. We think it's only right."

This time she was met with nods of approval and a gentler murmur of chat.

She continued, "We know there will be some of you who would personally like to attend and I know there are some pupils who will want to be there too." More silent nodding as she stood bolt upright, changing her demeanour. "Okay, that's pretty much all I wanted to tell you. Any questions or problems then please let us know." Joanne took a couple of paces backwards, re-joining the other SLT members in a line.

Will Cawthorne headed up the central aisle to the main doors and locked them open using the footholds. He appeared to be the only member of staff who could do this correctly, with ease. As Joanne turned towards Sheryl to have a quiet word, Tom Cawthorne took it upon himself to dismiss the meeting.

0830hrs

Outside the main entrance of school things were heating up and not temperature-wise. Those who were demonstrating against the fact that the school had remained open after the death of a pupil were now getting frustrated. Seeing a steady stream of staff coming into the school, albeit later than normal, demoralised them. They saw their purpose diminishing with every vehicle that drove in through the wrought iron gates.

They had considered blocking the entrance by closing the gates and securing them with an ad hoc padlock. As the group increased in size, so too had the police presence. Tensions were running high as each side manoeuvred to take the moral high ground. As the time drifted towards the start of the school day and registration the number of students approaching increased.

The number of demonstrators had reached the forties and the four police officers were struggling to keep the main path clear. Plumes of exhaled breath rose into the chilled morning air as the adults jostled each other to gain a better position. The path, although only a couple of metres wide was bordered by freshly cut grass so the uniformed presence were fighting a losing battle, positional-wise. The approaching students, already a little morose, were confused or panicked by the frantic movement of the adults at the school entrance. Some stopped. Some ran past using the bordering areas, crunching through the cold, glass-like blades of grass as they strangely saw the school as a safe haven.

The tension created by the sudden surge of students towards the adults led to raised voices amongst them. The near presence of the youngsters made them avoid the use of any harsh language but tempers were fraying.

The parents were getting nowhere so Euan Ramshaw, normally a quiet, understated man, suddenly took the initiative and pulling a couple he recognised, Thomas and Ellie McCutchen, he started to form a barrier across the grass. "Come on you guys, we need to stop the kids getting past!" he said as he grabbed his wife, Catherine's arms and stuck them out. He got the McCutchens to do the same forming a chain which covered the entire width of the grassed area. This coupled with the large group of demonstrators in and around the pathed area stopped the students dead in their tracks.

As the backlog of young people grew the police officers struggled to clear the path. Dayna Thomas, the sergeant in charge of the group decided drastic action was needed. "You guys need to move back onto the path!" She moved to stand in front of the two couples blocking the grassed area.

Catherine Renshaw pulled away from her grasp. "We aren't moving for anyone!"

"Okay, you leave me no choice. You are all under arrest for blocking a public right of way." She gestured to her three officers. "Okay you three take them to the van and hold them there."

Diane Kent was a Community Support Officer and knew the four individuals concerned personally. She hung back as the two constables, Dan Clemence and Eddie Gray ushered the four protestors away.

"Come on Ladies and Gents, let's move out of the way shall we." Dan Clemence took control. At six feet four he normally didn't get argued with.

As the three officers and four protestors moved towards the main entrance the floodgates opened and even with the large number of protestors there was no way to stop the dodging, fleet footed youngsters. The odd protesting word did nothing to slow the excited hoards.

Dayna Thomas allowed herself a little smile as the young students poured in through the main entrance. The remainder of the protestors admitted defeat and stood in small groups chatting and gesticulating. As the small group of police and the arrested protestors moved toward the large white police van, it's yellow and orange diagonal stripes seemed to shine in the fresh morning sun.

Members of the press started moving towards them, snapping pictures and filming as they did. Questions were being asked, voices raised as they intensified.

"Are you arresting these people?"

"Where are you taking these parents?"

"Are these people under arrest?"

The police officers ushered the four parents into the rear of the van; no answers were forthcoming. Tomorrow's headlines were already being written.

Tuesday 21 May
1110hrs

It was a cool, dark spring morning. The rain had died away leaving a chill in the air. As the dark clouds hovered over Ashton the feeling was one of dread. Nelton Bridge cemetery, located on the eastern edge of the town was a pitiful scene. The family and friends of David Milton gathered at the entrance to the small chapel. Black the predominant colour. Handkerchiefs and tissues in abundance.

A churchyard was often a scene of pain and misery but today those feelings were tenfold as the imminent burial service of a young, teenage boy approached. The parents of the young lad were stood at the doorway, greeting all those who entered: some with a handshake or a quick hug, others with an exchange of tear-filled admissions of past experiences.

As the last of the mourners filed into the chapel, father Ian Major gave a final greeting to both parents before he mounted the steps to the pulpit. A hush fell over the near silent congregation as he opened up the funeral service with a traditional prayer.

"Oh God, who brought us to birth,
And in whose arms we die,
In our grief and shock
Contain and comfort us;
Embrace us with your love,
Give us hope in our confusion
And grace to let go into new life;
Through Jesus Christ.
Amen."

Ann Milton began to sob quietly. She had struggled over the last week since the untimely death of her son. Her grief knew no bounds. A parent should never bury their child. Medication had dulled some of the pain over the past few days but the service had brought up all her bare emotions to the surface. She was burying her only son. A sweet, kind young lad who never got into trouble, was bright and intelligent if a little introverted. Gone!

The service continued and then came the turn of Ronnie Milton to give the eulogy. His assent of the steps to the altar was very slow and measured. He tried to take in his surroundings. The dark, gloomy apse to the rear of the altar looked very foreboding. The various plinths and statues seemed to contain moving appendages. He turned to face the congregation and quickly grabbed hold of the lectern to keep his balance.

He looked out over the sea of faces, his friends and various members of his family. He noted that this seemed the only type of occasion he saw certain people. His gaze took him to the left of the crowd and his eyes stopped roaming as they landed on the font. It was just twelve short years ago that David, the apple of his eye, had been christened there. He remembered the day clearly as if it were yesterday. Similar crowd to today he suddenly thought, minus the staff and students now filling one side of the aisle.

His gaze returned to his family, wife Ann and David's older sister Rebecca. He shuddered and suddenly came back to the present as his daughter gestured for him to start.

How long had he been up there at the lectern, looking down, he had no idea. He reached into the inside pocket of his jacket and pulled out a folded sheet of paper, carefully opening it up. He followed this by fishing a pair of specs out from another pocket and began:

"Today is a day I never wanted to see, stood in front of a coffin with my beautiful boy inside. Words can't begin to describe the grief we, as a family, are going through. I know that everyone here is suffering too. I can look around and see family, friends, guys from his amateur radio club and of course the school he loved to attend. People who came into contact with our David knew him as a quiet, polite young man. He was a great son, helped his mother out around the house. He would take our Jess out in all weathers, come rain or shine that dog and him would be running around the park out the back of here," he gestured towards the rear of the church with the fields beyond. "They would stay out all day and night if they could."

Ronnie glanced to his right seeing if his gaze could penetrate the stained glass window to the park beyond. Hoping, dreaming that his boy was out there now with his dog.

A deep sob from the front row brought him back to reality. "That dog won't leave its bed now. They came into our lives at the same time..." His voice trailed off.

He flipped the sheet over, briefly reading the contents before looking up. "I wanted this to be a joyous occasion, a chance to talk about all the good things David was and did in his life but despair kind of drags you down. I know every parent must think the World of their child but David was a great kid. He had a heart of gold, would do anything for anyone."

He looked around and noticed a few people nodding and the odd smile. He deviated from his painstakingly prepared script, identifying those who had responded to his last comment.

He pointed to a lady at the far left of the front row, his sister, "Jane, he helped you bake all those cakes for your charity drives"

"Uncle Tommy, when you weren't very well last year he took your old dog Scamp out for a walk when he had Jess."

His gaze returned to his close family on the front row, "Mam, how many times did he come round and cut your grass, even during the winter when it didn't need doing just so he could spend some time with you." His mother, sat with a hanky permanently on her face let out a half laugh, half sob as she acknowledged her son's comments.

"I could go on all day telling you about his kindness. He had a heart of gold our David. He would do anything for anyone and he didn't ask for anything in return. He was the best son you could ever wish for. I will miss him a lot."

Tears started flowing at this point and it seemed to spread through the congregation. "We will all miss him."

With that final remark Ronnie stepped down from the lectern and slowly made his way back to his seat. He quickly put his arm around his wife Ann's shoulders and held her as she continued to weep.

The service continued with some hymns, favourites of the family and then Father Ian Major started preparing for the coffin to be taken to the churchyard.

1145hrs

Sat in the back row, members of the school staff prepared to go outside, gently sliding along the pew to the end next to the aisle.

"Come on Sally," Joanne Tindell said. "Let's go and get some fresh air."

"Thanks Joanne, it's a little stifling in here" replied Sally Cowan.

"I know this is difficult for you as you were there at the end." She gave a compassionate smile.

"It must be the same for you Joanne, you watched the poor boy fall?"

They passed through the massive oak doors into the sunshine and cool breeze beyond.

"It's been a difficult time all round for everyone concerned. Losing such a young life."

Pete Thornton led Jackie Howarth outside to join them. Jackie, a close working companion of David Milton, was visibly shaking.

Pete put a comforting arm around her shoulder, "Come on Jackie, try to keep it together. The family will be out soon."

"You're not the most sympathetic of guys are you Pete?" Joanne said.

"Don't worry Joanne, he means well," Jackie responded.

Sally moved in closer to the other three. "You didn't hire him for his good looks did you Jo?"

The three ladies laughed quietly as Pete shrugged his shoulders and straightened his tie. "I'm not that bad Sally, thanks very much."

This was followed by some more titters and then their little spell of innocence was broken as the rest of the mourners started to appear from the main door of the church.

1155hrs

Gary Cole had just finished setting up and testing the sound on the camera when the congregation started coming out of the church. He passed the microphone to Josh Thorpe, his long-time friend and reporter on BBC North East. They worked well together, they knew how each other worked and it made the job seem a lot easier. "Here they come Gaz, let's get a quick shot of them coming out the church."

Gary shouldered his camera and hit the record button as the rest of the mourners came out of the church. They both quietly watched, respectful, as the church emptied. The coffin came out at the rear, borne by four men, walking slowly. The light weight not unnoticed by those watching as the task of carrying the deceased was normally undertaken by six people.

Josh Thorpe waved to catch the attention of the police officers who had turned up, in dress uniform to represent the local force.

Chief Constable Alex Craig only had time for a quick word, "Hi guys, are you going to get this on the evening news?"

"Yes Alex," Josh replied. "The chief programme editor says we will get between 60 and 120 seconds, second up."

"Good to hear, we need this story up there on the main news to highlight this growing problem in schools."

Gary had continued his filming turning their greeting into an interview. Neither man paused, flawlessly continuing the thread of their conversation.

"So Chief Constable, do you see this as a one off event or are you concerned it may be the start of a trend?"

He flipped the microphone head back towards Alex. "I am concerned yes. I am hearing stories like this from other schools in the area, although nothing that has produced such a tragic outcome as the loss of poor David."

"What have you got planned to counter this slide towards carnage?" Josh posed.

"I wouldn't call it carnage but we do seem to have a growing problem and we as a force have started putting measures in place." He paused gesturing towards the other two police officers just out of shot. He beckoned them over. "Sergeant Thomas and CSO Kent are part of a new initiative, getting into schools more often and talking to the students and teachers."

The two officers were now in shot and they both forced smiles as their senior officer spoke about them. The Chief Constable continued, "Sergeant Dayna Thomas has lived in the Ashton area for over six years now and CSO Diane Kent has lived here all her life.

Both are well known in the area and we feel this can only help when forming new and developing long-standing relationships."

With the party line now completed Alex Craig turned to see the coffin being placed over the grave and made his farewells. "I wish to go and pay my final respects now to the Milton family but if you have any more questions, these two fine officers should be more than happy to answer them." With that he turned away and walked towards the gathering group of mourners.

1213hrs

Father Ian began reciting the final part of the burial service. The two junior police officers approached the edge of the crowd at the graveside, Josh and Gary continued filming with a mixture of sadness at the event and hope that their piece would make the nationals.

Friday 24 May
1520hrs

It was definitely a frosty atmosphere as members of staff trooped into the main hall at the end of a very busy day. David Milton's death the week before had left some members of staff mentally drained and struggling to cope with just the everyday activities of work. Tension had been building all week and it was obvious that some staff did not want to come into school at all. This meeting was an open one; people could air their grievances as they had in the previous few days.

As the final few came in a hush settled over the meeting as Joanne Tindell stood, walked to the front centre and turned to face the expectant crowd. She had been very busy over the previous couple of days with visits from various teachers, the governors and a host of parents. Things were coming to a head and tough decisions would have to be made.

"Good afternoon everyone, thank you for attending this meeting today, I know it has been a very busy and emotional week for all of us." She started a slow walk up the centre of the hall, continuing as she went, "I feel we are entering a very difficult period and much though I would like to find positives to tell you now, I can't."

With those final words hanging in the air, she turned facing the backs of her audience. "I appreciate that some of you or indeed most of you see this place becoming a dangerous place to work." She started a slow walk back to the front. "I could try to enforce changes or manipulate you, bend you to my will," the last words came out in joking voice. "I won't." She reached the front again and turned abruptly, scanning the faces in front of her. Some were friends she had known for many years. "I will give you five minutes or so to chat amongst yourselves or if you wish, come and speak to myself, or any of the SLT, please do. Then I would ask for a vote to decide if we should stay open!"

A sudden murmur spread through the gathering, it rose in crescendo. Joanne Tindell held her right hand up and gently asked, "Quiet please." She looked around as a hushed silence fell. "If you need more time to think about it overnight we can adjourn until tomorrow morning?"

Two hands went up. She pointed at John Reynolds, one of the longest standing teachers in the school. "Joanne, I think we all have a good idea what we want," he glanced around and gestured with his arm. "We have been talking about it for a few days now." Others nodded in agreement.

A smile crossed Joanne's face and she pointed across to Jenny Sayers, one of the school's Biology teachers just as she was standing.

"I agree with John, we have waited long enough." Jenny said in a firm, resolute voice.

"Okay then," replied Joanne, "I will go and make myself a coffee and on my return we will go to a vote." With that she strode purposefully down the hall and away to her office.

1535hrs

Will McCormack stood up at the front of the hall, clipboard in hand. He looked very tired, his tie was a little askew. It had been a long and difficult day but now decisions would be made, the future would be a little clearer.

He watched as Joanne Tindell appeared in the entrance to the hall, she nodded and he took this as a sign to continue. "Ladies and Gentlemen," he spoke in a loud oratory voice. Glancing left he nodded to the head of sixth form, Angela Newsome, who stood up. "Angela will take a note of the ayes," and then to his right Tom Cawthorne stood up, "and Tom will note the nays."

Everyone present could feel the electricity in the air. This was unprecedented in the teaching world, holding a vote to decide if a school would close indefinitely or remain open.

Joanne stood in the entranceway, undecided whether to enter the hall or not. She wanted the staff to make up their minds without being swayed either way by her presence. She looked around the hall, noticed the tired looking curtains hanging loosely in the windows. Outside it looked a little dull. Rain had started falling.

A loud voice brought her back to the hall as Will spoke. "So Ladies and Gentlemen, the vote is 'Do you wish the school to close?' Simple as that," he looked around the expectant faces. 'Now please raise your hands clearly if you wish the school to close forthwith."

A low buzz filled the hall as the odd hand was raised, more followed until it became difficult to see an easy winner. Joanne Tindell took a few steps forward frantically trying to count the hands she could see.

At the front of the hall Angela Newsome was slowly and methodically counting the hands on her side of the room. She paused and moved to a more central position whilst making a note on her clipboard of her first count of 20. Angela commenced counting the second half of the hall as teachers eagerly glanced around trying to make a guess as to which way the vote would swing.

It was too close to call and everyone knew it.

To Joanne at the back of the hall it seemed to drag on far too long. She had played her hand and was determined to keep the school open but she needed the support of her staff. As she scanned the gathering the abrupt retreat of Angela Newsome to her starting point forced a sharp intake of breath.

She looked directly at Angela but her face gave nothing away.

Will nodded at Tom. "And now the nays - who want the school to stay open."

Tom Cawthorne had already started his count of the nays as the first hands had shot up. He counted as quickly as possible and had soon finished but then recounted, moving his waving hand in the opposite direction.

Happy that his two tallies concurred he asked staff to put their hands down. The two vote counters moved together, comparing totals.

Joanne Tindell strode purposefully towards them, trying to put on her best smile. Tom caught her eye and proffered a wink, she knew that was the result she had wanted.

She reached the pair and quickly glanced at their written results: ayes 40, nays 46. Close but decisive. She also had the members of the SLTs votes in hand if things had gone the other way. She didn't need that ace now.

Tom and Angela backed away to give Joanne centre stage. Her beaming smile gave the game away to some of those watching who knew her thoughts on this very important matter.

"Ladies and Gentlemen, the votes are in as they say." She savoured the moment. "The ayes were 40 and the nays 46." Some controlled cries of anguish accompanied by subdued squeals of joy. "This gives us the result that the school remains open, I want to thank," she paused as Tom tapped her on the shoulder and then whispered into her ear.

After a few seconds she resumed. "Is everyone happy with the way they voted?" She now glanced nervously around the room. "Tom reminds me that sometimes people vote the wrong way due to the way the question is worded."

Members of staff looked left and right but no hand was raised so Joanne continued quickly, "We stay open then."

A few hands suddenly shot up and took Joanne by surprise. She quickly calmed herself realising this was from those staff who had wanted the school to close. Losing a vote always sparked a response.

"If anyone is unhappy about attending work or if they have any other worries I will be up in my office for the next few hours, please come and see me."

Joanne started to walk back towards the main hall entrance but was stopped mid-stride by a challenging voice. Everyone stopped moving and listened in as Jackie Howarth spoke, "Miss Tindall, can you guarantee our safety?"

Joanne paused and turned towards the young woman who had posed the question. Jackie Howarth was one of Joanne's recently appointed Learning Support Assistants. She had a lot of respect for Jackie as she knew her background and that she had come from a tough Pupil Referral Unit as her last job. As she noticed that everyone within earshot had stopped what they were doing and were now listening for her response she decided that she must be honest.

"I'm sorry Jackie, I can't guarantee anyone's safety." Joanne looked around at the expectant faces before continuing, "I can only say that I will do all I can whilst you are in school to keep you and everyone else, staff and students, as safe as possible. I have already spoken to the police on this matter."

Jenny Sayers, a Biology teacher, was hovering on the edge of Joanne's vision and she added a comment, "Jackie it is our obligation as teachers to come into school and teach these young people regardless of the external situation."

Joanne didn't want the issue to become enflamed at this point so she decided to quell any further comments before the situation turned into a free for all. "I agree with you Jenny but I also sympathise with Jackie. I won't see anyone put in danger, not at any cost but we must try our best to keep going." She smiled at both before continuing "Jackie, if you want to chat more pop up to my office."

She took a couple of paces before stopping and in a raised voice said, "If there is anyone who thinks it's too dangerous to come into school please come and speak to me. I have a feeling we may need to adjust the timetable a bit over the next two months anyway."

She took a final glance at Jackie before striding purposefully away towards the main doors and onwards to her office leaving behind a quiet muttering in her wake. As she sat at her desk, Will McCormack appeared with two cups and a welcoming smile. "Coffee Joanne?"

"Yes please Will, you are a life saver."

"My pleasure."

He placed one of the cups on a pretty, flower-patterned placemat in front of his friend as he nodded towards the office door, "The queue has already started outside."

Joanne visibly sagged in her seat. She picked up the cup in both hands and took a sip. "Okay, send in the first one." She looked up at Will as he made for the door, "Can you stay and help me Will?"

As Will reached the door he turned to face Joanne, clicked his heels together and with a smile answered, "Of course Boss."

They both smiled as Will waved the first member of staff in. It was Jackie Howarth.

1550hrs

The staffroom was a buzz with chatter as many staff members had drifted in from the hall, wanting to keep the discussions going.

John Reynolds was one of the most outspoken teachers, wanting the school to remain open. “Listen, listen most of us here are of the same mind.” He gestured with his hands, palms down, bringing the gathering crowd to a silence.

Most of the tired, old blue armchairs had an occupant now, straining to hear what was going to be said next.

As a couple of other staff entered he waited, wanting more people to hear his comments “At the end of the day we are here to educate the young people who attend this school.” A lot of those in attendance nodded or mumbled consent but one or two were shaking their heads. John noticed this and spoke again. “I have to say that we also need to have a level of safety which is higher than normal, just to be more vigilant.”

This time he saw nods from those who weren’t sure of his previous comment. He pushed on, “Katy and myself have come up with some ideas of how we can move forward. Katy?” He indicated the young PE teacher, Katy Howard, sitting across from him.

“Thanks John. Ladies and gents, our idea is to create a group who are going to attend school no matter what and those staff will be the core of our team.”

John took up the lead, “We reckon if the outside situation worsens then the numbers will decline but we need a strong group to ensure those doors,“ he pointed through the main entrance, “never close!”

Ian Taylor, a staunch disciplinarian and English teacher stepped in. “We need a name?” he smiled.

John smiled back, “A name?”

“Yes, something catchy?”

A few moments of silence as those present thought.

Tommy Johnson was the first to come up with a suggestion, “How about the mad buggers?!”

This was met with a chorus of laughter and some applause.

“Sounds about right Tom,” John responded.

Another period of silence followed until Katy spoke in a tone which gave some gravity to their idea, “How does the ‘School Defence Force’ sound?”

A couple of those present nodded.

Jenny Sayers was eager to show her commitment saying, “Sounds good to me.”

Ellie Hayton wasn’t so sure, “That sounds a bit harsh to me.”

“Ellie, I think that’s what it might come down to,” Jenny replied.

The others sitting and standing around the staffroom main table were struck with a sudden realisation. The situation could reach this point in the future.

The change in mood was obvious to all. John Reynolds decided to break it, “Okay guys, we need to start making plans.” He dragged a couple of sheets of A3 paper out of his satchel. “I have already started looking at how we can protect the outside of the school from attack or vandalism.”

He spread one of the sheets over the centre of the table which showed a plan of the school. Some changes had been hand drawn. “I have marked where we can block off an entry from the outside.” He pointed to various areas on the plan.

Katy cut in, “We will need less classrooms too, with less staff.”

The conversation continued at pace as the enthusiasm of the group was drawn into the planning.

Saturday 25 May
0850hrs

The click of the kettle boiling coincided with the click of the magnetic door release in the staffroom. Katy Howard smiled a tired smile at John Reynolds, "Morning John."

"Morning Katy," he returned her smile. "You look how I feel."

Katy's smile turned into a cough, "Thanks John, you sure know how to make a girl feel good."

John laughed as he watched the smile return to Katy as the coughing subsided. "I reckon we are going to have a lot more sleepless nights before this is all over."

He nodded towards the freshly boiled kettle and Katy gave an enthusiastic thumbs up and swung her bag to the front. After fumbling with the zip a while she slid it open, delved inside and produced a packet of Hobnobs. John's eyes lit up and he made an over-dramatic gesture of making Katy the coffee.

Katy ripped open the packet as she placed it on the centre of the large table they were to use that morning.

0900hrs

The staffroom was filled with a general hubbub of chatter as the small group sat around the large conference table. John Reynolds sat at one end and Katy Howard at the other. In between sat an array of teachers, parents and the school caretakers. John tapped the reverse end of his pencil on the table a few times to gain everyone's attention. "Thank you, thank you, let's have some quiet now." The chatter died away as John took control. "Good morning everyone," he glanced around with a smile, making sure he caught everyone's eyes. "Firstly, Katy and I would like to thank you all for attending, we know it is your weekend time but after yesterday's vote we feel we need to move quickly. Katy?" he gestured along the table.

"Thanks John," she acknowledged before continuing. "Ladies and gents, our student numbers are dwindling but those that are still attending need a safe place to learn." There was some furious nodding from those around the table. "As the number of staff and students has decreased we have decided to reduce the size of the school, well the teaching area part of it. I will hand you back to my able assistant," gesturing back to John, "who has the plan on the whiteboard."

John Reynolds was a technophobe, he preferred the old methods of teaching; blackboard, chalk and a loud voice. Although the school had advanced to whiteboards and marker pens he still had the voice to carry his instructions to all corners of the room. Technology-wise he could handle emails, word documents and old style powerpoints but as versions updated he lost track and excel and PDFs were out of his range. Katy had formed a close bond with John as she helped him get to grips with modern technology. She had even introduced him to Facebook but he baulked at Instagram and Snapchat.

The PDF document that appeared suddenly on the whiteboard showed a plan of the whole school site, minus the adjacent sports pitches and Astroturf. The sudden appearance of an image on the staffroom whiteboard forced a number of the attendees to turn around, or sideways.

John picked up the electronic pointer and aimed it at the board, "Right then, as you can see...." Nothing. He shook the device and tried again, still nothing. He looked up infuriatingly at Katy then started looking around the room. Katy held out a hand on the table and John slid the remote across to her.

Katy couldn't get it working but John was off across the room and soon back next to the whiteboard with a headless golf club in his hand and a beaming smile on his face.

"Old school," he said happily.

Katy now began her description of the changes they would need to make to keep the school safe whilst reducing the size of the teaching area. John pointed and interjected as the pair continued to explain their plans. As they finished the presentation a hushed silence fell over the staffroom.

“Any questions?” Katy concluded.

There was a long drawn out silence that left the two protagonists looking at each other questioning themselves.

“Any ideas for improvement?” John ventured.

Jenny Sayers spoke first “What about during the night?” She gestured to the three caretakers sat opposite, “Do we just leave the site and hope it’s still standing here in the morning?”

Jimmy Nelson, the oldest and therefore the ‘wisest’ of the caretakers responded, “We are willing to have one of us spend the night but were hoping a member of the teaching staff would too?”

“Where?” Jenny asked.

Jimmy glanced at his colleagues and got a nod from his boss, Phil Dawson. “We are thinking of closing Gym two and using it as a sleeping area.”

Alex Small chipped in, “I have a two-ring camping stove that I’ve brought in and Phil has got a spare TV.”

Jenny smiled. “Sounds great,” she looked around at the others. “Maybe we can set a rota?”

Katy and John seemed quite happy to sit back with the former taking notes.

“Spending one night here every week or so won’t be too bad,” Ian Taylor ventured.

John chipped in, “Be a nice change from the wife and kids, eh Ian?”

The others laughed.

Ian’s face took on an undignified expression. “How dare you John,” he threw the others a quick grin. “Put me down for every Wednesday night,” he chortled. “Might get to watch some footy too.”

More laughter from those gathered around the table.

“I could manage one night every other week if I work around Ben’s shifts?” Jenny added.

“Same for me,” John put in. “One night during the two-week cycle.”

Tommy Johnson half raised his hand. “I can do one night every week, I don’t have any family to worry about.”

John leant forward, “That’s really good of you Tommy.”

Again Tommy’s hand went up, “Can I bring my dogs in though?”

This set everyone off laughing again.

Phil Dawson answered, "Why not Tommy, as long as you pick up their poo."

This response kept the laughter going.

"You know me Phil, you come out now and again with me and the girls down the river or the woods, and I leave no poo unpicked!"

Phil slapped the table in response, "You do mate, you do."

0912hrs

A knock at the door stopped the laughter in its tracks and all heads turned towards the door. Through the glass pane in the door the face of Ellie Hayton could be seen, grinning as she stooped to look through into the staffroom.

Katy Howard jumped up and headed over to open the door. "Hi guys, great of you both to come."

She let them both in and showed them to two empty seats on the side of the table occupied by the caretakers. They noticed that everyone sat opposite were teachers. Chance, perhaps?

John Reynolds leaned over to shake both of their hands, "Welcome to the meeting Billy, Ellie."

"Have we missed much?" Ellie asked, looking a little hurried and flustered.

"Sorry we are late," Billy added as he slid out of his huge jacket.

"Not much," John replied. "We've decided to have two members of staff spending the night in school just to keep an eye on the place."

"Good idea, can we help with that?" Billy ventured.

"No Billy, we'll stick to school staff for now, thanks though." He didn't want Billy to feel unwanted but it would be difficult enough trying to explain something happening to a member of staff during the night, let alone an outsider.

Ian noted the look of frustration on Billy and Ellie's faces so he added, "I think we will be needing your building skills quite a bit over the coming weeks Billy anyway, that can be your input."

Billy smiled, "No probs, I have brought all the spare wood and offcuts I could lay my hands on for now."

"Excellent."

"Just need to know where you need blocked off?"

Katy stood up and went to her bag as she explained, "We went through a plan just before you arrived about sealing off part of the school," she continued rummaging, finally pulling out a plastic wallet with some papers in. She opened the wallet, clicking the catch and took out a few sheets, passing them to Billy and the caretakers.

The three men took a couple of minutes to look through the sheets, twisting and turning them.

Katy slid back her chair, glancing between the three men she said, "I think I had better put the kettle on."

0940hrs

The group had just finished making their plans when there was a knock at the door.

Katy jumped up, "That might be John."

She walked over to the door and pressed the green release button whilst pulling the door open. She gave the late arrival a big hug, "Hi, Uncle John."

John Richardson beamed a smile back at his niece, "Sorry I'm late, traffic." He was in his fifties and a very handsome man. Having worked in education around the country he had finally decided to retire and return to his home town. It didn't take long for his old school to come calling and ask him to join the board of governors which he accepted without pause.

"Don't worry, we've pretty much decided the parts we are going to close down and we have agreed to do it over half term."

John headed towards the table, "Sounds like you guys have things sorted."

John Reynolds rose from his seat and shook hands with his old friend and teaching colleague, "You still alive then old man?"

"Ha, ha, says you." The two men laughed as the others sat at the table realised they were old friends. Jimmy Nelson was another old friend and work colleague of the pair, "How's life treating you John?"

John Richardson clapped him on the shoulder as he sat down next to him, "I was drinking with you in the club on Saturday Jimmy, not much has changed since then."

“That’s what you said then but you still look absolutely knackered.”

John shrugged, “I though retiring from teaching would make life easier,” he glanced around the others sat around the table, “I was wrong there.” He gave a short laugh and slapped his hand gently on the table. “What have you guys got planned then?”

The others quickly glanced at each other before Phil Dawson took up the challenge. “Okay then,” he moved the school site plan in front of John. “This is our plan.”

John looked astounded, “You have been thinking a lot about this then.”

As Phil and Jimmy started to go through their ideas, John Richardson listened intently and interjected on some of their points. As a school governor he could give the go ahead, as their representative, to any changes and hopefully get the rest of the board of governors to agree.

1012hrs

“Okay guys, I am happy to say I agree with the planned changes,” John Richardson said as he smiled at those sat around the table. “I am meeting with the other governors on Monday night and we will ratify things then.

There was an audible release from those gathered.

John continued, “Once you get the nod what are your next steps?”

John Reynolds spoke up next, “We are going to do everything over half term.”

Katy commented, “It will coincide with the timetable reduction that SLT are working on today.”

“Good idea,” the governor said. “What about funding and resources?”

This time Phil was ready with the answer, “Most of everything we need is in the supply shed, sat waiting and I have two eager assistants.”

The two men next to him muttered under their breaths causing everyone at the table to chuckle.

Some of those present started to get up and stretch, loosening off tired muscles that had been taught for a while. The blinds were opened by Jenny and light streamed into the room as they gathered up the paperwork and put away the used cups.

"Right, I am off then and will leave you to your rebellion. I will contact you on Monday night John and confirm the governor's support." With that John Richardson rose from his chair and headed to the staffroom door.

"Good luck to you all and let me know if there is anything else I can do for you." The others acknowledged his departure. "See you at dinner tomorrow Katy," he threw her a parting smile.

"See you tomorrow Uncle John." With that she blew him a kiss and he was gone.

Sunday 26 May
0600hrs

It was early. It was six o'clock on a Sunday morning and this was reflected in the sombre mood present in the shift briefing room at Northumberland East Police Station. The new shift looked very tired and this was the prelude to a twelve-hour shift. Extra work and extra hours were taking their toll on the countries police workforce, especially in the north of the country where many forces were undermanned anyway. Extra patrolling of schools and other educational premises along with the increased number of youths knocking about on the streets had put everyone on high alert.

"Okay ladies and gents," Sergeant Dayna Thomas said as she entered the briefing room to stand in front of Bravo shift. "Let's get the day started."

"Do we have to Sarge?" came the response from Police Constable Eddie Grey, sat in the third row of chairs.

"Yes, PC Grey, you chose this career," she paused allowing a few sniggers before continuing, "and now you are stuck here."

"Noooooo." he replied.

With one short exchange the mood in the room had lifted and Dayna was thankful of her easy-going relationship with Eddie and indeed the rest of the shift who had worked together for eighteen months now since her promotion to Sergeant.

The laughter died away as Dayna completed the roll call. Each name answered, she shuffled the papers she held and prepared to speak whilst taking a final look at the officers sat in front of her. Eddie and his sidekick Dan were the best team she had. Dan had been in training with Dayna, he was tall, thin and athletic, a contrast to the short bulky Eddie. They were very different personality-wise too. These differences are what made them such a good team she thought. They could work out any given situation. She felt guilty for what she was about to do but knew it was the best use of her resources.

"Okay, so listen in for today's plan. The council have devised some no-go areas within the town that we can only have vehicle coverage in, which means no more foot patrols."

Moans and grumbles came from the shift but Dayna wasn't going to respond.

"Quiet. Two main areas have been identified: County has the area to the west of the train station and we have been allocated the area immediately to the south and east of St Paul's." She ignored more moans from the officers and continued, "So the area south of Bridge Street as far as Hamilton Lane."

She moved across to the large street map just behind her and to the right. Picking up an old pool cue as she moved she quickly gestured to the area of concern. "Here is the River Esse with the bridge funnily enough heading onto Bridge Street," she paused waiting for some laughter, as more came she quickly continued. "Here is the school and just to the south, the church."

As she spoke her cue was following her words now drawing a wide oblong shape following the main street east to a perpendicular street going south before shortly turning west and heading back before quickly stopping back at the church.

"Any questions?"

Diane Kent, sat in the front row, was a Community Support Officer and she held up her hand.

"Yes, Diane?"

"Are we going to get any support?" Diane asked.

This was met with nods of agreement from the others present.

"Not at the moment," Dayna quickly added.

Moans of disapproval followed.

"We might hope for something in the future but at the moment everyone is stretched."

The earlier feeling of joviality rapidly dissipated. The briefing room suddenly felt like a cold place, the walls suddenly seemed to be closing in on the beleaguered occupants. The large white-faced clock on the wall seemed suddenly to tick louder and slower as reality set in. There would be no support, everyone present realised that. Dayna pushed on to try and clear the mood.

"Okay, teams for today are as follows: Bravo One and Charlie One as yesterday."

Dan interrupted, "Oh oh, here it comes."

"Thanks Dan, Alpha One you are to patrol the area I indicated earlier and this is designated as Red One."

Silence fell for a while as those present in the room took in the information.

"Red One, great name!" Eddie quipped.

"How about some extra pay, let's call it danger money?" Dan Clemence chipped in.

Dayna looked a little bemused, "All you get is normal overtime, if you earn it?"

"What are your orders for these areas?"

"Excellent question Bobby," Dayna said to one of the PCs at the back of the room. "We just have to visibly patrol these areas more often than the rest of our patch." Dayna left the lectern and began to walk among the officers of her shift. "Headquarters wants to know immediately of any illegal activities in the zone."

The officers present were now nodding along. The faint glow of sunlight from the recent dawn coming through the blinds lay stripes across the space. Everyone the Sergeant passed had been striped. They listened intently as she continued to explain the newly posted procedures the police authorities deemed necessary to combat the growing surge in the crime rate.

"Before you ask, there will be some instructions posted on the station bulletin board, shift response boards and on our website. I suggest you all have a good read through them but in summary we need to look out for an increase in the following areas: graffiti, under-age drinking, vandalism and intimidation. We need to break up large groups of youths, taking names where necessary and identifying ringleaders.

Dayna had returned to the dais and now had her audience captivated. There were some pensive expressions in the crowd but the message was getting through. She continued, "Be on the lookout for acts of intimidation and violence but most importantly command needs to know the scale of these offences. This will dictate overtime policy, extra recruitment and possible military intervention!"

"Military intervention?" Dan uttered in disbelief.

"Yes Dan, if things get too out of control."

"Surely we won't be needing them lot?"

"Command seems to think there might be a time when it is necessary."

Those final words hung in the air as the shift prepared to start work.

0828hrs

"And here we are in Ashton on a beautiful Sunday morning with nothing better to do," barked Josh Thorpe.

Four hundred yards away his fellow reporter, Adele Hoy, heard him through her earpiece, "Are you ever happy Josh?" She chided.

"Never," he continued sorting his tie. "Not when they keep sending me up here."

"You love it, Josh Thorpe – the roving reporter, getting the stories as they happen."

"Very funny," he responded. "Why are we both here though, practically within spitting distance of each other?"

"Urgh, are you spitting?"

"You know what I mean."

"Okay you two, cut the chit chat." Moira Laing the News Producer entered the link.

"Sorry Boss," Josh responded.

"Morning Moira," Adele cut in. "Are we going live soon?"

"Yes Adele, just a quick update on the new police policy on the no-go areas."

"That won't go down well around here." Josh injected.

"I know but it's what we do, inform the public of the news." With that Moira closed her end of the link.

Adele was checking through her lines when Josh interrupted her, "Adele, I hope the locals don't kick off when they hear this news?"

As the national news link came to an end and prepared to switch to the local stations Moira Laing sat pensively in the North East newsroom. Seven years in the station with the last two as producer on the news she had never felt so nervous. It was not about the people she was working with no, it was the news they were about to deliver. Like everyone else paying close enough attention she had watched as the situation had deteriorated and it had now reached a point of no return. This morning's item could take things over the edge.

She was jolted back to reality by a prompt from the floor manager. Being a true professional she immediately sprang into action, "Josh, check ready at school?"

"Josh ready," he replied.

"Adele, check ready at First Row?"

"Adele ready," she replied.

"We are going live in 30," Moira informed both reporters and their respective teams.

"Moira, I have a family packing up to leave just around the corner from the school, should I grab them for a quick chat?" Josh asked.

Moira thought quickly, saw the lack of time for a live chat and also remembered the last 'live chat' they had broadcast contained some choice words. The condemnation from one of her execs was still ringing in her ears days later. "Not live Josh but grab a few words with them and we can put it into our next slot."

"Okay Moira, will do."

"We are going live in five, four, three, two, Josh, go." Moira linked from the main headlines, read in the studio to the first live report with the flick of a switch.

Josh began, "Thank you Margaret in the studio. As you can see I am here again outside Ashton High School as some very important news has just reached us from the local Police Headquarters on the other side of town." He paused as he knew photos of the Police HQ were being shown in a split screen for the viewers.

"The statement claims that the police will be paying more attention to acts of violence, intimidation and low level crime, especially involving groups of youths." Again he paused slightly as he knew the pictures on the screen would be changing to a map and he was being told in his earpiece when they were changing to a map. "But in conflict to this the police have also effected 'no-go areas' as shown on the map. These areas will only have vehicle patrols which means no foot patrols. I will now hand you over to Adele Hoy who is with the Thomson family. Adele."

"Thank you Josh, so I am here in First Row in Ashton with John and Edna Thomson," she gestured to the couple standing next to her as the camera panned back to include them in the shot. "Good morning to you both."

John Thomson responded with a vague Scottish twang, "Not so good I'm afraid."

Adele recovered quickly, "May I ask where you are going?"

"Well, we have the car packed with the most important of our belongings and we are heading back up to Scotland," John replied with a lovely lyrical tone to his voice.

"Back to Scotland," his wife, Edna, repeated.

"And why are you heading up to Scotland today?" Adele questioned.

"We can't stay here any longer, it's far too dangerous," John answered very directly.

"Too dangerous," his wife repeated.

John quickly sought to explain his previous statement thus negating the next question from Adele, "The wife and I don't feel safe living here anymore. Just recently we have had windows broken, the car was damaged and we got shouted at walking up the road minding our own business."

"It's not right," his wife added.

"I am sorry to hear that, do you have somewhere to stay?" Adele queried.

"Yes, we have friends up in Lockerbie. We are originally from there." John explained then shook his head. "It was the terrorist attack on Flight 103 nigh on 30 years ago that gave us the opportunity to move down here and now it's out of control kids forcing us to move back."

Edna added, "It's a strange old world."

Adele, prompted to end the feed in her earpiece, turned back to the camera as it zoomed back in, "There you have it, terrorists on one hand and juvenile delinquents on the other, both producing fear in people in equal measure. This is Adele Hoy for BBC North East in Ashton."

After the live link closed down Adele and her small crew walked back up towards the school where the van was parked. Her grip Gary Cole, walked beside her, looping up the microphone cable, "Can you believe that Adele, surviving Lockerbie and now having to go through this?"

“I think he’s been through a lot more besides.”

“What makes you say that?”

“Did you not see the Army Veteran badge on his tie?”

“No, I was to the side, didn’t see it.” Gary thought for a moment then continued, “Don’t you think he would be able to cope with a bit of vandalism and verbals?”

Adele smiled, “Of course I do, he looked the type to come out all guns blazing, but not his wife, she looked very scared.”

“Sure, he’s looking out for his wife,” Gary acceded.

As they arrived at the van they saw Josh and his team approaching from the neighbouring street.

“How did it go Josh?” Gary asked.

“Great, we got a couple of minutes on tape of a young family from Snowdonia Way,” he gestured, “who are leaving to move into the country, away from what they see as impending doom.” He trailed out the last word, mimicking a famous saying from ‘Dad’s Army’.

“It’s not funny Josh,” Adele cut in.

Josh thought before responding, “I wasn’t joking though you guys. That is what they say is coming. I heard your piece with the Thomson’s, same thing, moving away because they are scared of what is coming.”

Adele put her arm around his and gave him a little hug, “Sorry Josh, you are right – we’re all doomed.”

Gary spoke up after the tittering had died down, “What about the young family then, what’s their story?”

“Peter and Steph Cairns, couple in their 30s, two young kids, eight and four, in fear for their safety. Moving to live with friends up in the Cheviot area.”

Gary was shaking his head.

Adele looked around her colleagues, “We all have a very important job over the coming days and weeks, telling people what is happening here.”

Josh added and this time with no jest in his voice, “And I think it’s going to get very testy around here!”

1300hrs

Kayleigh Rogers sauntered along the street, it's variety of shops stretched out before her: the PC Repair shop run by the Asian brothers whose surname she could never quite pronounce, Charlie's Chippa, although Charlie had long since gone, Smart 'n' Clean, the dry cleaners and then her place of work, McColl's Estate Agents. Four years she had worked here now and she was very proud of her local knowledge and the ties she had to the town. Being in her 30s now, unmarried and no kids, she had put a lot of her time and effort into this place. You could say her soul too, if estate agents had them.

"Hi Tommy," she said to her colleague as she crossed to her desk. "The other two gone for lunch?"

"Yes Kayleigh, I let them go a few minutes early as the shops are so busy this time of day." He looked up timidly, "Was that okay?"

"Of course, it's not going to get busy for a while yet." She smiled at her young co-worker, putting his mind at ease. He was in his second year in the trade and Kayleigh was doing her utmost to show him the ropes. She had spent half her post school life working in the trade; four years here and four years in a couple of other locations. But this was where her heart lay, her hometown, streets she knew and people she cared about. The Psychology degree had not gone to waste entirely or the two years working at Lidl. The full time wage had given her her own flat and the start she needed to her adult life.

She checked the bookings programme on her desktop, three more properties needing to be valued before being put up for sale and five new owners looking to rent their properties out.

"It appears the desertion is continuing Tommy."

Tommy Adams, sitting opposite, ruffled his hair, something he seemed to do when people entered into conversation with him. "You're right, I've just been looking at the ongoing monthly figures and they back you up, sales up eight per cent and rentals up eleven per cent." He shrugged.

"What started as a trend is quickly becoming a major exodus," Kayleigh said.

"Good news and more work for us," he smiled limply.

"I know, but I don't enjoy working on a Sunday Tom."

"This is the first time Mr McColl has asked us to work on a Sunday though," Tommy responded.

"Yeah, but if this trend continues unchecked, I don't think this will be the last Sunday we have to work." The phone on her desk rang; Kayleigh waited the obligatory three rings then picked up, "McColl's Estate Agents, Kayleigh speaking, how may I help you?"

At first only a few people noticed the changes. Some people saw the odd friend or colleague leave whilst some businesses may have noticed a small down-turn in profits but the situation was changing.

People sort a safer place to live whether they thought it temporary or long term, they weren't sure. They prepared for the worst and prayed for the best. Ashton was akin to a long extinct volcano, rumblings here and murmurings there but not many people taking notice of what was below the surface. The police had a good idea of what was coming but they sat on the proverbial fence. More vigilance but no-go areas left them with a confused and frustrated workforce.

Wednesday 29 May
1000hrs

"Sshhh, quiet you lot!" Brad called in a hushed tone. The inside of the building was dark and gloomy; dust floated in the air from their disturbance of the surroundings. "Tasha, make sure the main door is locked again, we don't want to be disturbed."

"Consider it done Brad," Tasha Stanley replied.

The five youths stalked around the open area, careful not to disturb anything. Whispers punctuated the silence and the odd scrape of a chair or table being knocked slightly. Suddenly, the main lights came on, one after another.

"What the fuck!" shouted someone in the dark.

"What are you doing?" Brad shouted in the direction of a now smiling Louis.

"I found the lights Brad, look here on the wall," he said excitedly pointing to them.

"You idiot!" Tasha hissed loudly. "You'll have the coppers on us."

Jack Mills strode behind the bar with an air of confidence, "Don't be daft, the coppers don't come round this part of town anymore," and with that he tapped at the keypad on the electronic till, covered in a fine layer of dust. It didn't respond.

Brad walked up and sat on one of the bar stools, slapping his hand on the bar, "Suppose you're right there Jack mate, I'll have a pint of lager then," he said with a big grin.

Jack still struggling to open the till looked up with a smile, "My pleasure young man." Looking under the counter he found a pint glass, held it up to the light and giving it a pretend clean with his sleeve he placed it under the adjacent Fosters pump and pressed the button to release the drink.

After the pint finished pouring Jack placed it on the bar in front of Brad and said, "And that will be," he paused for dramatic effect, "absolutely free young man."

They all laughed and the rest of the gang gathered around Brad at the bar asking for various drinks.

Drinks poured, they all stood and looked at each other and Jack raised his glass of beer, "To the Killingburn Road Posse."

"What kind of a name is that for a gang?" Jonjo spat.

Tasha intervened, "I like that."

"Why though?" Argued Brad.

"Well, we live off the Killy Road, don't we? It seems to be where all the reprobates live," Jack responded.

Louis seemed happy with that, "Jack's right, I like it too. What do you think Brad?"

Brad was mulling it over staring at his now empty glass. Jack grabbed his glass and started to fill it with lager again, "Got to be better than what they called us at school, the SENKs, the have nowts or the poor brigade?"

Brad took a sip from his freshly poured pint ending up with froth on his nose, which produced a couple of muffled sniggers. They stopped abruptly with a quick glare from him.

Louis moved over to the dartboard at the end of the bar nearest the group. He picked up a piece of chalk and started writing on the blackboard to the side of the scoring area.

KRP KRP KRP K
R
P

Louis was the most intelligent of the group and he enjoyed Art as a lesson in school but joined up with Brad and Jack as he grew bored with his own peer group. It had got him into a few tricky situations with school staff and the law but after a while, Brad and Jack had accepted him. He became their thinker or planner as Brad had labelled him.

"I like that one," Brad finally spoke up.

Louis immediately cleared a space on the board and drew the diagonal design to a larger scale.

K
R
P

"That's the one," he said as he walked over and slapped Louis on the back. "I think we should start leaving our mark around the patch, starting with the outside of this place."

Tasha walked over to her discarded backpack and took out various tins of spray paint. "I never liked the name anyway, 'The Miner's Tavern'. What colours do we want to use?"

Jonjo, who had sat quietly at the bar jumped to the floor from his stool. "Red, white and blue," he ventured.

Brad looked from Jonjo, smiling, across to Jack then Louis and Tasha who were both stood at the dartboard, "Red, white and blue it is. Well done JJ. Okay you two," he said looking at Tasha and Louis. "Get outside and start marking this place up," he smiled. "Then we'll go and see our turf."

1130hrs

The old rust-streaked white van pulled up to the kerb with a bump. The owner had long stopped wondering how the vehicle was still able to move let alone carry all the equipment he needed to keep his building company going. The lettering on the side had long since faded, but if you looked close enough you could still see:

'Coulson Building Firm – 01670 820208'

'All your building needs in one phone call.'

Harry Coulson had always hoped it would be 'Coulson and Sons' but it hadn't happened and he felt a small twinge of regret. His wife had produced a daughter but the older she got the more hours he needed to work to keep her in the custom she thought she deserved.

Harry turned off the ignition and jumped out of the van, his able sidekick, Pete Davis, doing likewise on the other side of the cab.

"Okay Pete, you start getting the boards ready and I'll check the two addresses." With that Harry took his trusty notebook out of the front of his overalls and squinted at the scribbled writing.

He approached the second address on the list and checked the windows were closed and the door was secured. With everything in order he gestured to his colleague who came across with the tool kit, tape measure in hand.

"Pete, is this the one you did the measurements for?" Harry asked.

"Yes Boss, two doors, two downstairs windows and four upstairs," he gestured over his shoulder. "Same as the other one you looked at."

"Great, that means all the wooden sheets we've brought should fit perfectly," he smiled. "If you've done your measuring properly?" With that he smiled at Pete who just sighed back at him.

"Cause I have, double and treble checked the measurements. I know how tight you are with money." It was his turn to let out a sly smile.

Harry noticed a small group of youths walking across the road from the direction of The Tavern, his local, thinking they should be in school but he wasn't surprised. A lot of kids had been kicked out of schools recently and now they just aimlessly roamed the streets, causing mischief on occasion.

Pete started carrying the first sheet of boarding over as Harry got his drill ready. Boarding up the two recently derelict houses shouldn't take long.

Jonjo spotted them first and pointed out to Brad. "Look Brad, those blokes are going to board up some houses, see."

"Nowt to do with us Jonjo, people scarpering all the time round here," Jack cut in.

"He's right mate, nowt to do with us," Brad responded.

"No, but my old fella was saying these people bugger off and leave all their kit behind," he pointed towards the house where two men were starting to attach a board to the downstairs window. "They only take their essentials you see. I mean if you're doing a runner you don't start packing TVs and Play Stations do you?"

"He might be fucking right there Brad, you can't exactly fit a 50-inch flat screen into the back of your poxy car can you?" Jack said excitedly.

Brad thought for a few seconds, "You're right lads, supplies in the pub won't last forever and we need to start stocking up on essentials," he said rubbing his hands together.

Tasha queried, "You mean TVs and Play Stations are essentials?"

Brad barked a laugh, "No stupid, we get the food and booze." He glanced around to see the pained expressions on the faces of Jonjo and Jack so continued, "Of course we'll take the bloody TVs and Play Stations as well."

They all laughed.

Louis was first to come up with a plan. "Okay then let's scare the shit out of the two Bob the Builders and we can come back tonight for a proper look in the houses."

"Good idea Louis," Jack said.

Brad spotted the decorative pebbles in the plant pots at the edge of the grassed area they were in. "Let's stone the fuckers!" And with that he grabbed a loose handful of pebbles and started hurling them one at a time towards the two builders. The rest of the gang quickly joined in.

Pete was just drilling in the third bolt in the bottom left corner when the first missile hit the boarding near the centre. The sound caused him to drop his drill and jump back to avoid the spinning drill bit. A second missile nearly hit him and was accompanied by a bout of laughter from the assailants on the far side of the road.

"Hoi, what you doing?" Harry shouted but that only seemed to increase the amount of missiles heading in their direction.

"What the hell are they up to?" Pete shouted above the constant drumming sound as the pebbles struck brick, wood, concrete and then flesh.

Harry winced at the pain in his arm after the stone struck him, "Let's get out of here Pete. Grab the other board, quick sharp." He gestured to the smaller board they had carried over for one of the smaller upstairs windows.

Pete grabbed the board and started to drag it towards his friend when he took a double hit. A missile hit his left shin and a split second later one struck the side of his head. He stumbled but Harry caught the edge of the board nearest to himself and quickly lifted it up higher to cover them both. He listened as more missiles rattled off the board and he looked at Pete as he saw a small trickle of blood running down his temple.

"Come on mate, let's head back to the van," Harry said and the two men using the board as a shield started moving back towards their van. Once there they discarded the sheet of panelled wood onto the path and quickly got into the front seats.

Harry fumbled slightly, still in shock, taking the keys out of his pocket. "Bloody hell, what's all that about?"

"No idea mate," Pete put his hand up to the right side of his head. He felt the stickiness and quickly took his hand away looking at it red and slick with blood.

"The little buggers got you!" Harry said as he finally put the ignition key in and turned the engine over.

A couple of missiles pinged off the outside of the vehicle as Harry selected first gear, gunned the engine and released the handbrake. The van lurched up the road heading away from the slackening barrage. He started slipping on his seat belt and gestured to the glovebox compartment, "Grab the first aid kit Pete and I can stop around the corner and see about that gash on your head."

"Cheers Harry, it doesn't half hurt and," he paused mid-sentence, abandoned his search for the first aid kit and pointed out the left hand side of the windscreen. "Will you bloody look at that?"

Harry followed his friend's indication and as he slowed the van they stared in disbelief. Parked off to the side of the road, in view of the whole estate and the events that had just occurred sat a police car. In the front seats you could clearly see two officers. They waved at Harry and Pete and gestured that they had seen the events that had just happened.

Harry could just shrug and Pete pointed to his head wound as they drove, bemused, past the police officers.

"We should have gone over there and sorted them kids out Eddie," Dan said frustratingly.

"You know what our guidelines are Dan, observe and take note. We don't go in and inflame the situation."

Dan wasn't happy but his colleague and friend was right. "Do you know any of them?" he asked.

Eddie was from Ashton and had been to the high school quite a few times and worked with the Child Protection Team too so he knew quite a number of the local kids.

"I know two for sure. The big blond lad is Brad Jones and the girl is Tasha Stanley. I think one of the other lads could be Jack Mills, the one in the cap."

"I'll make a note of their names and we can get that info back to HQ." Dan replied, "Shall we follow them?"

"No, we'll just pass on the info. We should check on Harry and Pete though."

"Yep." Eddie started the patrol car.

1204hrs

Hunger started to catch up with the group of teenagers. They were about to head back to the Miners Tavern when they saw a man fixing a trailer to his car. He was obviously in a hurry packing items and preparing to leave.

Jonjo recognised him at once, "That's the Nevis boy's Dad."

Brad was intrigued, "Seems to be in a bit of a hurry, doesn't he?" He started walking towards Bob Nevis. "Going somewhere Mr Nevis?" Brad shouted.

At first he appeared to ignore Brad but then thinking better of it and not wanting to get into a discussion with the tough looking teenager, he gave an over-elaborate nod.

Just as the group of five youngsters neared Bob Nevis' car and his increasing packing activity the door to the house opened. A mother and her two sons appeared. None of them seemed to be happy or enthusiastic about what lay ahead of them. The two lads, each dragging a backpack with them were complaining to their mother until they saw the gang standing in a semi-circle around their father's car.

The slightly taller one of the two who was also the oldest by a year swung his backpack over his shoulder and strode over to them. "Hi Brad," he nodded. "Tasha, Jonjo, how are you guys?" Billy Nevis asked as he nodded to the two remaining members of the group, not sure of their names.

"Just wondering where you Nevis boys are off to?" Jack interjected.

The younger of the two brothers, Terry, stepped forward to answer that question, "Dad is dragging us down to Lincoln to stay with our Auntie Laura."

Billy chipped in, "It's a shithole Brad, nowt to do down there."

Their mother, Emily Nevis, looked shocked at her oldest child, "Billy, is there any need to swear?"

Brad sniggered, "Quite right Mrs Nevis," he turned to face Billy. "Naughty, naughty Billy, no swearing in front of your Mam and Dad."

Both Bob and Emily Nevis now shifted uncomfortably. Brad noticed this but before he could react the younger of the Nevis brothers interrupted him, "What are you guys up to then?"

Jack took centre stage now as he walked up and sat on the bonnet of the Vauxhall Vectra which was the pride and joy of Bob Nevis, "We are the new proprieties of the Miner's Tavern."

"Proprietors," Louis corrected him.

"Proprietors then," Jack responded, not too pleased at being corrected in front of the others. If truth be known he wasn't best pleased at being corrected at all. He had never really got on with Louis; thought he was a bit snobby and too clever for his own good.

Emily Nevis looked shell-shocked. She had worked in The Tavern for the past four years and the landlord deciding to close up and leave had been one of the reasons the Nevis' had decided to leave.

"You can't be the new owners?" she stammered.

"Ah, Mrs Nevis you forget, possession is nine tenths of the law," Jack smiled.

"And we possess it," Brad followed up as he jangled the pub keys, found earlier in the office, in front of her.

She recognised the small, brass miner's lamp keyring. "Disgraceful," she said as she tried to usher her children towards the open back door of the car. "Come on boys, we are leaving."

Bob Nevis just stood open mouthed at the audacity of the youths stood in front of him. Part of him just wanted to get in his car and drive away but the other part of him wanted to do something about the smirking youngsters. Fight or flight?

His wife made the decision for him, "Come on Bob, get the boys in the car and let's get going." She had noticed his indecision.

Again it was Billy who spoke up, "Can we guys come with you?" He asked as he glanced across at his now smiling brother.

"No, no, no, we won't have any of that talk!" Bob Nevis walked towards his sons and gave them a gentle push towards the car.

"Now wait there Mr Nevis, don't you think your lads should have a choice in the matter?" Brad said forcefully.

"They don't have a say in the matter. I am their father and I decide what's best for them."

Jack slid off the bonnet and passing the open passenger door he slammed the back door shut, "And here's me thinking we lived in a democracy." He walked over to the brothers and put a friendly arm around each of their shoulders, "So how does a democracy work then Louis cleverclogs?" He looked over to where Louis was standing.

Louis was a little irritated by the 'cleverclogs' reference but also saw it as a compliment, backhanded maybe, but a compliment nonetheless. "People vote to decide on a matter and the most votes wins," he beamed a smile at the boy's parents. "Simple."

"Okay," Brad said, "let's vote. Those in favour of the lads going to Shithole, oops, apologies Mrs Nevis, Lincoln, raise your hands."

Bob and Emily, catching on to the unfurling scene before them, both slowly raised their hands.

"That's…one, two votes." Brad made a very deliberate motion of counting them slowly and out loud. "Now those who think they should stay in lovely, old Ashton?"

Immediately, seven hands were fired up into the air. Some even stood on tiptoes to ensure their vote could be seen.

Brad continued his commentary in a victorious tone, "The staying puts win by seven votes to two."

Bob was getting angry now and he quickly strode over towards his sons. As he approached, Jack moved forward to stand slightly in front of them, still with his arms around their shoulders. Bob gave him a gentle push back and grabbed the arms of his sons and started to drag them over towards his car.

Brad positioned himself directly in his path and adopted an aggressive stance. He stood six feet tall, he had been a regular gym user for a few years now and a member of the local boxing team for longer. He feared no one, except his mother. "They ain't going anywhere Mr Nevis," his voice carried an audible threat that wasn't lost on any of those present. "And I think you owe Jack an apology as well."

Bob Nevis found himself in the worst of positions, trying to protect his family whilst being faced down by a teenager. He made the mistake of underestimating the power and ability of Brad. As he reached out and grabbed his collar Brad's right arm snapped out a punch so fast that anyone watching would have had to press rewind and slow-forward to see it again. Bob Nevis cannoned backwards landing at the feet of his younger son, Terry, and there he sat in shock and pain. Blood started to trickle from his now broken nose and his wife let out a half muffled shriek.

The Nevis boys were now in a quandary. Happy at first to go with Brad and his gang they both now felt guilty about what had happened to their Dad.

Brad took the doubt from them as he stepped past Bob Nevis and turned the boys around, adopting the same position Jack had only seconds earlier, arms around their shoulders. "Your Dad will be okay, that was only a little tap." The boys still looked a little startled and Terry glanced over his shoulder as they left the scene. "He grabbed me first remember and pushed little Jack," he said as if to justify his brutality.

The gang of seven now walked back towards their new establishment.

Mr and Mrs Nevis would complain to the police but it wasn't exactly kidnapping and the police inspector said his officers would keep an eye on them as the parents still wanted to leave.

1520hrs

Back in the Miner's Tavern a new arrival had turned up. Nathan O'Connell had walked up to the front door and announced he wanted to join the gang. Apparently news of their 'taking over' the establishment had already started to spread through the local community via gossips and social media, most of the latter initiated from within the gang by Louis.

As the Nevis brothers sat drinking what seemed to be a never ending supply of lemonade from the pumps Brad paced back and forth in front of the bar as he listened to Nathan's updates from the outside world. Jack and he had been out of the loop for a while and Nathan had been in the school recently so his news was interesting to say the least.

Brad stopped pacing, “So you reckon more than forty kids have been kicked out of the school?”

Nathan was reclining across a number of leather padded bar stools, “Yes mate there are teachers leaving too, because of all the trouble in there.”

“Do you know who these kids are?” Jack asked.

“Some, not many.” Nathan responded. “You know I’m a traveller so I don’t spend so long in one place, especially that bloody school.” Nathan was tall and wiry and Brad had already thought he would be a useful guy to have around. With his background as a traveller he knew he would be tough enough.

“Could you find out for us, which kids have been booted out?” Brad asked.

“You mean go back in?”

“Yeah. Just to find out who has left and where they live, they might make good recruits for the KRP.” Brad said proudly.

Nathan sat up straight, “The KRP you say?” He dropped to the floor and gestured up above the bar at the recently sprayed sign, “The Killingburn Road Posse.”

“Yes, that’s our tag.” Jack showed a similar vein of pride as Brad had.

“Suppose it wouldn’t do any harm would it. Old Tommy Johnson is always leaving his computer unlocked in the Zone so I will have to get put in there” he smiled. “What’s in it for me then?”

There was a pause as the others were taken aback by the fact that Nathan had made a demand before Brad stepped in front of him. “You can stay here with us in the pub, be a member of the gang and share in the spoils.”

Nathan’s turn to think, “Sounds good to me. You’re not going to get me to take part in this induction thing you’ve got going, are you?”

“No, you can miss that.” Brad conceded.

“That’s not fair Brad,” Terry Nevis piped up. “Me and Billy have to do it.”

“Tough, he’s going back into school and getting information for us.” Brad motioned back to Nathan, “He can also have a good look around and see if they have made any changes to the place.” Brad turned back to face the majority of the gang who had all been listening in to the conversation. “I think we might be paying that hellhole a visit in the near future.”

Tasha waited for the laughter to die down before she spoke next, “Any other news Nathan?”

“Oh yeah, something that might be of interest to someone who is thinking of breaking a law or two in the near future.”

“What are you talking about mate,” Jonjo put in.

“Well my Da is a regular visitor to the cop shop and he overheard something really interesting.” He paused for affect, looking around and making sure everyone was focussed on him. “The cops aren’t patrolling this area anymore!”

“Bollocks,” came the instant reply from Jack.

“No, he might be right guys,” Tasha said.

Brad laughed. “I think he is. I saw a cop car earlier when we pelted them two builders and they didn’t raise so much as a porky finger to help.”

“So there shouldn’t be anyone to stop us going back to them houses and having a look around?” Jonjo queried.

“You’re right Jonjo, we’ll wait till dark though, just to be safe.

1610hrs

Standing quietly in the narrow lane behind the ‘Med Tan’ tanning salon, the eight youths kept vigil over the major shopping area of the town. Their purpose was to initiate their two newest members, the Nevis lads. Billy and Terry were nervous but that’s what Brad wanted. He needed to know that in a tricky situation they would stand their ground. He had tasked them with stealing a woman’s handbag. A robbery with violence.

As they stood looking for a likely target Tasha gave a startled cry, “I know her.”

The others followed her pointed finger.

“That’s Miss Howarth isn’t it?” Jonjo said questioningly.

“Sure is,” Brad confirmed, “and, she’s your target.” He turned to look at the Nevis brothers.

Billy glanced straight at his brother, “You ready Tez?”

"Sure am, let's go." It was bravado though as Terry was petrified and hoped his brother would take the lead as he usually did in difficult situations.

To the gang watching from the side-lines they saw the boys make a confident approach to their target, but both the brothers were truly scared at what they were about to do. Inside though they were more scared of what would happen if they didn't do it. The ridicule and physical repercussions. A simple task, grab the shoulder bag and run.

"You distract her and I'll grab the bag, okay Tez?" Billy said in hushed tones as he split from his brother's side and walked towards Jackie Howarth.

As they got within a few feet of her, she looked up and recognition dawned on her face, quickly followed by fear as she noticed the aggressive nature of their approach. She abruptly stopped and in anticipation she clutched her bag close to her chest.

Terry spun to the left and Jackie Howarth turned to face him. Billy made a grab for the bag but he wasn't strong enough to tear it from her grip. Terry saw his brother struggling to free the bag and noticed that Miss Howarth had now turned to face him. He glanced quickly across to the watching gang where he saw Brad give him an example of a shoulder charge. He quickly turned back to see the continuing struggle between his brother and Miss Howarth and just lunged forward, throwing his whole body weight, little that it was, behind the move.

As Terry connected, Jackie Howarth lost balance and hit the ground quite hard. She put her hands out to protect herself from the fall, which released her hold on the bag. Billy pulled the bag but it was still looped around her arm.

He leaned down and taking hold of the strap he said, "Just let go for God's sake, just let go!"

Jackie looked up into his eyes and saw the fear there, reluctantly she lifted her hand and Billy pulled the bag free. With the speed of the attack no one nearby had any time to react as the two lads sprinted off towards their friends, Billy holding the bag aloft like a trophy.

Monday 10 Jun
0845hrs

As the early morning sun filled the main entrance block of the school, the head teacher, Joanne Tindall, stood basking in its rays. It was true that education in the country was in a terrible mess but her team and she had fought off imminent closure and here they were re-opening for the final half term of the year. She felt very proud to be part of this team. If they could make it to summer then they could re-group. Government intervention in the whole problem across schools could then give them a new start in September after the long summer break. She dared to hope.

Her reverie was interrupted, as usual, by the appearance of Will McCormick arriving at her side.

"Morning Boss," he handed her a cup of coffee from the machine in the canteen in a disposable cup.

"Morning Will," she popped the lid off and took a deep smell of the coffee's aroma.

"Is this your first cup of the day?"

"Of course it is," she replied glancing at her watch. "How about you?"

"My third."

"How many do you drink in a day Will?"

After a quick pause for thought he responded, "At least twelve."

"Twelve!"

"Yep."

"Ever thought what would happen if you stopped your caffeine intake?" she chided.

Will chuckled, "Probably sleep for a year."

Joanne laughed, "Well don't expect me to pay you for that year," she playfully slapped him on the arm. "Come on then, show me the changes you've done over the past week."

Will opened the main door for her as two late arrivals dodged past them both with subdued 'good mornings'. "After you," he gestured outside. "Thought we would start with the external buildings and then do a lap of the main building." With that he turned slightly right and stopped in front of the impressive two-storey Science Block.

"Completely closed down and any dangerous items have been transferred into the main school." He moved a few feet further along and pointed to the Performing Arts Block, "Same here, completely closed down and all dangerous musical instruments have been moved into the main building."

Joanne chuckled. Through all the years she had known Will, his sense of humour had been a constant. He never failed to make her laugh, whatever the situation. "I hope that doesn't include your singing?"

"I resent that remark," he responded as he gently took her arm and turned her towards the Sports Hall. "Where we are stood will now be the new parking area and to further aid security we have three of the local lollipop persons coming to man the main school entrance during the day." He pointed to the main gate but quickly put his arm back down when he realised quite foolishly that Joanne would know where it was.

"How much are these changes going to cost us?" she enquired.

"That's a tricky one Joanne, the council are helping us out with some of it and as you know the government is negotiating with the teaching unions to see about cutting the pay of those teachers who are refusing to work. That should free up more funds."

She sighed, "Now that's a minefield I'm glad I don't have to deal with."

"There is talk of the Army and or the TA being deployed to hot spots!" Will mentioned.

"Yes, I heard they were on permanent standby."

Will gave her a quizzical look.

"My neighbour is a Captain in the TA and he was telling me about being on 24 hours standby. Fancies himself as a bit of a Captain Mainwaring," she chortled.

"Don't tell them your name Pike!" Will mused. "With all due respect to our lollipoppers I would rather have the Army or TA watching over us, especially at night."

"Same here."

A look of incredulity passed between them before Will shrugged and continued with the guided tour, "Now the big changes have taken place in the PE Building." They both walked the short distance into the main Sports Hall and Gym One.

Will motioned to his right where Gym Two used to be, now all boarded off. "Gym Two is now a staff sleeping area and of course during the evenings and nights the staff here have full access to the showers and changing rooms." He led Joanne to the left and they stood in between the various doors of this end of the building.

"Changers on the left will be checked and cleaned thoroughly after last lesson and again every morning before school starts."

"How many staff will be camping out in Gym Two? Do we know yet?"

"Three or four have said they will spend Monday to Thursday nights in here and we've been thinking of a rota maybe?" Will replied.

"Sounds like we might not need the rota?"

"We thought two other staff every night would make a good night shift, six in all." Will said, obviously having put a lot of thought into this. "Maybe a weekend shift too?" he shrugged.

This was something totally new and alien to teaching staff and it was happening all over the country.

"Okay, I will leave that in your capable hands," she smiled at him.

Will nodded in recognition.

"Any home comforts for them?" Joanne asked, knowing how boring it would be.

"Yes," Will walked a few extra steps to the end entrance, pointing. "As you can see the staffroom is just over there and we have put a lock on the external door. Inside there we have access to some basic cooking facilities."

Joanne interrupted, "Can't they just cook in here, somewhere?"

"Ha, if only it was that easy. Fire regulations don't exist for this building and I only had a week to organise this."

"I see. You've done great Will, so far," she teased. "What else?"

"They have a kettle over here, big screen TV which IT have hooked up to the local BT line. We have put a radio base station in here and added six pagers to it. You will be getting yours later!"

"Thanks," she responded sarcastically.

"Mobiles will be the main line of communications with a member of SLT on call every night, you're not included in that by the way," Will added with a smile.

"I don't mind being on the call out roster."

"That's okay, if you get called you know it's something we can't handle." Smiling as he continued, "We have a special night shift comms page on the intranet which we can access from home with alerts when needed."

They both moved outside the PE Building back into the blinding sunlight, shielding his eyes where Will had a quick glance at his watch which revealed first bell was about to ring. They headed back to the main building. Will quickly covered the other changes explaining how fire exits had been changed, with some locked for extra security, all with the agreement of the local fire service.

1155hrs

For nearly two weeks the gang known as the Killingburn Road Posse had been living in the Miner's Tavern, coming and going as they pleased. Stealing on the streets, ransacking empty houses - even at one stage car-jacking, but they were starting to get bored. Some of their more essential items were running out, namely tabs and booze. Some scuffles had broken out but Brad had mainly kept a lid on things.

"You got the last of the tabs Jack, it's not fair that you get the crisps too," a very agitated Jonjo explained.

"Let's face it Jonjo, I'm just faster than you are," Jack laughed.

"Fuck off and hand some over, you can't eat five packets anyway."

"I can eat as many packets as I fucking well like and you….."

"Quiet!"

The room fell silent as Brad stood up from his seat in front of the TV. "You're like a pair of old women." His gaze now fell on Jonjo and Jack, "Jonjo stop the whining, Jack give him two packets of crisps for fuck's sake."

"But…" Jack started.

"Now!"

Nathan had been sat next to Brad watching the news and he clicked the up arrow on the volume and grabbed Brad's arm, "Here it is Brad, the school story I was telling you about."

Brad slowly returned to his seat and gave a bemused shake of his head intentionally so that the others could see his annoyance with their behaviour.

Nathan tugged on Brad's sleeve, "Here, listen."

The reporter was stood outside a school in Danford, West Yorkshire. Smoke could still be seen drifting up from part of the school building behind her. "The local fire service have put out the main blaze but they are still fighting a number of residual blazes on the grounds, as you can see behind me. The school only closed down two days ago amid scenes of carnage after two large groups of youths attacked staff and police with stones and home-made petrol bombs."

The newsreader in the studio was nodding along to the reporter's comments before proffering her a question, "Thanks Kate and what is the situation like in the area of Danford itself?"

"Well Soriya, before the school closed there was a semblance of control. The police were keeping the gangs in check but then the closure forced too many young people onto the streets with not enough provision for their well-being or education. A few students were passed on to other schools but the majority had nowhere to go and more importantly nothing to do."

Nathan turned to Brad with a mischievous smile on his face and said just one word, "Chaos!" He hit the mute button.

Brad looked back at him, "What are you thinking gypsy boy?"

"Simple," Nathan replied. "If we can force your school to close down think how many recruits we could get then?"

Brad turned back to look at the silent screen, the news continued showing more scenes of disorder in schools around the country. Brad wasn't the most intelligent of individuals but he was a good thinker. With Jack looking on, jealous of this newfound friendship in the hierarchy of the gang, Brad rose to his feet. He gave Nathan a little fist pump again unknowingly hurting his best friend Jack's feelings.

"Okay guys, listen in," he looked around the pub's lounge ensuring everyone was paying him attention. "We have a few jobs on this afternoon with the house clearances and gathering our donations from some of our 'friendly' local shops but I want everyone in here for five o'clock sharp." He raised his arms in the air turning so he caught everyone's eye. "We will be having a war council!"

1704hrs

During the early afternoon Brad and Nathan had spent a long time chatting before they called in Jack, Louis and Tasha to help them make plans. It was obvious that they had already decided what to do and were just being gracious to these three. Louis and Tasha didn't mind; Jack did.

Now the whole gang, 17 members strong by this time were gathered on a variety of chairs, benches and small tables, eyes glued to the crude felt pen drawing on the pub wall in between the two main windows. Brad stood to one side, pool cue in hand, Nathan the other, likewise equipped. At a nod from Brad Nathan commenced the war council.

"Welcome guys to the KRP War Council. Can you all see this excellently drawn map of Ashton High School?" He bowed as a smattering of applause and table slapping followed his introduction. "Our task is a simple one, to inflict as much damage as possible on the school, and it's staff, to force it to close down. The result being our gang will increase in size, dramatically, and then we can aim for bigger things. Much bigger things."

Some of those listening clapped whilst others just sat back, awed by the declaration.

"I will hand you over to our illustrious leader who will go into more details. Mr Jones," he gestured across to Brad who took a short step forward, assuming control.

"Okay guys, the plan is simple, a three pronged attack with all three happening at the same time to cause maximum damage." Woops and hoots followed this announcement. Brad regained quiet, the swishing of his pool cue helping with that. "So team one will drive two cars through the main gate and smash them through the front school entrance. Team two will go over the south fence, break in and set fire to the Science building whilst team three will go over the back fence and cause as much damage as possible to the back of the school." Brad paused, looking around at the mixture of shock and satisfaction on many faces. Some he could not read, including Jack's.

The first hand went up from a massive young man sat on one of the benches.

"Yes Tank," Brad responded, pointing towards the giant with his cue.

"What do we do if other kids get in the way?" Tank asked.

"No worries mate, all attacks commence at eight o'clock, there will be very few kids around at that time. Next," as he pointed the cue at Gaz sitting at the front.

"Where do we get the cars from Brad?"

"Cheers Gaz, that leads nicely on to the final part of my presentation today. You will split into your teams now to get the things together you need for the attack. Jack and Nathan are in team one, me and Tasha in team two and Jonjo and Louis lead team three."

Brad spent the next couple of minutes splitting the gang into teams; two to team one to help the drivers, two to his team, the burners and the remainder to the stone-throwing team three.

"We've got a lot to get ready tonight guys, with cars, ladders, petrol bombs, stones and more so meet up now with your team leaders."

A nervous atmosphere had been created and a sense of anticipation filled the room.

Tuesday 11 Jun
0742hrs

As the sun's penetrative rays dislodged the early cloud cover, the temperature began to rise. It was going to be another balmy day in Ashton but by the end of the day there would be a hell of a lot more to worry the residents.

With almost military precision the three groups of teenagers arrived at their start positions. Brad's team of four, carrying two boxes of Molotov cocktails, arrived unseen at the southern edge of the school and were hidden by a patch of small bushes. The two cars, driven by Jack and Nathan, were parked in between the shops and tanning salon where the gang had nigh on two weeks earlier launched an attack on Jackie Howarth. She had recovered now and being a strong individual had returned to work. The final group had worked their way along the River Esse and turned east towards the school. The problem they had was that it was all open ground with very little cover so even before they had reached the rear fence they had drawn some curious looks from some of the school staff. This team had most of the gang members, ten in all. Although led by Jonjo, Louis had given him some good ideas on where to put their people as they approached the fence. The group split in to four pairs, each sharing a backpack full of stones. The final two members were put on the two extremes, the corners of the school perimeter fence keeping watch, although they also had pockets full of stones to cause some damage with.

Brad and Tasha had spent some time looking through the gaps in the fence into the massive Science block but had still seen no signs of life. Brad was quite happy with this as together with Tasha and the assistance of Gaz and Shovel they were going to unleash a fiery hell on this part of the school.

As the time for the attack to begin grew closer, Jack was getting more and more nervous. He was in the lead car with Tank who held a small box containing the two Molotov cocktails they had been given to use. Jack had wanted more but Brad had insisted that together with the damage the car would do, two should be enough. Jack hadn't been happy but acquiesced.

Both drivers and the other two team leaders each had a Motorola portable handheld radio. These, together with a lot of other items, had been stolen last night but they had forgotten to steal a charging station too and were now unsure how long the power in the radios would last.

As eight o'clock approached, Brad took out his radio and prepared to send the start message. His palms were sweating and the radio felt cold in his grip. He played the words over in his head and smiled as he thought how an Army commander must have felt before launching an attack in a battle.

"This is Gang Leader. Drivers, start your engines." They had decided on not using names over the air just in case someone in the authorities was listening in. "Team two and team three prepare to launch attack when you hear the signals from team one." He paused, turned and smiled at Tasha then finished, "Out."

Tasha returned his excited smile, "Time to light up."

"Just give it a few secs to make sure Jack and Nathan get the cars moving okay," Brad said as he held out a calming hand.

0758hrs

Inside Ashton High School the second day back after half term seemed to be starting okay. Assemblies were being planned in the main hall for all students now that the SLT had an idea of how many were still attending. A few of them, including Joanne Tindell were setting up a PowerPoint on the drop down screen in the hall and checking the right amount of chairs with the morning caretaker, Jimmy Nelson.

Upstairs, in the Humanities and English corridor, some teachers were preparing for their lessons. After all, exams were still being held.

John Reynolds had been popping in and out of classrooms ensuring everyone present was getting ready until he was stopped in his tracks in MFL classroom one.

"John, have you seen these lot out the back?" queried Orianna de Suza, an amazing MFL teacher from Spain.

John had already moved onto the next room but checked back, "Seen what?"

Orianna gestured to him and he followed her to the rear windows of her room, "These guys have been stood out here for ten minutes, they look a little mischievous."

John quickly took in their numbers and then motioned for Orianna to follow him. They quickly arrived at the end of the corridor, at the window at the top of the stairs.

"I noticed these four earlier." Pointing towards the group including Brad he continued, "And look, they are still there?"

"Looks like they have some boxes with them and the others had backpacks!" Orianna stated, some trepidation in her voice.

"You know, you're right," John turned to head down the stairs. "I'm going to let SLT know. You keep an eye on them for me please, I'll be back in a tick."

With that he was gone, down the stairs and straight into the hall. It only took a few seconds to locate Joanne Tindell and as he walked towards her, he raised his arm. Joanne smiled as he approached and then he embarrassingly brought his arm down. "Sorry, force of habit." They both smiled.

"What's up John?" Joanne asked.

"Well, not to alarm you but we've seen two different groups of kids hanging around outside the school perimeter fence, one around the back and the other behind the Science block." He gestured generally with his arms as he explained.

"Yes, we knew about the Science block group, I've sent Will over there to check it out. He has taken the block keys so he can have a sneaky look at them from inside without raising suspicion."

John became slightly more worried saying, "He should be careful, they have some boxes with them. Not quite sure what they are up to?"

Joanne headed towards the entrance John had come in through. "Come on, show me the other group you saw."

Parked behind the tanning salon Jack gunned the engine. Parked where he had full view of the school entrance the adrenalin was coursing through his body. Sat in the back seat was Tank, clumsily hanging on to the two Molotov cocktails, a nervous expression on his face.

He looked to the left, road clear, then slowly pulled the car out onto Waterloo Way. The school entrance quickly appeared on the left. He quickly checked the rear view mirror, saw their second car right behind him and gave Nathan a distinctive nod. He swung the car through the narrow entranceway and accelerated towards the main school building, tooting the horn three times. The signal.

The car bumped up the two steps and crashed through the main façade which was 90 per cent glass. It made one hell of a mess but with no handbrake applied it gently rolled back and prevented Nathan in the second car from swinging right to his attack point which would have destroyed the rest of the main entrance.

On Jonjo's command, team three started launching their missiles at the massive array of glass windows on the rear side of the school. Several broke within the first few seconds.

Joanne and John reached the top of the stairs as the first windows at the rear were broken but Joanne now walked toward the side window and immediately saw the small group huddled next to the fence.

Gaz, Shovel and Brad all held two Molotov's each. Tasha had a lighter in her hand and she moved along the line, lighting each one as she went.

Joanne saw flames.

"Oh no, fire bombs!" she screamed.

John grabbed the radio from his panic stricken friend, "Will, get out of the Science Block, we think they've got petrol bombs!"

As soon as Gaz saw his second Molotov lit he stood, turned and threw one at the building, quickly followed by the second. Both of them struck wall but the flames spread down the brickwork like a rolling river as the flammable liquid coursed down. Shovel was more assured in his aim and both of his broke through windows into the darkness beyond. Brad took his time with his first throw and his followed one of Shovel's through a first floor window. The second burnt his hand slightly and was thrown too quickly to have any aim, it missed, again hitting the wall.

Will heard the first window smash and then the whoosh of both flame and heat. He glanced back through the window he had just been looking through to see a flaming bottle flying towards it. He instinctively jumped to his left into the doorway as the bomb broke the window and landed on the opposite side of the classroom. The blast of heat took his breath away and he rolled over and sat up to see half of Chemistry Two engulfed in flames. As he was preparing to get up the second petrol bomb came through the window landing ten feet short of him.

Nathan, having no way past Jack's vehicle, allowed his to roll back and he applied the handbrake. He knew the Science building to the left was being attacked and then the neighbouring Arts block so he turned his gaze to the building opposite them, the PE Block.

They both threw.

There didn't look to be much damage but job done they climbed back into their stolen vehicle and prepared to scarper.

More than half of the windows had now been broken at the back of the school when a strange thing occurred. The staff from the main hall and the first floor classrooms were putting up a fight. They were gathering up the fallen stones and started to throw them back. Those thrown from the first floor were particularly dangerous as they had the advantage of height.

The group of eleven youngsters were actually being forced back by the ferocity and fervour of the staff's response. Brad had moved his team up twenty or thirty yards and they followed the same procedures as last time but Brad caught Gaz by the arm and slowed him down. He didn't want to see any petrol bombs wasted after all the time it had taken to prepare them.

"It's not a cricket ball Gaz, "Brad remarked. "Just lob it at the window, the glass will break."

Gaz did as he was told and a broad grin crossed his face as both his bombs crashed through the same window into one of the two music rooms. Brad again struck with a fifty percent hit rate but flames were pouring out of the various windows they had hit so he was happy with the results.

The heat now coming from the two buildings was quite ferocious so the four of them backed away and then made for the rear of the school to meet up with team three.

Will was crawling through the dimly lit corridor of the Science Block, thick smoke seemed to fill every space he could see. He stopped to wretch again, gasping for breath when he felt a hand on his shoulder. He rolled onto his side and through the gloom he saw the big, smiling face of the caretaker, Alex Small.

"Come on Big Man, let's get you out of here." The big, genial Scot lifted him up. "Don't think we want deep fried Will McCormick on the menu."

Will smiled, "You'll have your deep fried Mars bar though?" Another bout of coughing left him helpless as Alex half carried him back out towards the fresh air.

Jack was livid, the car wouldn't start and although they had caused some damage to the main doors, due to his stalling of the car Nathan hadn't managed to do any more damage to the front of the building.

Tank had gone.

Jack looked in the backseat and saw one of the petrol bombs. He pulled it out and with a crazed look he took out his lighter and put the flame to the edge of the cloth hanging out of the bottle's neck. He looked at the main entrance and as anger filled him for his lost education he ran to the two steps and brought his arm back to throw.

As fate would have it his lead leg, the left one, slipping on a large shard of glass and as his body was thrown to the left, the bomb slipping from his grip. He crashed onto the lower step looking directly at the astonished face of the head teacher. It was as if the whole incident had moved into slow motion; Jack gave a cruel laugh but he simultaneously noticed the pure horror in Joanne Tindell's eyes.

Out of the corner of his right eye he saw the flaming glass bottle come in to view and crash on the top step. The heat produced in that instant was so intense it fused Jack's eyes closed. He wouldn't see anything ever again but he felt every split second of burning agony as his whole body was engulfed in flames.

At that moment Nathan screamed Jack's name, his voice louder than he had ever thought possible. He looked on horrified as Jack somehow rose to his feet, moving in the direction of his voice. After only a few steps he fell to his knees, flames leaping from his body in oranges, purples and blues. Without a sound he collapsed face first onto the hardened concrete of the main yard.

Will and Alex reached the doorway to exit the Science Block just as Jack Mills collapsed and perished. Will was motionless, unable to move but Alex sensed more danger from his right as he saw three youths stood around the second vehicle. He had served with the Royal Fusiliers in Afghanistan and had seen some terrible things out there; it did not faze him. They ducked back inside the block entrance.

Nathan knew there was nothing he could do. He jumped back behind the steering wheel as Tank and Tubs both strangely clambered into the back of the car. Still looking towards the body of Jack he selected reverse and backed out through the main gates. Instead of heading to an area near the pub as previously planned, he went right and took the first right after the school.

Brad and his group had met up with the stone throwers and were reliving their triumphant attack when they heard the screaming engine of a car coming towards them. They all looked across and saw a single vehicle coming along the school park path, Nathan behind the wheel. Brad had a sudden feeling of dread.

The chaos caused by the attack had galvanised the staff into a quick clean-up operation, the Police, Fire and Ambulance services were on their way. Apart from Will there were a few cuts and bruises to be dealt with. There was Jack of course, but Joanne made sure that he was covered with a blanket from reception, a strange wispy smoke still exuding from his remains.

As police and paramedics were checking over the injured and taking initial statements a car pulled up outside the main entrance. One by one, those present turned to look as Brad and three other lads got out and walked in through the pedestrian entrance.

No one said a word as they approached the body of their fallen comrade.

Brad glanced up looking directly at Joanne Tindell, an uneasy truce assumed.

No one else moved.

The four gang members rolled the body of their friend up in the blanket that had been covering him and then at a nod from Brad they lifted him slowly and started walking back to their vehicle.

Brad gave Joanne Tindell a final look over his shoulder.

She sensed pure malevolence.

1720hrs

The rest of the gang had kept well away from Brad.

The death of his best friend had hit him very hard.

Jack's remains had been put in the pub garden and once there Brad said he wanted no-one to go near them. He had brooded all afternoon, refusing to eat as the other's had. His only accompaniment, a bottle of vodka which he had just about finished. Anger bubbled inside him. He suddenly rose, striding purposefully to the leftover Molotov cocktails and scooping one up walked to the main door. He stopped and looked over his shoulder, the grief evident in his face, "No one goes anywhere until I get back."

With that he walked outside.

The devastation caused earlier in the day had been cleaned up. Very little debris remained although the scars of burning were still evident. Many of the staff had worked late, long after the emergency services had left to make sure the school was safe to open in the morning, not knowing how many pupils would brave attendance.

Sally Cowan gave out a verbal sigh as she surveyed what had been the scene of carnage earlier in the day. She stood in the main entrance, now partly boarded up although some of the glass panels had been replaced in the afternoon. As she walked down the stairs she inadvertently veered around the blackened patch of ground where young Jack Mills' life had ended. A shudder ran through her body at the vivid memory. She had seen the drama unfold from her viewing point in the SEN classroom.

Sally got to her car and as she crumpled into the front seat her thoughts went out to the family of Jack. She thought of her own two daughters, sat at home with their Dad, tea cooking, awaiting her arrival.

Brad had brooded on this action but had found the loss of his best friend a powerful weapon to fend off any guilt. He had been sat opposite the school entrance for ten minutes, hidden from view. At last a car approached the entrance to leave.

Sally got to the entrance and indicated right to head for the bridge. As she pulled to a complete stop looking both left and right she saw the dark, hooded figure walk in to the middle of the road directly in front of her. She saw a flicker of light in their right hand. A strange bottle in the left. The two were brought together. A flicker of flames now on the bottle. Sally had a sudden realisation of what was about to happen. The utter hatred in the dark eyes staring out from under the hood. She tried to scream but nothing came out of her mouth.

Brad raised the bottle and threw it with all his might through the windscreen of the car.

Sally had no chance.

Brad Jones turned right and walked slowly back to the safe haven of the pub. He glanced only once over his shoulder seeing the car engulfed in flames.

Revenge for Jack.

Thursday 13 Jun
0908hrs

It was a blazingly hot day, early mist had been quickly burnt off by the unrelenting sun. The streets of Ashton were relatively quiet. Those attending work or school had already made their way to their various locations. In the entranceway to Ashton High School a multitude of figures stood, some chatting, some stood silent in prayer or private thought.

A small display stood to one side of the pedestrian gate, its main feature was a large framed photograph of Sally Cowan. This was the spot two days ago where the brutality and vengefulness of a fifteen year old boy had ended her life. Half a dozen candles stood either side of the picture and many attending held candles, some cupping their hands around to protect the precious flame.

The air was calm and still; no candles flickered as if God had decided that this occasion in this location required it. The vigil had been going since the start of school with a varying number of attendees. Some of those staff members closest to Sally still attending school had managed to change lessons or have cover provided so they could attend. She was very well liked and her death and the manner of it had caused a lot of grief and anxiety.

Joanne moved swiftly through the temporary car park heading towards the main entrance. In her wake was Will McCormick, Ian Taylor and Mary Summers. She paused only briefly to see that repairs to the PE Block were nearly completed. She slowed to a more mournful pace as she reached the gate. She gazed around at those attending the vigil, knowing that some would hold her responsible as she had kept the school open - but most knew her and saw her resoluteness.

"Good morning and thank you all for attending this vigil," she gestured to her left. "Jean and Robert, we are so saddened by your loss. Sally was such a beautiful person and had a heart of pure gold." Those present were nodding and smiling as she spoke. "There wasn't anything she wouldn't do to help the children in this school. She will be a huge miss."

Joanne took a breath and some of those present noticed a change in her stance and when she spoke next, an edge to her voice. "For all we mourn and will continue to mourn our friend and colleague I want to make this clear. This school will not close! No matter what it takes we will stay open and we will educate the young people of this area and it will be in honour of our dear friend Sally that we do this."

The sombre attitude on that path was replaced by resilience. With her speech over, Joanne and her entourage moved among those attending the vigil offering kind words and compassion.

Will's mind drifted to the tasks ahead as he exchanged pleasantries with Sally's family and friends. How could he ensure nothing like this happened again? What contingencies needed to be put in place to protect the school and its staff? Would their homes and families be in danger? What he couldn't believe was the total apathy of the local police. He had spoken at length to both the Chief Inspector and one of his favourite ex-pupils, Sergeant Dayna Thomas, but all they responded with was current policy. Watch and inform.

1158hrs

Brad looked up, shielding his eyes as the sun breached the clouds and filled the area with bright sunlight. Around him stood all the members of the Killingburn Road Posse, numbering in the twenties now as more new recruits joined the cause.

He looked down again at his best friend. Jack was laid out in the middle of the beer garden on a pile of logs and cardboard boxes. Despite the surroundings he looked very serene, hands folded over his chest and a white sheet covering his body. Nathan had placed a penny over each of Jack's closed eyes, an old family tradition he explained, dating back to Roman times.

The clock tower on the town hall started to chime the midday accord. As the twelve chimes designating the hour started, Tasha used a lighter to set ablaze to the end of the torch they had made, an old table leg, wrapped at one end with a towel and covered in rum. It blazed brightly as the flame flickered purple, orange and yellow. As the chimes neared the end, Brad glanced across at Jonjo who was counting them off on his fingers.

Brad smiled.

Jonjo reached ten then glanced up in confusion having run out of fingers.

Brad counted the eleventh chime on his left hand then slowly put the torch to the funeral pyre on the stroke of twelve. It took a few seconds for the pyre to get going but soon flames, crackling brightly, started to engulf the body of the young man lying there.

Brad thought it strange in a way, burning the body after it had been burnt to death but it was a pact Jack and he had made recently when they realised things were going to start getting dangerous. He threw the torch into the growing flames and took out a sheet of paper from his jeans pocket. He opened it up.

After a quick nervous glance around the gathering he started, "We are here to see our friend and comrade, Jack Mills, pass into the next life. It's not something you think about doing at our age but me and Jack were chatting about this not long ago. He had been playing 'Invasion' on his computer and told me about Viking funerals. So this is what he gets."

He looked up to note the reactions from those around. Most had heads bowed, Nathan had his eyes closed, as if in prayer. Brad smiled at that as he continued, "Jack and me go back a long way and we have always had each other's backs. I suppose that couldn't always be, as I might have been able to do something to prevent his dying."

Brad grabbed another can of lager and popped it open before holding it up to the sky. "To Jack," he said in a loud but trembling voice.

The rest of the gang repeated his toast and Nathan added, "Hope your journey is a good one mate."

Brad smiled at Nathan before continuing, "Those who knew him have to add an item that reminds us of Jack, I'll start."

Brad took out the two toy soldiers he always carried with him and gently threw them into the flames. Others started to take out things they had prepared: a Toon baseball cap, a toy car, a comic, a games joystick. Brad watched intently as one by one this strange collection of items followed his into the flames, and then Smooth leaned over and dropped a ten pound note onto the pyre. Brad gave him a strange look.

Smooth explained, "I owed him it, from a bet we made."

Brad chuckled knowing that was one of Smooth's favourite lines, 'I'll bet you a tenner.' He looked at Smooth, "He won again?"

Smooth gave him a rueful smile.

With the formalities, such as they were, completed, the gang continued their plans to get pissed.

1336hrs

The area around Bridge Street and the connecting Waterloo Way and Esse Lane were now starting to resemble a media scrum. Vehicles jostled for position and they were huge. Outside Broadcast Units normally consisted of a large wagon, sometimes articulated, and various dismounted items including satellite dishes, antenna, reporting platforms etc. They all wanted to get that special shot so cameramen and women were wandering around the paths and roads looking to see if they could get the perfect background shot before parking up their vehicle, claiming that spot.

To say it was a hive of activity would be an understatement.

The locals at first thought of the positives, the increase in local revenue and custom but thoughts soon drifted to the negatives: notoriety, long term effects on tourism and such like. Who could tell what the future held but it seemed that for the moment they were in the spotlight.

The local hairdressers and Rags to Riches, the only posh clothes shop in the town, were making a roaring trade. It seemed a number of the residents were expecting to appear on TV, and wanted to look their best.

The day itself appeared to start as normal but slowly through the morning after the live broadcast of the vigil for Sally Cowan, the mass media had started to arrive. No one knew if it was the vigil itself, the tears from family and friends or that final comment from Joanne Tindell that whatever happened the school would stay open - regardless of the reason and similar troubles in various locations around the country - it appeared that the town of Ashton was becoming the countries measuring stick for the massive rise in troubles based around education.

1621hrs

After a long and hectic day in Ashton the town seemed to be settling down. As people finished work and set off for their homes one final disturbing event was to put everyone on tenterhooks for the foreseeable future. At first it seemed like nothing, a lone Army Land Rover casually moving along the town's main street. Travelling from east to west it drove very slowly, nearly bringing traffic to a standstill, especially as it drove past the school. It stopped and pulled over just before the main bridge over the River Esse. Half a dozen soldiers jumped out, two of them crossed the bridge and two moved to the side of the bridge and started putting out cones and then a barrier. Some of the locals stopped to ask questions but were quickly ushered away.

Captain Peter Terry and his radioman remained next to the Land Rover as the others completed their tasks. The media teams noticed this too and cameras were rapidly trained in their direction. The sun was creeping ever closer to the horizon and the colours covering the land forged by the hills beyond took on a deep red glow. Captain Terry grabbed the radio handset, "Hello, Alpha One, this is Charlie Zero Two, message over."

There was a crackle and a pause from the VHF421 radio after he released the pressel switch. Then came the response, "Alpha One, send over."

"Charlie Zero Two, the bridge is secure and the route is clear as planned, send the convoy in, over."

"Alpha One, Roger, Out."

It only took a few minutes before a line of Army vehicles followed the route previously taken by the Land Rover. Again, they drove slowly, engines loud, a distinctive show of force to those who were watching and those who would hear about it later. The media around the school lapped this up, live broadcasts flashed around the country and the globe.

The vehicles came to the bridge, Captain Terry and his radioman both threw up a salute, as the lead vehicle had their commander on board. Lieutenant Colonel Peter Alderson BEM had been given the task of quelling the problems arising in this little northern town. Although he had pre-meditated a showy arrival he did not bring as many troops as some had advised. He used to be a local, he knew the people. He knew a larger force would be met by a similar sized show of defiance. He needed to try and keep things as small scale as possible, numbers-wise.

As the convoy crossed the bridge they took an immediate right parallel to the opposite bank. In time it would lead to another bridge back over the river and into the grounds of Esse Castle. This was to be their base for the foreseeable future. As the last of the vehicles as being parked up the Commanding Officer walked over to the main entrance to check all was well. Peter Alderson was a highly intelligent, well-educated man who had taken to Army life as would a duck to water. His men adored him as he was as straight as an arrow but didn't tolerate any bad behaviour. He was tall, good looking for his age and had a certain charm too. He loved nothing better than getting stuck into work with his men, this was his most endearing trait. Soldiers like nothing better than someone who leads by example, from the front; Peter Alderson was that man.

Captain Terry alighted from the last vehicle and walked over to the CO, "Good evening Sir," as he threw up the expected salute. "Did everyone get here okay?"

"Yes Tez, all present and accounted for. Make sure the guys get squared away with accommodation and get the chefs to prepare an evening meal." He glanced over towards the house situated on the edge of the large grassed and partly paved area they had been allocated. "I believe we are staying with the groundskeeper in his spare room?"

"Excellent Sir, I'll make sure your kit gets stowed in there."

"Thanks. I am going over to visit the police station, see if they can give us an update."

"Okay Sir, looks like your driver is waiting for you over there," he gestured to a short wheel based Land Rover with a slovenly looking soldier leaning on the bonnet, fag in hand. "Good luck."

Peter Alderson gave a shrug and shot his subordinate a final question, "Why did you give me Smith as a personal driver again?" This was accompanied by a sarcastic smile.

"To improve the man's attitude and outlook and to enhance his Army future," Pete Terry smiled.

"What do I get out of it?"

"A driver," this time a snigger escaped from his mouth.

"Okay, Captain Peter Bartholomew Terry, you can have that one, but I expect a nice bottle of Burgundy to go with my evening meal tonight."

Peter Terry sprung to attention before giving an outrageous salute, both men laughed, "Consider it done Sir."

With that the CO gestured to Smith to get rid of his fag and start the vehicle. This would be a long, busy evening.

Saturday 15 Jun
1020hrs

The earlier golden sunrise had heralded what was going to be a beautiful day. An early mist had burned off the River Esse and the views from the upper floor windows of the Premier Inn were stunning. South, the river meandered its way to the nearby coast if you could ignore the rows of pit houses on the east bank. To the north it flowed steadily under the narrow archways of the bridge leading into Ashton, onwards towards the picturesque Esse Castle on the same eastern bank as the town and opposite the caravan park.

Becky had lived here all of her life, in Ashton. Not academically gifted she had left school at sixteen and was lucky enough to find work straight away with the Premier Inn. She mostly enjoyed the work, the wage wasn't too bad and there were some added perks. Some of the male guests were very charming and very generous when guilt ridden after a naughty night. Most were married or in a relationship and that suited Becky, she was only 19 and intent on having some fun before she thought of anything serious.

She drifted through some of the more pleasant memories as she finished changing a quilt cover in her final room on this floor.

Her radio crackled into life on the trolley she had parked in the doorway, "Becky, its Jacqui, are you nearly finished up there?" a slight pause before her boss continued, "It's getting a bit busy down here and we could do with some help?"

Becky picked up the handset, she didn't like using the radio, she though it very strange especially with everyone owning a mobile phone nowadays.

She clicked the call button, "Becky here, I am just finishing up in room 24, I will be down soon." She quickly put the radio down.

"Okay Becky, as quick as you can." It then went silent.

Becky looked out of room 24's window for a few more seconds before straightening the quilt a little and heading to collect her trolley. Once the cleaning trolley was safely locked away in the second floor cleaning cupboard she headed down the stairs. Staff weren't allowed to use the one elevator, in case guests needed it.

When she threw open the swing door into reception a scene of customer carnage hit her.

It was frantic, packed with all manner of people.

She glanced across to the reception desk where her boss, the day manager, Jacqui Shaw was on the PC and the main receptionist, Carl Thomas, was checking through the key cards.

Jacqui saw her and beckoned her over, "Becks darling, would you help with booking guests in so I can check what rooms are available or not?"

"Of course Jacqui." Becky slid past her boss and sat behind the PC, hand on the mouse ready.

"Mr Simms has asked for a room for a week so I am going to see if we can move some of the short term guests around to free up some long term bookings, not just for him but for others who will probably want the same." She half smiled, aware that it would be a difficult task.

Becky put on her best smile, "Okay Mr Simms, are you here on your own or is there anyone else in your party?"

Larry Simms, a national reporter by trade worked by himself but he quickly understood how busy the hotel was. "Don't you have any single rooms?"

Jacqui was studying the board behind reception seeing if she could juggle some free space for long term bookings. She had quickly realised earlier in the morning that the recent troubles had brought more visitors to the area than usual. She didn't want to turn away guests though.

"Yes Mr Simms, we have one or two but if there is anyone you could share with I would be most appreciative?" Jacqui replied to his question.

Larry Simms gave a smirk to her response which was not lost on her. He quickly looked around behind and someone caught his eye.

He waved, shouting, "Bob, Bob Hemmings."

An older man, dressed in a smart jacket and open-necked shirt waved back.

Larry waved him over through the crowd. When Bob got within earshot he asked him, "Do you fancy sharing a room for the week Bob?" he gestured backwards with his head, "They're a bit busy in here and running out of rooms."

Bob finally fought his way to his colleague's side, "Sharesies, okay."

Becky gave him a thumbs-up and set to work with the mouse.

Jacqui gave him a thankful smile.

As Bob slid his small backpack onto the counter he looked thoughtful, as if trying to remember something important. "Let me get the room this time and you can get the bar bill at the end of the week."

Larry laughed.

"Yes Larry, I remember last time we bunked up in Belfast," he nodded slowly, knowing his friend remembered, "I got stung with the bar bill when you got 100 per cent back on the room from your lots expenses."

Larry looked perplexed. "Didn't your rag give you 100 per cent of the bar bill?"

"No," was the terse response from Bob, "They only gave me half, said it was too excessive!"

They both laughed.

The rest of the morning was going to be just as busy at the Inn. It appeared most of the countries press and television crews were going to be descending on this quiet part of the World.

1544hrs

John Middleton was slumped in his favourite armchair, daydreaming. The tatty, old leather chair had been his for years but his wife had banned it from the house. It didn't fit in with her 'chic' looking ideas in the living room or anywhere else for that matter.

He was okay with that.

So here it sat in the rest room behind the main office of the Esse Caravan Park. The only problem was that this had been his first chance to relax all day, and it was nearly teatime.

People had been arriving in their droves over the past two days. Ashton had become something of a Mecca for all kinds, not just the normal holiday makers but journalists, TV crews, bloggers, you name it and they were heading this way.

He knew one of the girls who cleaned rooms at the Prem Inn and knew it was the same there. The infamy of Ashton was spreading.

A call from the office brought him back to his senses, "John, can you give one of the customers a hand with their connections please?"

It was his wife Elaine's voice, so up he jumped and quickly strode back into the office. A quick glance up at the wall clock showed he had been away for only fifteen minutes and hadn't had the chance to grab a coffee.

His wife noticed the look and picked up a vending token from the box they resided in, flipping it to her husband of 18 years, "Get yourself a coffee love," she smiled. "Looks like you need it."

John flipped open the counter and small door below it and ignoring the pleas around him he walked up to the hot drinks machine, slipped the token into the slot and pressed 'Latte'. He was rewarded about 40 seconds later with a small, grey plastic cup full of his steaming coffee. He took a sip. It seemed to instantly revive him as he placed the cup on the counter and turned to face the avalanche of comments coming his way.

"Okay gentlemen," he said in a raised voice. "Please, oh and ladies too," as he gave a cursory nod to a middle-aged woman stood just inside the door.

The noise died down.

John looked across at his wife who was dealing with a customer, "Where are Jenny and Max?" Jenny was their 17-year old daughter and Max was her older boyfriend. He helped out at the caravan park as a paid assistant but Jenny was in sixth form so was only available to help mostly at weekends. She had only just finished her first year and was hoping to go on holiday with Max but they had both been roped in to help on the site, due to the invasion.

Elaine replied to John's question, "I sent them over to the camping site as it's getting busy there too."

"Okay, let's try and sort out the dramas here then." He turned back and looked at the man standing immediately in front of him, "Hello Sir, how can I help you?"

A tall distinguished looking gent in plain trousers and an opened-necked shirt looked flustered, "I need a hook up?"

John was ready to throw in a quick joke but after a glance towards his wife, who frowned, decided against it. "What vehicle do you have and where is it parked?"

"It's a campervan and I am in slot 18 but this gentleman," he gestured to an older gent who looked more of the caravanning type and was stood next to him, "he is in slot eight and is hooked up to the single power point." The campervan man gave an exasperated shrug.

"I see the problem sir, slots one to ten and eleven to twenty are opposite each other and they all have two points, so one each." He changed his gaze to the caravanner and then back to campervan man. "Now eight and eighteen only have one connection between them due to an intermittent fault," both men nodded in agreement. "I can lay a cable from this main building to you Sir in slot eighteen." This incurred a shrug form campervan man, "Or I can give you a double connector junction box?"

The two men looked at each other and then both posed a question.

The man with the campervan asked how the bill would be split and the caravan man asked, how it could have not been foreseen as a problem.

"Okay, gentlemen, question one is," he looked at the first man, "We put the meter on both connection points and it gives you a direct reading of how much electric you use." He now glanced across at the second man. "We aren't normally, well, this busy so have avoided this problem in the past," he shrugged as he finished.

"Can't you fix it permanently?"

"We have had it assessed and the costs involved are enormous as they involve digging up the broken cable, retrieving it, laying a replacement cable, heavy machinery needed to do that, the list goes on.

The caravanner smiled, "Understood."

By way of further apologising John mentioned that they had never been this busy before so it was the first time this problem had reared its head. The two men prepared to leave.

John checked on his wife, "Elaine, can you cope on your own for ten while I sort out the dual connection on eight and eighteen?"

She nodded whilst still dealing with another new customer.

"I'll check on the kids too." With a smile he led the two gentlemen out of the site office.

1800hrs

In homes across the country people tuned in to the news at six o'clock hoping to hear a feel good story to lift their spirits. Instead they were bombarded with more doom and gloom.

Unemployment had reached a new high.

The incumbent Labour Party were about to get another vote of no confidence in the House of Commons.

Fuel prices were rising (again).

And to round it all off the violence in schools was increasing; 124 incidents were reported last week showing a ten to twenty percent rise for the fourth week in succession. The problem was increasing rapidly and the powers that be didn't seem to have any idea how to stop it or even slow it down. As the education system in the UK span inexorably out of control there were some suggestions ranging from closing down all educational establishments to placing small armed units within each one, but they wouldn't work. The problem wasn't in the schools, it was the young people who had been forced out of the schools due to behavioural issues. Where did the fault lie? With parents? With schools? With government? Blame was thrown far and wide but finding a solution was a long way off.

Tuesday 18 Jun
0814hrs

It hardly seemed like a week ago that so much carnage had been caused at the school. As the sun beamed from its rising place beyond the eastern horizon, the effect of being inside the newly glazed main entrance was akin to being microwaved. Well that's what Will McCormack thought as he sweltered in his usual attire of suit and tie. His collar felt a little tight and he pulled it open a little expecting a great plume of steam to emanate through the gap.

The previous few days had seen much activity in and around the school since the earlier attack. Repairs had been carried out, paint had been applied, windows replaced. This all happened with little effect on the continued running of the school. Lessons were taught. Meetings progressed. Clubs continued.

Like any other part of life, scars would fade, events would stay in the memory but life would go on. Joanne Tindell vividly remembered the events of last week. Seeing someone burn to death is something she wishes she could delete from her mind, but she couldn't. The images stored like photographs or a video in her brain's 'hard drive' had resurfaced frequently and not just in her periods of sleep but in some waking moments too. This was one such moment as she stood in the entrance bleached in the sun's rays. She could feel the heat through the glass edifice as she had the tormenting heat from the moment after the glass bottle had broken, less than ten feet in front of her. When she had gotten home that night she found that the front of her legs were pink, like sunburn, but she knew inside that it was from the fireball that had consumed Jack Mills. She shuddered at the memory but then she snapped back to the present.

"Are you okay, Joanne, are you okay?" Will was speaking to her as he looked into seemingly vacant eyes.

Joanne's immediate response upon regaining her senses was a well-prepared smile. Will had seen it many times. Not a smile of pleasure but one that responded to his question.

Will glanced around to where Joanne had been absently staring and he placed a gentle hand on her shoulder. "I don't suppose it is something that anyone could forget." He turned to look back at her, "No matter how much they were to try?"

This time, a proper smile. One that said, 'Thanks for understanding, thanks for being my friend.'

Will took this as a sign that all was well again and so he moved next to her and faced towards the open doors unerringly as they waited for their visitors to arrive. It was a couple of minutes before the first of the governors turned up. Joanne put on her best smile as Jimmy Duffy walked up the steps before shaking hands with both Joanne and Will and then being led to the conference room by the latter.

He was quickly followed by their old friend and ex-colleague, John Richardson. Evelyn Williams turned up next; she was a woman with a large personality to match her large physique. She lived to intimidate people and would always look to get her own way. 'Big, belligerent and brassy' was how Will had described her before Joanne had officially met her, the newest member of the board of governors. All Joanne could think of when she saw her or was thinking about her was the female quizzer from 'The Chase' on ITV who funnily enough was called 'The Governess.'

Several teachers passed by greeting both Joanne and the recently returned Will before the final member of the board arrived. Carrianne Edmondson was a lady of undetermined age. She was a long-standing member of the community who some saw as a do-gooder. She was devoted to the high school although she was on the board of another school in nearby Ingleside. She had the time and energy to put into any of the work required at both schools but more specifically Ashton.

Joanne greeted Carrianne and then guided her into the school, heading for the main meeting room. With the ever faithful Will at her side Joanne scrutinised those now sat around the large mahogany meeting table. A gift from a previous head it would not look out of place on the 'Antiques Roadshow.' The addition of jugs of water and empty glasses would not have improved its value on the programme but to the assembled group they were a godsend as the day had started hot and sticky. Even with the windows open the air was stifling.

Coffee, tea and pastries adorned some tables to one side and those present had taken advantage of them already, to excess some might say.

Apart from the governors, the others present were the SLT consisting of Peter Thornton (Yr9), Sheryl Townsend (Yr10) and Tom Cawthorne (Yr11). The sixth form head, Angela Newsome, had chosen not to remain in school during this troubled period. Joanne and Will covered her role with the limited numbers of sixth form who remained in school.

As the nine individuals took their seats and settled in Joanne checked her watch, 0828hrs. She knew the year ten assembly was being covered by John Reynolds and that Mary in the main office was fielding all SLT phone calls so the meeting wouldn't be interrupted or that those present would be missed. SLT meetings didn't normally take place during school hours for that reason.

She sat and started to relax.

As refreshments were being consumed and those present glanced around at each other it was the ever-forceful character of Evelyn Williams who broke the ice.

"Well everyone, I wish you a good morning and as we are all very busy people I shall move straight to the point." She glanced down at a cardboard file she had laid out in front of herself, "We have been approached by several people who have shown an interest in coming to work at this establishment."

There were mixed looks of shock and bemusement on the faces of the other governors and members of the SLT as Evelyn continued, "There are four teachers, a caretaker and two...well what can only be described as security staff." She paused and looked up.

"We'll take them," Will stated before anyone else could respond.

Joanne was quick to step in, "Will, no. We can't just have people come in to the school like that."

"I can assure you they have all been fully vetted and I have checked out the teachers personally," Evelyn added.

There followed a silence punctuated by the munching of a choc au pant in the capable hands of Pete Thornton and some noisy, if delicate, sips of tea by Carrianne.

Joanne was deep in thought, Will kept glancing to his left to try and deduce what her thoughts were.

It was Tom Cawthorne who broke the silence, "The teachers would definitely come in useful as I am sure the caretaker would to help out Phil and his crew."

Sheryl entered the conversation next. "I wouldn't say no to a couple of security guys around the school either."

Joanne looked around at her staff. Pete nodded his approval. Sheryl and Tom seemed happy enough with the possibility of additions to the dwindling staff team. Her gaze finally rested on her most trusted advisor, Will. "You think we need this help Will?"

Although he had already shown his hand with his earlier outburst Will thought a little more deliberately about it, as it appeared his yeah or nay would prove decisive. He spoke out aloud as he mulled over the pros and cons, raising his left hand, palm up, "On the one hand our staff to student ratio is too low and the staff we have coming in are tiring quickly." He put his left hand down and raised his right hand, likewise, palm up as if weighing something. "On the other hand we don't know these people and will we be seen as just escalating things?"

Joanne spoke next as the silence prolonged uncomfortably. "It's not a nuclear arms race!"

"No, but is a race of sorts," Will input.

As time passed, John Richardson had been sitting quietly listening as the discussion ebbed and flowed, never seeming to near a conclusion. He had had enough and slapped his hand down on the table. This startled some of those sat near him, in fact everyone to some degree. "Enough!" he looked around those present ensuring he had gained eye contact with everyone and then spoke slowly and more deliberately, "What is it we do? What is our main role in this community?"

An awkward silence followed.

Evelyn spoke next, "We educate the young people of this town?"

John responded, "Correct Evelyn, but we do it in a safe environment and that's where we are falling short at the moment."

Some around the table nodded in agreement as John continued.

"We don't have enough staff for the number of kids we have in school so I think we should take them up on their offer."

After a short period of reflection Evelyn posed the question, "Are we all in agreement then, we will accept the help of these people?"

Several nods and mutterings followed, as everyone seemed to be in agreement. It was strange getting outside help but some of those present just viewed it as a sort of supply role for those coming in. Joanne had been thinking about the practicalities of the situation and spoke up next. "We will get some short-term contracts drawn up. Evelyn, what can you tell us about them?"

Evelyn opened up the folder she had on the desk in front of her and read out some details. "We have Ken Thomas and Mags Allinson from St Peter's in York, they teach Maths and Humanities." She took a quick glance around those sat at the table to confirm they were listening to her before continuing, "Bob Dunleavy, an English teacher from Carlisle and a young PE teacher from Glasgow called Euan Robshaw. The caretaker has worked in this area before, his name is Neil Weston and he…."

She was interrupted by Will, "I know Neil quite well. He worked here for a while when we moved two tier."

"Correct Will, as I was about to say, about four years ago," Evelyn chastised him.

"Sorry Miss Williams," he nodded meekly acknowledging his interruption.

Evelyn smiled and prompted him to continue.

This was why Will didn't like attending the monthly meeting of the Governors. Evelyn was a very intimidating person. He recovered his poise before continuing, "Neil Weston is a great guy to know, ex-forces but he doesn't stay static too long." He looked around the table trying to glean if his prior experience of Neil would be enough to confirm his secondment to the school.

"I worked closely with Neil and he was a great support to Phil Dawson when we had to develop the infrastructure after losing the year sevens and eights. He is an ex-Army Engineer and has a very particular skill-set that would enhance…" he paused as he tried to find the right words to finish his character reference for his friend, "I'll just say it, the defence of the school."

"Is that what it has come to?" muttered Jimmy Duffy.

"I'm afraid so Jimmy," Joanne interjected.

Will went on, "He knows the school, a good number of the staff and the area."

John came back into the conversation at this point. "I remember Neil, he's a good guy, reliable and that military knowledge is just what we need right now. Whether we like it or not we face some tough times ahead and men like 'Watto' are going to prove invaluable. The security guards will also be very useful at controlling access and responding to any," he paused, "incidents!"

There was a prolonged silence as those sat around that old, Victorian table, glistening in the half-light, pondered on John's harsh insight into their situation.

Evelyn cleared her throat to speak next bringing a number of those present back to reality. "Okay, so we are settled I think, these seven individuals would enhance our current manning levels." She checked there were no objections before continuing. "Now that should bring us to the end of this meeting, unless anyone else has something to add?"

There were a few seconds of quiet before John Richardson spoke, "What about us, the governors?"

"What do you mean John?" Jimmy Duffy responded.

John looked directly at his fellow governor, "How many of us are going to stay in the school through this troubled period?"

Evelyn Williams immediately looked down, avoiding any eye contact. Jimmy Duffy looked bemused, firstly at John and then around the table.

Carrianne Edmonson allowed a little smile to herself before she responded, "You can count me in John."

John nodded at her, "Thanks Carrianne, knew we could rely on you."

"I will need some time to attend Ingleside."

"That's okay," he glanced around smiling at the permanent school staff. "I'll be here permanently and I'll bring my sleeping bag too."

Some of the others giggled and Tom spoke up, "Does that mean we might tempt you into taking a couple of lessons?"

More people joined in the laughter.

"If you are short anywhere Tom, you can put me down." John managed a big smile as he finished, "Be gentle with me though as it's been a few years since I've wielded a blackboard rubber."

Joanne tapped him on the arm, "It is whiteboards now John."

John just shrugged at that but then looked directly across the table to where Jimmy and Evelyn were sitting. "How about you two?" He knew he was putting them on the spot and he also had a good idea what their response was going to be.

Jimmy spoke up first, "You know I can't spare the time John, Town Council, Church, my diary is always full."

John switched his attention to Evelyn, raising his eyebrows to try and garner a response.

"Sleeping bags, skill-sets, defence of the school, what do we think is happening here?!" Evelyn screeched.

"War, Evelyn," John was ready with a quick response. "War is coming to Ashton High!"

0914hrs

A little later in a different part of town the sound of repeated banging had woken the inhabitants of the hostelry formerly known as the Miner's Tavern.

Brad shouted down the stairs, his voice hoarse but still powerful, "Will someone get the fucking door!"

Jonjo, a light sleeper, was already there undoing the last deadbolt. He shouted back, "Sorted Bossman!"

Outside were gathered a motley group. Three lads were lounging around one of the outdoor tables, smoking and enjoying some cider, cans from the local Nisa. Two guys, presumably who had knocked, stood immediately in front of the door, smiling like Cheshire cats. Off to the side, sat at another of the picnic-style tables was a gorgeous young girl, about fifteen or sixteen Jonjo thought.

He returned his gaze to the two hyperactive guys stood in front of him. "And who the hell are you lot, waking us up this early in the morning?"

The two stood at the door answered first, "I'm Bang and he's Smash" the smaller one spluttered.

"I'm Smash and he's Bang," his friend corrected him.

They were nudging each other until the second guy put and arm around his mate's neck. "It's Smash and Bang stupid, you can't say Bang and Smash."

His friend retorted, "Why not?"

"Because I say so, it's Smash and Bang."

Jonjo held up his hand to stop them, "Enough, what do you want?"

Smash and Bang continued to nudge and push each other ignoring the question. They were obviously some kind of strange double act.

It was the young girl who stood up and spoke next. "We are all here to join up with your gang," she walked towards him, past the wrestling duo. "Are you taking recruits?" she asked as she walked in through the door.

Jonjo was mesmerised by the beauty of the young woman as she passed right in front of him. On closer inspection he noticed her piercing blue eyes and some intricate tattoo work on her neck and left arm. He smiled, impressed, but as the other arrivals started to shuffle towards him he regained his composure. "Come on in then," he ushered the five guys towards the entrance. "It's not my gang by the way, it's his," he said pointing to Brad who had now made it down the stairs and was sucking on a bottle of water.

Stood in vest and shorts, Brad was a formidable sight to the new arrivals. He had been a regular gym user for a few years now and he was over six feet tall to boot. As the six new arrivals formed a loose line in front of him he looked them up and down. He saw potential and he couldn't fail to notice the gorgeous flame-haired girl at the end of the row. He let his eyes linger a moment longer than he should have and smiled.

"Welcome everyone, welcome to the Killingburn Road Posse. So introduce yourselves, starting with you lassy." He pointed the water bottle he held towards the girl at the end.

Not shy, she quickly answered, "My name is Nelly, I'm from Sunderland and I've come up to this godforsaken shithole cos I've heard things are hotting up around here."

As other members of the gang joined them in the bar there was a shout from the back, "Not a fucking Mackem!"

Again, Nelly was quick to respond, "Yes, but I'd rather be a Mackem than a bloody coal-shovelling Geordie!"

Brad laughed and the others joined in. He turned his attention to the three guys who stood together in front of him, "What about you three, where are you from?"

They glanced at each other, aware that everyone else was now looking at them. They quickly leaned in and whispered to each other before the smallest of the three took a step forward to speak.

This amused Brad as he had noticed the other two were both taller and broader than their elected spokesperson but he waved him on to speak.

"My name's Chazza and before any of you think of taking the piss out of my wonderful Scouse accent," he said this with a flourish as he slowly turned to take in everyone who was watching him. He gave a gesture pointing a thumb at both of his pals, now stood behind him again, "These two are my bodyguards, Terry and Phil and they love a good scrap."

He finished there and turned around instantly to face Brad. His friends were now slightly in front of him, one on each side. He placed a hand on each of their shoulders and smiled.

Brad walked forward and stopped just in front of them. He put out his hand and Chazza took it and they shook hands. Brad looked at Phil, then across at Terry, "Your guys are welcome, grab yourselves a seat." He gestured to a table just behind them. "You join them Nelly." He winked as she immediately moved and sat at an empty table adjacent to the lads from Liverpool.

Brad fired a parting shot, "Keep an eye on your valuables lads, we have three Scousers amongst us now." The group laughed out loud in response as the three Scousers gave a mixture of one and two fingered gestures to those around them. Meanwhile the two remaining newcomers were looking around excitedly, knowing they were next to be introduced.

Brad took two large sidesteps so he was now standing in front of them, "You two seem like a lively pair?"

Before Brad could continue though he was interrupted by one of the lads, "I'm Smash and he is Bang."

"We are Smash and Bang," his friend echoed.

"Good tags, where are you from lads?" Brad asked.

Smash answered, "We come from York."

Bang continued, "It's a bit boring there."

Smash again, "We smashed two windows on the train on the way here," he laughed.

Bang, "That was cool." He too laughed.

"Well you two sound like you are here for some fun."

"Oh yes," Bang smiled.

"Definitely," Smash countered.

Brad ushered them to another empty table, "Grab a table lads."

Smash drifted towards Nelly's table but Bang grabbed him and pulled him to the empty table Brad had shown them whilst flicking his head towards Brad. Smash grinned at Brad as he took his seat.

Brad surveyed all the members of the KRP in front of him ensuring he made eye contact with each one. "It's great to see you all here. We have some planning to do but I can promise you that you are going to be causing a lot of damage around here." He thrust his arm in the air and his voice rose in volume. "Be prepared to get stuck in over the next week or so until everything is ready."

Those gathered in the pub, listening to him, hanging on his every word started cheering and hooting, some banged their fists on the bar or the tables they were sat at.

"Okay," he looked around catching the attention of two of his lieutenants, "Tasha and Jonjo, get some drinks sorted, we need to celebrate our new arrivals."

1910hrs

The bar was quiet which wasn't unusual for a Tuesday night, but more so than normal. Apart from two regulars sat at the bar there was an older patron playing on one of the two ancient fruit machines stood in the distant corner. Dayna Thomas placed her hands on the bar, she felt just a little nervous.

The young barmaid came straight over to serve her, obviously a little bored and knowing that Dayna was Police, didn't want to vex her. "What can I get for you officer?"

Dayna visibly slumped. She hated being treated as a police officer when off duty, "Rum and Coke please."

"Single or double?"

Dayna paused, caught unawares by the question, "Make it a double please," she smiled.

The barmaid prepared the drink which gave Dayna a chance to have a look around. She wasn't a regular here but she noticed that it had at least been redecorated since her last appearance. It used to be a dive but then again most of the pubs and clubs around Ashton were. Diverse some called it, shite she called it. The bar's surface was sticky, so in fact was the floor next to it. The carpet ended leaving a one metre tiled area against the bar, for spillages she assumed. Never really much aggro here as it was such a quiet pub, just a few locals.

Her drink was placed in front of her and the barmaid smiled, "That's three pounds twenty please."

Obviously being a police officer didn't get you cheap drinks Dayna thought as she fished in her pocket bringing out a couple of notes. She handed over a five pound note but just before the barmaid could snatch it from her hand Dayna pulled her hand back and quickly changed it to a tenner.

The barmaid looked flummoxed but Dayna had noticed in the mirror behind the bar that her company had arrived and he would be wanting a drink.

"A pint of Guinness for the Armies finest?" she asked.

Malcolm Fuller walked up behind her, placed his hands on her shoulders and gave her a friendly kiss on the top of her head. "Don't mind if I do Sergeant Thomas," he moved to stand next to her. "Nice of you to remember," he said nodding towards the slowly pouring pint behind the counter.

She smiled, "Well you seemed to drink enough of it if memory serves me right."

"Touché," he responded with a bow.

With the drinks paid for they sat at a table next to the window across from each other and started to chat as old friends do. They had been good friends as teenagers, in fact they had been each other's first lovers all those years ago. Malcolm's joining the Army had slowed the relationship and his posting overseas had put an end to any future they could have had but they remained friends, writing occasionally or meeting up on Malcolm's rare visits home on leave.

"How are the Police coping with all this trouble then?" Malcolm asked after they had caught up on all the news of their friends and relatives.

"Not great really, we have one big gang who we are monitoring at the moment but the powers that be won't let us intercede."

"Why not?" He asked with interest.

Dayna leaned forward slightly, lowering her voice, "Apparently Headquarters don't want us to initiate a confrontation and look like the bad guys, beating up kids!"

"Really?"

"So they say," she drained her glass. "I just think they don't want to look bad in the press and they have no idea how violent this bunch are."

Malcolm scooped up her empty glass with a smile, "That probably explains why we are here then, we don't mind looking bad in the press." He chuckled as he went up to the bar.

They would chat more and drink more long into the night.

Thursday 20 Jun
1030hrs

A busy Thursday in Tesco's. Lots of parents, especially Mothers having finished work or just collected their kids from school. The staff hated this shift. Payday and end of school combined. In this current era Thursday was not so much a weekly payday as it had been in the past but call it tradition or habit, a lot of people still got their weekly shop in at this time. Some also thought that they would avoid the weekend rush but the lucky people who worked at Tesco's knew better.

Bridget Thomson was one of those reliable workers, who management didn't mind dumping the heavy shifts on. "Here we go lassie," she smiled across at her colleague Annie Simms. "Hold on to ya hats!"

Annie smiled back, not a happy smile though. "We'll be okay today old woman."

"Hey, less of the old woman you, ya wee snaggy."

"Snaggy?" Annie responded quizzically.

"It's a turnip ya bampot," Bridget chuckled.

"You Scots have a language all your own, don't you."

"Aye lassie, that we do." Bridget suddenly walked towards her young friend and moved her gently backwards. Annie hadn't noticed the four fast moving family trollies until they hurtled past them, a dozen youngsters in tow.

Chazza made a honking noise as he glided by, standing rigidly on the rear axle of his trolley, throwing up a salute towards the women as he did so. The four trolleys moved on up the first aisle and just as Bridget was going to step back to keep an eye on where they were headed, Annie pulled her back towards her.

Brad winked as he pushed his trolley close to the woman, "You're looking good Annie."

She mumbled an incoherent response as Brad followed the rest up the aisle with Tasha and Nathan flanking him.

Bridget smiled her thanks but immediately asked the question, "You know that boy?"

Annie followed Bridget as they both started to walk up the aisle, keeping their distance from the large group of youngsters.

"He went out with my younger sister, Ruby, for a while." She looked across at her mentor and friend shrugging slightly, "He was very possessive, a bit of a nutter she said."

Bridget linked arms with Annie, "At least she had the sense to get rid of him ay?"

"He didn't go easily though, kept on calling and texting her for ages after they split up."

"Poor lass."

"She was scared to go out with anyone for a while after Brad. She keeps her dates secret now, even from me!" Annie sounded upset as she said the last part. They followed at a distance for some time before they stopped. Bridget pulled Annie behind the tea bag section.

"Thought so, three trollies getting booze," she pointed, "and the other two getting microwave meals from the fridge behind. Is this that gang that's been on the news recently, the ones they think killed that poor teacher?"

Annie replied, "Yes, the Killingburn Road Posse they call themselves. Brad's their leader."

"I'm just going up to the tills to warn them off, you keep an eye on them." Bridget stopped then added, "Pretend you are doing something though, in case they see you."

"Don't worry old woman, I'll be fine," she smiled.

It wasn't long before the gang members had gathered up all they wanted and under Brad and Nathan's guidance they headed towards the exit. A line of ten tills stood firmly before them, each manned by a Tesco employee, eye-catching in their blue-checked uniforms.

Nathan organised it so they only used two tills, making it easier to pay. The staff and other customers were overawed by the presence of such a large number of youths who most knew were members of the gang. Most of those Tesco employees were relieved that their tills hadn't been chosen. Two of their colleagues didn't have that luxury. Customers who were queueing up seemed to drift to the right and find other queues to join and one of the stores managers stood to one side ushering them out of the way. He looked smart in his three-piece suit; it was either black or a very dark blue but he wore a striking blue check waistcoat which matched the shirts of his colleagues. All eyes were now on the group as they started to unload their trollies.

Nathan tried to organise it by ordering the drinks through till one and the food through till two. To pre-empt any problems he passed his ID to the lady at the till who gave it a quick perusal, probably thought it was fake but nodded her approval anyway.

The manager was looking very twitchy and a little worried as he approached Brad ready to ask a question.

Brad beat him to the punch, removing a large amount of notes, all twenty pounds in denomination, from his jeans pocket, "Don't worry your highness, we can pay." He waved them in the air much to the amusement of the rest of the gang.

Bridget walked up to the gesticulating Nathan, waited until he paused his directing then asked, "Will you be needing bags for all these items young fella?"

Nathan thought before replying, "Nope, we'll just load them back in to the trollies and wheel them up the road," he looked around at the others, enjoying being centre stage. "We only live around the corner." He smiled.

The manager was nervously hovering next to Brad and having had his last question hijacked he blurted out another. "Can we get the trollies back please, when you've finished with them of course?"

Brad looked taken aback but politely responded, "Certainly chief, as soon as we have finished with them." He smiled and then took a longer look at the strangely fidgeting man in front of him.

Brad leaned over and nudged the manager, "Malcolm Irving it says on your name tag." He smiled at the man who was near trembling now. "I like your waistcoat Malcolm, do you think I could get one?"

Malcolm Irving's heart rate increased to the point where he thought his heart might explode, "I don't think we have any spare in the store," he replied meekly.

"Well how about yours Malcolm? I'm sure you can get another one sent here?"

Backed into a corner, figuratively speaking, Malcolm took off his jacket, passed it to the newly arrived Annie. She held out a crooked finger for her boss to hang his jacket on. He did so, bemused at the situation he found himself in. All eyes were now on him as he slowly unbuttoned the smart, tartan waistcoat and pulled his arms free.

Brad gave him a smart bow as he took the waistcoat from his outstretched hand. Due to being a little self-conscious about his weight, Malcolm Irving quickly snatched his jacked and put it back on.

With everything passed through the till, Brad handed over close to seven hundred pounds to pay the bill. "Keep the change love," he glanced around to catch the eye of the manager, "and here's another twenty to pay for a new waistcoat for your boss," he finished with a smile.

Nathan passed through the cashier's desk and made the point, "We don't want anyone to think we were committing a crime or anything!"

As they reached the main entrance, Brad and Nathan heard shouting from outside.

Andy Peel was in a foul mood after another busy day at work. The last thing he needed as he put his pound coin into the locking mechanism on the shopping trolley was more moaning from his kids. The ten-minute journey to the supermarket had been fraught enough. He clicked the coin in and out popped the lock and he reversed the trolley out of the trolley park, quickly catching up to his wife, Natalie.

"Nat, can you explain to your children why they are here?" he hissed.

"Come on Andy, don't take it out on them," she replied.

"Take what out on them?"

"You know what, that bloody school," she lowered her voice to a whisper as if her teenage kids had never heard a swear word before.

Andy Peel took a moment and looked at his wife of eighteen years. She was just as beautiful as when they had first met over twenty years ago when they had started university together. Maybe a few lines here and there and a wave of grey running through her long black hair, but she had that smile that could disarm him immediately, and it did again.

He stopped pushing the trolley and sighed glancing around at his children. Joe was fourteen and a great all round sportsman whilst his daughter Ellie was more academically gifted. He loved watching them grow and understood their frustration.

"Tell you what guys, your Mam will make three meals a week. We'll go out for one and us three choose a meal for one night each. How does that sound?"

Ellie replied first, "That sounds great," she looked to her Mam for confirmation. "Do we have to cook it too?"

Natalie Peel laughed out loud, "None of you three are being let loose in my kitchen."

"Okay darling, I'm happy with that," Andy beamed.

Again Ellie responded, "No Dad, I think we should at least help Mam?"

"I agree," Joe added.

Andy shrugged, "Okay, that's decided." He now posed as if he was in deep thought. The rest of the family recognised this as a prelude to what a husband/father would think was a monumental statement.

He began as the others watched on in amusement. "Okay so we are all involved in choosing meals each week," he waved his hands as if expecting everyone to have read his mind. "We all need to choose ingredients so we all need to come shopping every week!" He shrugged to show he had made his point, grabbing the trolley and slowly setting off towards the entrance.

The rest of the family followed, each inwardly smiling.

Joe thought differently, "I could just order mine online and get it delivered to the house?" he said very pleased with himself.

His mother soon returned him to reality, "It's normally a minimum spend of twenty-five or thirty pounds Joe?"

Andy gave him a quick hug, "Good try Son."

It was Scruffy and Tasha who were making all the noise outside the supermarket as Brad got through the automatic doors. He saw the two abandoned trollies in front of him, "What the fuck's going on?" he spoke in his menacing voice as he looked to the left where he saw a few of his guys gathered.

Tasha was at the front of the group, "Hey Peely, remember me, Tasha Stanley?" She was stood directly in front of the Peel's trolley and with the presence of the other gang members the path was totally blocked.

Natalie gave her husband a sidelong glance, "You know these kids?"

Before her husband could answer Tasha broke in. "Hey Missus, we're not kids." She slammed her hands on the front of their trolley.

"Take it easy Tasha," Andy Peel roared back.

Tasha took a step back which filled Andy with confidence but then glancing behind the group he spied Brad Jones approaching, not looking too happy.

He reacted instinctively, turning to his wife and putting the car keys in her hand, "Nat, take the kids and go back to the car, now!" He emphasised the last word but in the few seconds it took to register their imminent danger, the situation was lost.

Brad pushed his way through the crowd to stand next to Tasha; the latter suddenly pulled the trolley free of Andy Peel's grasp as he was taking backward steps.

"Well, well, look who we have here?" Brad smirked.

There was a prolonged silence as the situation seemed to overtake the Peel family. Tasha slowly pushed the trolley to one side. Faces appeared at the shop window, the manager and two of his members of staff.

Strangely it was Smash who broke the silence and tension that was rapidly building. "So who's this then Boss?" he said gesturing to Andy Peel. "And who are these two lovely ladies?" He unknowingly stroked his hand through his hair, smiling.

Brad folded his arms taking complete control of the situation while Natalie noticed that her husband's previous confidence had dissipated. She glanced down at the car keys in her hands then up at the large young main standing menacingly in front of her. Brad seemed to recognise her fear.

He responded to Smash's question, "This my new pal Smash, is Mr Peel, teacher of Maths at Ashton High School."

Brad was in his element and had everyone present hanging on his every word, "He is the sixth best Maths teacher in that shithole of a school," he said as he slowly stepped towards him.

Andy Peel felt he needed to try and regain some stature so responded quickly and without thinking, "Ha, there's only five Maths teachers at the school, always has been."

Brad leaned in close to his ear and with one word he took all the wind out of Andy's sails. "Exactly!" Brad now stood in front of Joe Peel and leaned back in his stance holding out his arms, "Look at you, pretty boy." He turned around to encourage some laughter then grabbed the burgundy school blazer, "Look at the badge, fancy school that one."

"Leave me alone!" Joe retorted.

Brad stepped back beside Andy Peel. "The boy's less scared than you Peely but I notice you don't send him to our old school. Not good enough for you?"

Andy Peel was now in a quandary. He looked to the right where his wife was stood, visibly trembling. He gestured with a flick of his head and eyes towards the family car. She looked down again at the car keys in her hand.

Andy took the decision from her, turning and putting his left arm around her and his right arm around Joe. Ellie was already a few paces behind them.

Brad quickly moved past them, blocking their retreat and gestured to Smash and Bang to join him.

The Peel family were now blocked in, ten yards from their car and even further to the supermarket entrance. Andy quickly looked around across the car park but there seemed to be no one available to help or even call out to.

Brad was in his element and playing to his audience. "Tell you what Peely, you weren't that bad a bloke at school, apart from those bloody detentions you kept giving me."

Cornered, Andy Peel was ready to fight and responded dispassionately, "You never showed up for them anyway!"

"True," responded Brad. "Anyway, I'll give you an easy equation. In this hand." Brad held out his left hand, palm up, "is your family." He looked around ensuring everyone, particularly the Peel family, were paying attention to everything he was saying. "And in this hand," he put out his right hand, again, palm up, "is your car, that lovely black VW Touareg?" He gestured with his head towards the Peel's car. "You choose, one or the other?"

"No way," was Andy's immediate response.

"Well if you don't choose, we get both!" was Brad's response.

There followed a few seconds of quiet although everyone knew the outcome.

"Come on Peely, simple choice mate," and with that Brad held out his hand, waiting for the car keys.

Natalie Peel dropped the keys into Brad's hand.

Her husband made a grab for them, "No!" but Brad was too quick.

"It's only a fucking car Andy," his wife snapped.

Brad passed the keys to Nathan who immediately started organising the filling up of the large rear section of the SUV with their recently purchased goods.

Andy Peel moved his family closer to the building's wall thinking that the edge to the situation had gone with his concession of the car.

How wrong he was.

Brad still hovered in front of them, his evil mind working overtime. "Tell you what Peely, I have another choice for you."

Andy was now sweating profusely. He felt the rivulets running down his back. He wiped his brow with the sleeve of his jacket. "Haven't you got enough Brad," he said pointing to his car?

"Not quite," was the ominous response.

"So what is it now then?" Andy asked, dread in his voice.

"Simple mate, wife or daughter?"

"What do you mean, wife or daughter?" The tension in Andy Peel made his voice rise to a higher pitch.

Smiles appeared on the faces of those gathered around him.

Again, he desperately looked around for any kind of help or assistance. Nothing. He contemplated shouting and screaming but a small semblance of pride held him back, knowing it wouldn't work anyway.

Brad loved being centre stage. "I think one of these ladies should accompany us back to our place."

"No!" Natalie Peel shouted as she moved to stand directly in front of her daughter who was now crying in disbelief.

Brad continued, ignoring her and still looking into the eyes of Andy, "They could do a turn in the pub, you know," he paused, a big smile on his face, turning around so all of those surrounding him could see. "A song or a dance maybe?"

He stopped turning and returned his gaze to Andy Peel.

The rage inside Andy Peel was instant. Not a man who was taken to violence but he had been slowly backed into a corner. First his prized car had been taken but now this, this affront to his and his family's dignity. He exploded, "Who in the hell do you think you are?"

As no answer was forthcoming by a shocked Brad, he continued, "Some jumped up little school boy with your little band of followers!" He gestured to the equally stunned group who were gathered around him.

Andy moved sharply. Thinking that his response had removed the immediate threat to his wife and kids he set about resolving the ownership of his car.

Nathan stood at the back hatch of the SUV preparing the last trolley load of stores being loaded into the vehicle. Andy, now enraged, closed on him quickly spying that most of the goods were crates of beer. He ranted at Nathan and as the latter tried to pull the last trolley closer. Andy pushed him backwards. Caught off guard, Nathan tumbled over onto the concrete with a yelp of pain.

Brad had regained his senses and had moved to intervene, too late.

Andy shouted at the prone Nathan, "I bet you stole all that stuff anyway, you thieving pikey fucker?"

The last word had just left Andy Peel's mouth when Brad, approaching from behind, swung a haymaker that caught Andy on the right temple. He flew left cannoning off the rear doorframe of his VW Touareg and crumpling to the floor.

Brad had been half joking about the wife and daughter choice he had given his old maths teacher but the sudden assault on Nathan had provoked his immediate and devastating response.

A punch is always taken better when it is seen coming.

Pandemonium broke out as other gang members moved in to take a shot at the fallen teacher, a symbol of their negative outlook on life and an easy target. Simultaneously Natalie Peel leapt to her husband's defence, moving to block any further attack, screaming defiance.

Brad hesitated, showing some decree of respect for women. Tasha was not as restrained as she launched herself at the injured man's wife, grabbing her by the hair and pulling her clear as others waded in with kicks and punches to the stricken teacher.

Joe Peel reacted to the sudden surge in violence. He threw his weight into a shoulder barge which totally knocked the wind out of Terry Nevis, dropping him to the floor next to the slowly rising teacher.

Billy Nevis was close behind his brother but not being that adept at fighting he swung a loose punch that glanced of Joe Peel's shoulder. Joe's right fisted response sent the young lad reeling and he hit the ground not far from his brother.

Brad stood back watching the fun; he didn't need to prove himself and would only join in again if necessary. He watched Tasha and Natalie Peel swinging fists at each other wildly whilst both had a handful of each other's hair. He chuckled quietly to himself enjoying the spectacle of two females scraping.

Meanwhile Nathan was up and looking to respond to being caught off guard. Just as Andy Peel was getting to his feet Nathan fell on him, raining punches all over his body. Andy managed to fling out an arm which caught Nathan square under the jaw. He reeled backwards just managing to retain his balance. Frustrated he looked down at the Nevis brothers who were sitting, shocked on the parking lot floor, "What are you two doing sat on your arses, get stuck in?"

The brothers looked at each other briefly; feigning injuries they remained firmly rooted to the spot.

Nathan let out an anguished sigh as he moved back towards the action. What he saw only riled him more. The Peels were all on their feet, backs against the fought over vehicle. The gang had a final trolley stranded on the car park. He looked across at Brad who just stood at the back, arms folded, with a mischievous grin on his face.

Brad glanced across and caught the furious gaze of Nathan. He smiled even more and with a nod of his head gestured for Nathan to carry on.

Nathan looked around at who was available; he couldn't rely on the Nevis brothers in a fight so he turned to Smash and Bang. "You two, get the next trolley into the car!"

They grabbed the trolley handle simultaneously and edged towards the still open rear door of the black SUV.

Natalie, scratched, bruised and bleeding pulled her children out of the way and spoke in a near whisper to her husband, "Come on Andy and help me get the kids to safety."

Andy Peel stood resolutely in front of the open rear door of his vehicle, sensing the frustration of the young people surrounding him. He saw the two very young, bewildered looking boys hunched on the floor, the Nevis'. Two other lads, unknown to him, were slowly inching another packed trolley towards him. The lad he knew as a traveller was orchestrating things but he glanced right and saw sheer malevolence in the eyes of Brad Jones. He now realised, having had a brief time to think, that it must have been his punch that had knocked him down and left him with such a powerful headache. His vision was still a little blurred. Two girls, one of whom had fought with his wife, stood on the shop side with another lad.

He quickly turned and looked at his frightened family before taking a few steps towards them and standing between them and the gang.

Smash and Bang quickly finished loading the vehicle before flinging the final, empty trolley across the adjacent empty spaces of the car park and then climbed into the back. Nathan climbed into the front driver's side, Brad in the front passenger's seat. Tasha, bleeding from a bloodied nose, along with Nelly and Jonjo squeezed into the back seat.

1655hrs

The two detectives were approaching the entrance to the store when they saw the camera crew filming up the side of the building.

"What are those two filming now?" Billy Phillips asked.

His partner, Sangita Arajun, responded, "I know him, that's Josh Thorpe the TV reporter and I was chatting to the cameraman the other day at the hotel. Let me find out."

"Hey Ganesh!" she shouted. "What are you guys up to now? Nothing better to do on a Thursday night?"

Ganesh, the BBC cameraman kept filming but Josh Thorpe took a step back, behind and away from the camera's lens. "He pointed to where the camera was filming and shouted back, “Fighting over there, looks like gang members are attacking a family and stealing their car.” He quickly switched his mic back on and returned to his news report.

Billy reacted quickly, “Come on, let’s see who it is.” He started running towards the side of the building, past the entrance. He looked back to make sure his partner was following and then once to his right to see if the film crew were still filming.

As his partner and he rounded the corner a black SUV, possibly a VW nearly ran them over. Sangita stopped in her tracks as her partner swerved to avoid the vehicle. In the side windows she saw the smiling, laughing teenage faces as they drew alongside her and then the vehicle created a loud, screeching noise as it wheel-span away. The vehicle, a Touareg, meandered through empty car parking spaces and turned left onto the main road into town.

Billy continued on, now seeing what seemed to be a bloody and battered family against the building’s wall and two bewildered young boys huddled around some loose, empty trollies. Sangita radioed in the situation, calling for support and an ambulance whilst her partner rounded up the Nevis brothers, handing them over to two local PCs who had also just arrived from the opposite direction. He then he spoke briefly to the Peel’s.

The two brothers, subdued, sat on the path not a few feet from the family who had just been terrorised by their fellow gang members.

The film crew approached as Billy went to speak to Sangita who was diverting traffic away from the scene. He held out a hand, palm facing Josh and Ganesh, “Sorry guys, but don’t come any closer.”

“We just want a quick word officer,“ Josh replied.

“Not till we get the full story first and they need some medical attention too.” Billy ventured.

“Can we see them at the hospital?” Josh pleaded.

“After we’ve interviewed them,” and then in a quieter voice meant for Sangita, “and only if they let you.” He smiled.

Sangita looked flummoxed, “Attacking people in broad daylight, what next?”

Billy shrugged, “I know. Funnily enough they paid for everything they got in the shop, used cash.”

"Probably stolen," Sangita turned to look at the poor family as they huddled together, still in shock. "At least no serious injuries I suppose."

"Yeah, you're right, but I'm sick of these little thugs going unpunished." He started to look around and then looked back at his partner. "Come on, we're going after them!"

"Are you sure?"

"Yes, call for all the back-up you can, get them to meet us at St Mark's Church car park on Waterloo Way.

"The DCI won't like this," Sangita said worried.

"I don't give a shit," Billy vehemently replied. "We're going to chase them out of that bludy pub, scatter them and see where the little rats run to hide."

Sangita got on her radio as she handed the vehicle keys over to Billy. He started up the engine and they drove as quickly as they could through the busy rush-hour traffic. As they arrived at St Mark's they noticed two marked police cars parked near the small car park entrance and an unmarked vehicle on the other side.

The church was a beautiful, old building and as Billy stepped out of the car he glanced up to see the evening sun filtering through the massive stained-glass windows. He had been married here only two years previously and still wondered at the marvellous display of colour and light that the windows produced, especially on the inside. He thought about his wife, Claire and his newly born baby, Thomas. Was putting himself in danger like this a good idea? Was there a chance he could be leaving a widow to bring up their child alone?

He paused and glanced around as the other police officers got out of their vehicles. He knew them all: Corey, Des, Lynne, Dan and Eddie, not forgetting his pal and ex-partner Dayna.

No, they were going to do this and to hell with the consequences. Their instructions to leave the Miner's alone had been pure bureaucracy, nobody wanting a finger pointed at them for heavy handedness towards what amounted to be children.

Enough was enough.

He walked into the middle of the officers, giving one more quick glance up at the windows and his memories, then put on his sternest expression.

He clapped his hands loudly. "Okay guys," he looked around all the faces gathered around him. "I have just left a family bruised, battered and in total shock and it was these bastards!" He gestured with his thumb over his shoulder. "I know what the orders say, we have to leave them alone so we don't escalate matters but I want them nicked."

He paused glancing quickly from face to face, some expectant but all determined looking in their expressions.

"I understand if you don't want to go in as you'll probably get in the crap but I will try and take as much of the shit as I can. Who's coming with me?"

He smiled with pride as every hand went up except Dayna's.

"I know you outrank me Sarge and can stop us going in if you so order."

Dayna realised in all the adrenalin-fuelled excitement that she hadn't put her hand up. "Bugger that, I bagsy kicking in the front door!"

Sangita circled round to the rear entrance on the south side with Eddie whilst the latter's partner Dan continued around to the eastern side entrance where the beer terrace was situated.

He was with PC Lynne Edmonds, new to the job and the area. They moved steadily through the tables and chairs which were strewn around the terrace. Amongst them they saw lots of empty cans and bottles, fag ends in their hundreds too. They ducked and twisted past the huge umbrellas, some half closed, others open, and they arrived stealthily at the terrace door.

Dan spoke quietly into the radio, "Team three in position."

Billy, in overall control, responded. "Roger, team three, how about you team two?"

"Team two now in position," Sangitta offered before adding, "the stolen VW is here but locked."

"Thanks team two." Billy nodded at Dayna before speaking to the other teams on the radio, "Breach in three, two, one, breach, breach, breach!"

With that Dayna, having already pinned back the outer doors to the wall, kicked the single inner door, near the lock. It imploded.

Inside, pandemonium broke out.

Dayna was in uniform and so as soon as the door was smashed open those inside, shocked as they were, knew that is was some kind of police raid.

From the far corner of the bar a cry went up, "Five-o, five-o."

Brad was in prime position, stood centrally, just behind the bar where he had been organising their new delivery. He saw no weapons or riot shields and although the atmosphere around him seemed chaotic, he kept calm. It wasn't a full on raid, probably just a few plucky coppers he thought.

He threw the VW car keys back at Nathan, "Nat, you and Tasha out the back door and bring the car back around to the side." He quickly glanced around to give more orders; luckily most of the gang were in the bar, which seemed to have stopped the advance of the three coppers now at the main entrance.

He issued his next set of orders, "Tubs and Binky, get the side door open and hold it open. Take some of those crates with you." He pointed at the crates sitting on the bar tables near the door.

The three officers at the door were slowly moving into the bar area.

Brad vaulted clear over the bar and motioned to Louis who was next to the pool table, which was now adorned with a variety of cigarettes and snacks. "Louis, the pool cues - pass them around."

Louis as stunned as everyone else hadn't moved after the initial shock of the door being kicked open. He glanced around quickly seeing the three intruders to his right and hearing a scuffle at the side entrance. He turned, grabbing the first cue from the rack, throwing it across to Brad who caught it one-handed. He passed four more to Jonjo, Nelly, Smash and Bang. Others were coming to collect their own.

Brad stood twirling his pool cue as he walked towards the three officers.

Dayna, unphased, took out her baton and flicked it fully extended then took out her can of CS spray. Brad noticed a strange look of excitement on her face. It unnerved him.

Meanwhile, Nathan and Tasha had crashed through the rear exit knocking Eddie off his feet. Sangita had missed Nathan as he dodged past her but she got a hold of Tasha's coat. Nathan opened the car and just before he got in he looked back for Tasha.

She was struggling still with Sangita, "Go Nath, I'll be okay and catch up with you in a bit." She smiled as she faced off against Sangita.

Nathan got into the recently acquired VW and after sliding the fob into the ignition he hit the engine start button. The engine burst into life and after he selected first gear he quickly accelerated away, confident Tasha would be following as he drove around to the side entrance. He stopped in near enough the same place he had been ten minutes ago before unloading their goods.

Leaving the car running he moved towards the side door where he saw the large form of Dan Clemence pinning Tubs and Binky against the wall of the entranceway. He barged past Lynne and into the main bar area where he witnessed the standoff between his friends and the three officers all now armed, although the sight of the plain clothes detective holding a mop upside down made him smile.

"Okay Brad, wheels are ready, let's go!" Nathan shouted from the doorway next to the pool table, which contained all the non-alcoholic goods they had bought.

Brad turned smiling, "Jonjo, Nelly grab some of our stuff from the table and get into the car."

"What about you Brad?" Nelly asked.

Brad smiled even more, "I'll be fine. Get the rest out too, me and Louis will hold off these numpties. Smash and Bang, you guys grab some of the booze and get it out to the car." Brad gestured with his pool cue towards the bar where the boxes of booze were stacked.

Eddie Grey, slightly dazed, had slowly got back to his feet. He heard the crash of a chair hitting a table and saw his colleague Sangita lying prone under the table. He shook his head to clear it and advanced towards the female gang member he had seen earlier, fighting Sangita. Tasha threw another chair but it flew wildly past Eddie. He lunged forward grabbing her arm and spun her around quickly grabbing her other arm and forced her a couple of steps forward into the wooden lattice fencing. As she slammed into the fence he put his weight against her back, pinning her in place before he turned to check on his fellow officer.

"Sangita, are you okay?" He shouted.

A slow moan escaped from her lips as she rolled over onto her back, blinking furiously.

Eddie felt aggrieved that whilst he had been easily knocked over and partly concussed his young colleague had what looked like a bad injury. He pulled out his handcuffs and quickly locked one end onto Tasha's left wrist. He flung her arm around a very solid looking fence post and clipped the other cuff onto Tasha's other wrist. Tasha seemed very subdued now. All the rage was gone replaced by a haunted look. Fear.

Eddie noticed she had a pretty bad head wound, "I'll check out your head when I get back." He went to check on Sangita who was just conscious but breathing uncomfortably.

Nathan drove the car around to the front entrance and tooted the horn a few times as a signal to the rest. He had sent Smash and Bang on foot to leave space for Brad and Louis, also Tubs and Binky if they could get away from the huge copper he had seen them grappling with. He had no idea where Tasha was, he could only hope she was heading to the new location they had pre-planned in case this event had happened.

Tubs was face down on the floor and he felt the click of the cuffs as PC Lynne Edmonds kept her knee in the middle of his back. He was going nowhere. He glanced across and saw his pal, Binky being held in a vicious looking arm lock by the hulking big constable who had briefly fought with him. Binky didn't look too good. He had come off worse in the scuffle.

Nathan tooted the horn again.

Brad signalled to Louis to move around to the right so they could try and get to the main door.

The PC in front of Louis didn't move an inch. Corey Small by name and by nature was a tough little nut, a rugby player for the local force. A 'tenacious scrum half' the latest edition of the Northumbria Police Gazette had described him as.

Billy Phillips saw and heard what was happening and moved across to face Brad. He brought up his mop like a sword but Brad reacted quickly, slamming his pool cue against the mop handle and shattering it, sending Billy onto the floor.

Just as Brad was going to move in for the kill, Dayna moved to intercept him using her baton to block his next swing. Brad reversed his cue and blocked Dayna and then he brought his elbow across crashing into her face. She staggered backwards, instantly tasting blood in her mouth. She spat it out. Brad moved to deliver another blow this time with his cue but Billy was up on his feet swinging his half mop handle and howling like a banshee.

Brad just managed to block the strike.

Billy moved to cover the stricken Dayna.

Brad saw a chance and made for the entrance. "Come on Louis!" he shouted as he crashed through the main door.

Louis had been waiting for an opportunity to head for the exit but the officer opposed to him hadn't taken his eyes off him. As Louis made a feint to the right trying to dodge past his foe, Corey Small took a few rapid steps and dived in, rugby tackle style, taking him in the midriff.

They both hit the deck and Corey quickly subdued the winded teenager.

Brad looked back through the glass on the internal door, sighed heavily and then lunged through the open door, taking one more glance back to make sure Louis wasn't coming. He slammed the door shut.

Nathan wheel span the Volkswagen out of the pub car park and right onto Waterloo Way.

As they crossed the roundabout onto Esse Lane Brad looked around at those who had made it into the vehicle. "Where's Binky and Tubs and Smash and Bang?"

Nathan slowed the vehicle when he saw they weren't being followed. "I sent Smash and Bang on foot to make space for you, don't know about Tubs and Binky but I saw them tussling with a big copper in the side door."

Brad seemed a bit deflated by that news but then he started, "Tasha, where's Tasha?"

"She got into a scrap with a female five-o when we crashed out the back door," Nathan responded.

"Why didn't you help her?" Brad screamed, fury in his question.

Nathan lowered his voice to try and appease Brad. "You told me get the car Boss and that's what I did. Tasha said she would be okay and would catch up. Maybe she's at the YM already?"

Brad relaxed back into his seat, subdued.

The car followed the road around to the right and pulled off into the small car park behind the YMCA building; their new home. Brad got out of the car and immediately saw Smash and Bang running up towards him, out of breath and each carrying a case of beer under each arm.

He smiled, "Glad you made it boys," he paused glancing across at Nathan as he alighted the VW. "Some didn't!"

1825hrs

After having unloaded all their shopping and allocated guys to different rooms, Brad had retired to a quiet room at the back of the building. He had been on the scouting trip to the YMCA when he realised that their time at the pub might be short lived. He had already earmarked the office as a place where he could get a bit of peace and quiet.

He had just laid down on the camp bed when he heard a gentle tapping on the door. "Come in," he responded.

The door opened slowly to about a foot wide and the slender figure of Nelly slid in. She smiled and turned to close the door, sliding the small bolt to secure it, something Brad had forgotten to do.

He smiled.

Nelly responded, "You don't mind me coming to see you, do you? I wasn't sure if you wanted to be alone or not?"

"No, it's fine," Brad beckoned her in, quickly swinging his feet off his bed and standing up. "I wasn't going to sleep or anything, just needed to wind down a bit."

Nelly seemed to glide towards Brad, she was trembling slightly but to Brad she seemed at her most confident. He looked at her closely as she slowly closed the gap between them, from her long legs, tightly clad in faded denim to what he thought was a great ass. As his eyes continued upwards it only got more impressive with a slender waist and a fantastic pair of boobs. He liked her wide shoulders and slightly more than usual muscular frame. It was all topped off by that gorgeous face surrounded by her red hair in a bob style.

As he finished admiring her she was stood less than a foot in front of him. He could smell the scent of her as he took a breath in, a mixture of sweet sweat and a deodorant she had obviously used just before coming to him.

Brad spoke next, "I can't get rid of all this adrenalin."

Nelly replied immediately, "Neither can I."

She moved closer and they fell into a deep embrace. Kissing, their tongues started to explore each other's mouths. Gently at first but then the adrenalin took over and their kissing became frenzied. Their hands, after a few seconds of gentle exploration now worked furiously to tear each other's clothes off.

To a voyeuristic observer it would have been a wondrous sight. First Nelly's t-shirt, then Brad's, Nelly's jeans, then Brad's. Socks removed, there was a slight pause as Brad reached around clumsily for the back of her bra. Nelly chuckled slightly, pulled down the shoulder straps and spun it round one hundred and eighty degrees around her torso, easily unfastening it and letting it fall to the ground.

Brad was stunned, firstly by the sight of her perfectly formed breasts, second by the fact she had guessed he would struggle with the mechanisms of the bra and finally by her confidence.

They renewed their furious kissing.

When it was obvious they were both ready, they giggled as they then bent down to take off their own underwear.

Brad pulled Nelly down to the camp bed and in one motion he slid inside her. There was a pause, they both gasped and then Brad started a slow rhythm as Nelly hooked her legs around his back and helped to control his pace.

Brad had been with girls before but this felt amazingly different, Nelly seemed older and definitely experienced. He was still stunned by her confident nature and as he caressed the parts of her body he could reach he had the idea that she was much older than she wanted others to think.

After a short time their speed increased and uncontrollable moans came from both of them as the pure passion that was unfolding neared its end. Out of the blue and maybe out of character Brad suddenly slowed his thrusts and asked, "Are you okay, shall I?"

Nelly cut him off by pulling his head down so she could whisper into his ear, "Keep going, you're going to make me come."

And she duly did, as they both increased the intensity only a few seconds later they both locked together as their bodies shuddered though a climatic orgasm. Brad, unable to hold his own weight collapsed onto the sweat sheened body of the young woman lying under him.

Nelly held him tight as their panting slowed and they each recovered from the intensity of their love-making.

Monday 24 Jun
0907hrs

The view to the north over the school fields was beautiful at this time of morning. With the River Esse running to the left before arcing away into the nearby hills, leaving the castle as the primary attraction. The original parts of the castle, the keep and the main central tower dated back to Norman times. The additions of two more towers, extended and heightened walls together with the moat and drawbridge had rendered it almost impregnable. Many had tried; all had failed.

Joanne Tindell took heart from the history of the castle as she thought of her own school.

Impregnable.

Her early morning malaise was shattered by the rat-ta-tat-tat knocking on her door.

"Come in," she responded.

The door opened slowly with a slight creaking of the hinges. It had been opened slowly and carefully so it probably wasn't one of her SLT. She waited.

After a few seconds she heard a very tentative, "Joanne?"

Her reverie broken she span her chair around 180 degrees to face the intruder of her contemplative solitude. She could only smile though as the effervescent Katy Howard smiled back at her. Normally dressed in her PE kit of leggings and polo shirt her image this morning was in direct contrast, a white blouse with a black pencil skirt and matching jacket.

Joanne looked down and noticed how tall Katy appeared with high heels on instead of the variety of multi-fluorescent coloured trainers she usually wore.

She had only seen Katy dressed twice like this before: her interview and her first annual assessment.

She continued to smile as she responded to the interruption, "Hello Katy, how wonderful you look today. What can I do for you?"

Katy seemed to relax a little, "Morning Joanne, we are all ready, in the staffroom. Assembly has finished and the sixth formers are arriving in just under an hour for Fresher's Week so we should have enough time to get the meeting done by then."

Joanne's eyebrows raised, "You're hopeful!"

"Well there's not much on the agenda, the SDF have made some decisions and we just need to ratify them."

Katy folded her arms when she had finished speaking, a defensive stance if Joanne remembered the sessions on body language from her Head Teacher's course correctly.

She rose from her chair and gestured towards the door for Katy, "Is that all I'm good for now, ratification?"

As Katy opened the door for her Boss she quickly spluttered back, "No, I didn't mean it like that Joanne, I mean you are …"

Joanne interrupted her, took her arm and nudged her playfully. "Don't panic, I was only joking."

Katy relaxed again for a second time; she had known Joanne for coming up two years but still didn't quite get her dry sense of humour.

Joanne intended to put her further at ease, "You know I helped and supported with the setting up of the School Defence Force so I wouldn't have to get involved with the work it involves, as long as you run things by me so I am in the know. Still not happy with the word Force in the title though."

As they reached the bottom of the stairs and turned right up the main corridor Katy had a little chuckle.

Joanne laughed too, "What is it?"

They both nodded to a small group of sixth formers passing them before Katy replied, "You wouldn't believe some of the other names the guys, especially the caretakers, came up with before we settled on 'School Defence Force.' She shook her head.

"Well, what did you save me from?"

They stopped just short of the staffroom door as Katy lowered her voice, "Teachers Assemble, Educators United, The League of

Extraordinary Teachers, Trust In Teachers," her smile grew as she went on. "I mean the acronyms alone are scary!"

Joanne laughed out loud as she listened and just as she reached for the staffroom door handle she quipped, "I'm happy with the SDF Katy, it could have been a whole lot worse."

They entered the staffroom still sniggering as all eyes in the dull, darkened room turned to them, the seriousness of the meeting hit home.

Joanne spoke first, "My apologies Ladies and Gentlemen but a little levity once in a while is good for the spirit." She moved round to sit in a vacant chair. "Now let me know what your plans are for the remainder of this school year?"

The following 45 minutes proved very useful as the assembled group put forward their ideas to further secure the school and safeguard the staff, pupils and various visitors. To Joanne this seemed a very strange state of affairs. Her thoughts drifted back to her earlier view of the 'impregnable' castle. Was this what it had come to!

In conclusion, there were to be barred windows, some temporary and some permanent barricades. More security at the vehicle and pedestrian entry points and the installing of a new key card system for the main entrance which was ready to be installed later that day.

1014hrs

It had taken most of the weekend but the gang had settled into their new location. The shock of the raid, or more so the fact that the police had finally had the courage to enter the pub had caught them off guard but Brad and the others had been ready with a plan. From Nathan's advice they had prepared a second location, in this case the local YMCA building on the northern edge of the town, which had been abandoned weeks earlier. They had already moved some of their gear over there in preparation for their final assault on the school. A plan they had hatched recently but not gone in to great detail with. They knew the police were watching the pub intermittently and didn't want an offhand police check to ruin their final plans.

Brad was sat in the meeting room, nursing a cup of tea which had four sugars in it; his cure for the hangover he had. He had tried to get his ever-growing entourage to finish off all the booze they had, over the weekend. He wanted the members of his gang to have clear heads for the days ahead.

Sat around him were his trusted lieutenants: Nathan, Jonjo and Nelly. He looked at each in turn. Nathan had drunk just as much if not more than Brad the night before but he looked as bright as a button. Brad thought it was a gypsy trick.

His long-time friend and sometimes lover, Tasha, was not there as she had been taken into custody by the police after the raid on the Miners two nights before. He missed her constant presence in his life, especially over the last few weeks. His ever-faithful Jonjo had not lasted long with the drink, probably why he looked okay sat opposite him, big smile on his face.

At the end of the oblong table, to his left, sat the recently arrived Nelly, Brad's new lover, as of the previous week. She intrigued Brad. Although they had shared a bed he still knew very little about her. She looked older than the age she claimed to be, seventeen, but still had an innocent look that sometimes unnerved him.

Brad put down his cup and began. He went over the points of the attack and the preparation they needed to complete in the build-up. On reaching the end of his points he asked a question, "Okay guys, the plans are all in place for the attack later this week. Jonjo, any reports from our lookout posts at the skate-park and Snowdonia Way?"

Jonjo took out his mobile and quickly checked his WhatsApp. "All quiet over the weekend Brad but an interesting message from earlier this morning."

Brad leaned forward, his forearms resting on the table, keen to hear more. "What is it then?"

"Well, you know that company on the industrial estate who do secure locks, I think they are called Lockdown?"

Nathan chipped in, "It is Lockdown, my cousin used to work for them."

Jonjo continued his report, "They've been parked at the school since first thing this morning. The guys on lookout have just reported that they've started working on the main entrance.

"Shit," Nathan slammed his hand on the table.

Nelly asked, "What could they be doing?"

Nathan replied, "My cousin Joey told me he fitted security locks."

"What type of locks?" Brad asked hesitantly.

"Not key locks, either those keypads or swipe cards mainly." Nathan answered.

"Great," Brad said relieved, "we don't have kit to be smashing through more secure doors, the other things we can deal with."

After a few seconds of thinking whilst the others whispered to each other, Brad glanced at Nathan and made an immediate decision. "No probs then, Nathan grab a couple of the guys and the car and follow them when they leave. We need a copy of the codes or whatever swipey things they've installed." He gestured using a swipe card as he said this then continued. "We don't want the school to know we have access to the codes or swipey things though," he gestured again much to the others amusement. "Use money or threats, or both. Just make sure they don't snitch, not for a few days anyway."

"Got it Boss." Nathan stood up abruptly, his chair scraping across the wooden flooring making some of those present wince. "Should I go now?"

"Yes mate, soon as." He gave Nathan a thumbs up. "We haven't got much more to go over now, we'll see you when you get back."

With that Nathan was gone.

The others remained just covering a few things they had already put in motion. The shifts for the lookout posts, new members who had arrived over the weekend and how much more they needed in the way of supplies for the imminent attack and for afterwards. They planned to hold a big celebration with plenty of booze afterwards.

1100hrs

Located in the north eastern corner of the town of Ashton, the Northumbria Police Headquarters was a hive of activity on what was usually a quiet Monday morning.Events over the previous few days had brought in extra officers from neighbouring forces and extra shifts for those already working in the area. Tension was running high.

Two young PCs had just finished preparing the large meeting room when some more of the guests had arrived, in military fatigues.

Lieutenant Colonel Peter Alderson stood in the centre of the Operations Room, surveying all around him. By his side was the trusty Sergeant Malcolm Fuller who had served under the Colonel for over twelve years. Peter Alderson used him as his sounding board and always knew he would get a direct answer from the man.

Dayna Thomas glided through the Ops Room towards the two Army men and proffered her right hand by way of greeting, "Good morning gentlemen, I am Sergeant Dayna Thomas. Welcome to Northumbria Police HQ."

Sergeant Fuller didn't flinch, his eyes still scanning the room.

After a few seconds the Colonel took Dayna's hand, "Thank you Sergeant. I am Colonel Alderson and this is Sergeant Fuller."

"Nice to meet you both," Dayna smiled.

Peter Alderson removed his beret after he realised he wasn't going to be saluted by any of the police officers milling around him. "Can you show us to the meeting room sergeant?"

"Of course Sir, follow me." Dayna turned and strode off towards the other end of the Ops room where the Police hierarchy waited.

The police sergeant was a little disheartened by the curt, business-like response from the Army officer. She found him very handsome if not a little aloof. The Sergeant who accompanied him was striking in other ways, being shorter in height but 'very well put together' as she had fond memories of. The latter had not even had the decency to make eye contact. He seemed wary of the surroundings.

As she approached the glassed walls of the meeting room her mind switched back to the job. Opening the door, she moved aside to allow the two military guests in and gestured to two empty chairs. Malcolm Fuller winked at her as he passed close by, setting her a little more at ease. Closing the door behind her she introduced those present to the two new arrivals.

"This is Chief Constable Craig, head of Northumbria Police. At the end we have Assistant Chief Commissioner Dunbar and Inspector Andrews you already know. Gentlemen, this is Lieutenant Colonel Alderson and Sergeant Fuller from the Second Battalion, Northumberland Fusiliers."

With introductions completed Dayna took her seat next to Chief Constable Craig, her boss. The meeting had been organised through police channels in response to the rise in incidents over recent weeks.

The Army presence had been requested, not by the local county HQ but from higher up the chain, namely the man sat at the head of the table, ACC Dunbar. He felt the local police in Northumbria and particularly Ashton were struggling, especially in this area. When the Army were deployed in support of the police countrywide, it was Dunbar's idea to position Alderson's unit at Castle Esse.

From the Army point of view Lt Col Alderson did not want to be at the meeting. He had his own chain of command and would follow orders passed to him by the Brigadier who commanded him. He did understand that there was a need for cross-service liaison but as the meeting dragged on he quickly realised that the local Chief Constable, sitting across from him, did not want him to be here either. The general outcome of the meeting had reinforced those feelings.

The police would patrol more areas, they would detain any suspects and disperse any groups of youngsters. Alderson wanted to implement random searches and kick in some doors of some known offenders. To some extent his opposite number, Craig, had agreed but the ACC wanted to maintain the light-handed approach they had used up until now. He saw it as working, which would have confused those on the ground seeing incidents up close.

By the meeting's end Lt Col Alderson and Chief Constable Craig had developed a grudging mutual respect for each other, their respective Sergeants maybe a little more. With the ACC gone the four remaining attendees split into pairs and had a few final words for each other. The two Sergeants pretended to be tidying up after the meeting as their respective bosses walked across the still busy ops room.

"I'm Malcolm, by the way," he offered his hand.

She took it, squeezing it tightly, responding, "So you can speak then?" They both laughed and left the meeting room, chatting quietly.

At the ops room door the Army officer turned and thought a few seconds before saying, "I think I understand your position now, Alex."

Alex Craig smiled, "I'm glad one of us does." He let out a laugh before continuing, "We need to keep close comms Peter."

"I know, we will. My force is there whenever you need it, just call."

Wednesday 26 Jun
0700hrs

The town of Ashton sweltered under the early morning sun. The dew, little that it was, had long since burnt off after the early summer's dawn. The atmosphere was charged. Although it had been a quiet weekend and beginning to the week the memories of what had occurred over the previous few weeks were always there, simmering under the surface.

The police and Army patrols had increased. This, in combination with most of the remaining local population staying indoors, had made for a quiet period.

Was it the calm before the storm?

Had the gang been dispersed?

No one knew.

0707hrs

Jimmy Nelson rounded the corner and headed up the English and Humanities corridor, whistling as he went. Up ahead he saw his friend Neil Weston gazing north out of the large windows at the end of the corridor.

"You taking in the views Neil?"

Neil glanced over his shoulder and smiled, seeing his friend walking towards him grinning from ear to ear. "What's got you so happy?"

Jimmy laughed, "I spent last night at home," and he winked.

Neil laughed out loud as Jimmy came to a stop next to him, slapping him on the shoulder. They both looked out over the surrounding countryside.

It was Jimmy who broke the silence, "It is a glorious site. I never get tired of looking over to the castle."

"It is a smashing sight. Apart from those Army landrovers clattering over the drawbridge and up and down the approach road!"

"True, they do spoil it a bit."

"Apart from them driving around the town, it's all been a bit too quiet, you reckon?"

Jimmy turned to face his pal, "Do you reckon that's all the trouble over with then?"

"No mate," Neil shrugged, unable to hide the fear in his voice. "I still think there is a lot more to come."

Meanwhile, over in the PE building, the night shift were stirring: kettles boiling, sleeping bags being rolled up, eggs frying. Euan Robshaw walked out of the boys changing room drying his hair with a towel. After his shower he had changed into to his school kit comprising of dark blue shorts, a white Nike-swoosh t-shirt and a dark blue tracksuit top adorned with the school badge and logo 'sit docere discere,' 'to teach is to learn'. As he reached the sleeping area he bumped into Katy Howard who was heading for a shower herself.

"Morning Katy," he beamed, his fondness for her not going unnoticed.

"Morning Euan," she answered. "You been out for a run already then?" she smiled as she asked. She too was fond of the recent arrival who came as a breath of fresh air with his tall, slim build and a to-die-for Glaswegian accent. She didn't let on though, yet.

"Yeah, nice and quiet at six in the morning."

"I bet it is. Are there any people up and about yet?"

Euan thought a little before answering, "The odd shopkeeper or two, oh and a couple of Army patrols."

"Really, where?" Katy sounded inquisitive.

"A landrover coming over the bridge there," he gestured in the general direction of the main vehicle bridge into the town. "And, I passed a foot patrol going up the high street, guns and everything."

Katy looked bemused, "Guns, what are they expecting, World War Three?"

They both laughed and continued on their separate ways.

0730hrs

The YMCA was a hive of activity. To anyone watching, the Killingburn Road Posse looked like an army of ants. They seemed to be collecting the things together that they would need for the day ahead, a day they had been meticulously planning for. The 'Day of War' as Brad had called it.

He himself was just finishing writing on the massive whiteboard in the main games room. A huge hand drawn map of the school already adorned the wall, courtesy of Nathan. Now as Brad finished with some flourishing touches, he called his gang to order.

"Okay guys, gather round and let's go through the plan once more."

There were a few groans from around the room, a sign that maybe this had been done a few times already.

Nathan interjected, "Come on guys, quieten down and sit in your groups. Come on, move!"

All the gang members milled around for a few seconds before finally settling down into three groups of roughly equal size. Three lads sat off on their own.

Brad started, "We go in half an hour guys so just a last run through, like they did in the 'Dirty Dozen' that we watched the other night."

"We ain't singing like they did though Brad, right?" muttered Bang.

Brad smiled. "No Bang," he took a step forward so everyone could see him, dominating the room. He looked around to try and catch everyone's eye, lingering a little longer on Nelly and adding a sly wink for her.

"Okay then, it all starts at eight o'clock when Jonjo's lot attack the police HQ. By then Nelly's group will be here on the south side after coming through the churchyard. Your job is?"

Nelly replied with venom, "Burn out the offices on the first floor, especially the Heads!"

"Correct," Brad added. "What about your group Nat?" He looked across to where his trusted second-in-command sat with four others.

Nathan stood up, turning towards the rest, "We will approach from the west side after circumnavigating the park to the north."

This drew some ooohs from some of the others with his use of a particularly long word.

He continued, “Once through the fence we smash our way in using those sledges,” he pointed to a pile of equipment his team had gathered up. Two rather large sledgehammers were leaning against some other items stacked underneath including wire-cutters and a crowbar. “We set fire to the main hall and the food hall using their own curtains and blinds before joining up with the rest of you and having even more destructive fun.” He threw a fist into the air garnering some cheers from the remainder.

Brad had to step forward with his arms outstretched to try and regain some semblance of calm, “Okay, okay, calm it!”

The room slowly fell into a silence as Brad returned to the map. He had been indicating with a pool cue the different locations previously mentioned as they were introduced. Now it was his turn.

“My group, seven of us altogether are going straight through the main entrance. Our three scouse mates have obtained some dodgy looking Army uniforms and nicked some cool replica air pistols. With these we hope they can get past the security at the main gate and then in through the main entrance using our newly acquired swipey things.” A chuckle drifted around the room. “Enough. From there we go round that school and cause as much havoc and damage as we can.”

He waited, looking around at the rest of those gathered before finishing. “Those of you who were with us for the last attack have got to know that was just a little…” he paused, looking quickly to Nathan, “what is a little fight called Nat?” he asked in a quiet voice.

Nathan responded, “A skirmish.”

“That’s it, a skirmish.” Raising his voice again he continued, “The last one was just a skirmish, sizing the place up. This time we’re gonna raze it to the ground!”

There was a couple of seconds of quiet. Nathan realised that Brad’s way of speaking wasn’t as inspiring as it could be so he got the ball rolling by jumping to his feet and shouting, “Yeah!”

The others followed.

Whether Brad realised his friend had helped him out or not he gave Nathan a thumbs up.

"We are the K R P, we are the K R P." was now being chanted around the main games room from all those present.

Brad stretched out his arms, revelling in the glory.

This would be his day of vengeance.

0759hrs

Northumbrian Police HQ, Ashton. Shift briefing had just concluded and everyone was going about their daily tasks. Only a few staff were left in the briefing room. Dayna Thomas was gathering up the papers she had used to give the briefing. Dan Clemence and Eddie Grey were playing rock, paper, scissors to decide who would drive that day. Funnily enough, for a change, both wanted to lose.

Inspector Short had cornered his favourite CSO, Diane Kent and was trying to talk her into joining the force on a permanent basis, for the umpteenth time.

They all reacted when the first explosion occurred, shattering some of the windows along the corridor. Even with a well-trained police force, the sound of a massive explosion made everyone flinch.

Dayna Thomas reacted quickly, "Okay Dan, Eddie, get out the side exit and take a look. Be careful!" she emphasised.

With no one else of a lower rank she had to use Diane Kent for her next task, "Diane, nip down to the main desk and see what you can find out."

Inspector Gary Short looked at Dayna dumbfounded. "What the hell is going on Dayna?"

Dayna moved over to the window and took a quick glance in the direction of the vehicle park where the blast had come from just as a second loud explosion shook the station. She instinctively ducked at the rapport but she was soon back up, her eyes just above the lower edge of the window frame. "It's the patrol cars, they're on fire!"

Dan and Eddie reached the side exit and slowly opened the door. Unable to see much they moved outside into the small caged area where assailants were safely un-cuffed.

Eddie craned his head around the edge of the meshed fence to look through the vertical bars.

"What can you see mate?" Dan asked.

"A couple of cars on fire," his friend replied.

"Who's doing it?"

"Not sure Dan." Just as he was speaking he saw a petrol bomb fly over the back wall and land squarely in the middle of the vehicle park. Flames spread obscenely as it crashed on the concrete, engulfing two vehicles parked against the building. One of those was already ablaze and due to its proximity to the shattered windows Eddie assumed it was the site of the first explosion which had rocked the building. An unmarked car to the left parked against the outer wall was ablaze and again Eddie rightly assumed it had been the target of the second bomb.

Dan finally managed to squeeze around the corner and have a look, "Bloody hell, they are trashing our wheels!"

Eddie stood back from the bars, trying to clear his mind. "Do you think it's those kids again?"

"Maybe, but why just burn the cars and not the pig sty, as they like to call it?"

"Good point," Eddie responded.

"Shit, without wheels we aren't going to be much use to anyone are we?" Dan blurted out.

Eddie pulled him back into the relative safety of the meshed area.

Dan looked him straight in the eyes. As friends and partners of many years the recognition dawned on them both. "I got the keys," he said jangling the key fob in front of Eddie. "I'll go and get our ride and bring it round the front, you go and tell the Sarge the score."

Eddie's immediate response was to shake his head, "No way are you going out there mate."

Dan took a quick glance around the corner again, "Look, car Sierra-one-four hasn't been touched yet." Again he showed his friend the car key fob showing the letter and numbers - S14.

"Okay then, I know I can't stop you anyway but be bloody careful," Eddie conceded.

Dan slapped him on the shoulder, something he knew infuriated Eddie. "Just let Sergeant T know the score, maybe we can get more cars out of the firing line."

With that he hit the code in the exit to release the magnetic catch, went out and quietly as possible, closed it behind him.

Eddie leaned right up to the bars to speak to Dan. "You keep your eyes fixed on that section of wall," he said pointing. "That seems to be where the little buggers are stood behind."

"I will mate," he gave Eddie a thumbs up. "See you round the front in a tic." And with that he set off across the flaming car park. Eddie watched him for a few seconds before quickly going back inside.

0810hrs

As on the previous occasion, the gang's attack on the school began with a precision nigh on equalling a military campaign. Using short-range hand-held radios, Brad initiated the co-ordinated attack. He regretted the loss of his lifelong friend Jack; his rashness had slightly messed up the previous assault.

Nathan, his new confidant, had pretty much planned this attack and he led the second group, obviously knowing the plan inside out.

The final group was led by Nelly, who Brad now trusted implicitly even though he hadn't known her long. Their relationship had quickly developed and in the previous week had become intimate to a point where he worried about her well-being. He wanted her in his group where he could protect her but she was having none of it and insisted she was elsewhere.

Nathan had already led his group over the back fence on the western side of the school site and they were now in the process of forcing the fire exit door on the main hall. They also carried some containers of kerosene; they wanted the school to burn.

Scruffy had made a few attempts at using a stolen jemmy to force open the fire door. As he paused to take a breath, he glanced over his shoulder. Behind him stood Tank, a lad named after his size, naturally. In his hands, as he stood feet shoulder-width apart, he held a sledgehammer.

Scruffy took a step back, Tank nodded to him.

He took a step forward, spat on each hand in turn and then swung the sledge backwards in a slow arc. As he brought it forward with all of his strength, all those standing around him seemed to hold their collective breaths.

The hammer connected, full force, with the end of the jemmy and a loud crashing sound stunned them all. The jemmy flew out of the gap in the doorframe and nearly took Al's head off.

"Fuck sake Tank," Al screamed. "Take it easy will ya!"

"Soz mate." Tank gave him a rueful smile as he dropped the sledge next to the newly opened fire exit door, now partly hanging off its hinges.

Nathan pulled the door open and it fell off completely. "Tank, you're a big bollox," he smiled up at the big lad who was now grinning from ear to ear.

"Cheers Nat." He glanced around at Scruffy, Rich and Al. "Always wanted to do that."

The five of them slipped into the main hall.

Meanwhile Nelly and her four accomplices: Smash and Bang with the two recent recruits Josh and Macca were scaling the southern fence and then clambering up onto the Design & Technology storeroom roof. Previous experience from the gang's last attack had shown them how to bridge the gap and then break in to the Inclusion Room using short ladders. This room was on the end of the corridor which included the Duty Room, the Head and the Deputy Head's offices - all prime targets, with more incendiary devices being carried by the group. Access was quickly gained as, due to the hot weather windows had been left open.

Brad felt very nervous for once. This moment was the culmination of all the plans he had made since being kicked out of the school. Humiliated. Embarrassed. Mocked.

Payback was coming.

Brad had the largest group as they were going through the main entrance. He had the three Scousers dressed in stolen Army uniform, all armed with replica air pistols, a nice touch he thought. Also Smooth was with him to watch his back and two of the latest recruits to the cause, Ozzy and Bill, both big units, which is what he needed to force their way in through the well protected front entrance.

Nathan had tried to persuade Brad not to take on this entrance having seen the barricade and new security measures. But to Brad it was like a red rag to a bull and he had insisted on attacking there and also leading this group.

Simple plan. Burst through the vehicle entrance, take out the two security guards and access the main doors with their newly acquired swipe card. Ozzy and Bill were tasked with burning the PE Block, the other five would wreak havoc in the main building and try to join up with either or both of the other groups. Job done.

Brad took one more deep breath, stood up and casually crossed Esse Road towards the main vehicle entrance. Behind him, Terry, Phil and Chazza stood up and followed him, adjusting belts and berets as they went.

The two security guards on that morning were Bob and Terry. It was the former who turned towards the lads as they got to the barrier, "Where are you lot off to then?" He asked, opening his arms out as if to stop their advance.

Brad was too quick and grabbed the fluorescent yellow arm and pulled Bob on to the barrier as Chazza grabbed his other arm, pulling him over the barrier with a crash.

The second security guard made a break towards the school.

Brad ordered, "Phil, Terry - take him out!"

Five or six rapid shots followed as the two Liverpool lads fired off their air pistols.

The second man in fluorescent yellow crashed to the floor, wounded but not badly.

With the first man zip-tied to the barrier, the seven youths strolled into the open area in front of the school, passing the prone, moaning figure of Terry. Brad motioned for the two new guys to go to the PE Building and then he took a quick glance at the four who he would lead in the attack. A quick smile, another deep breath and then he moved, "Come on guys, we've got a school to wreck.

Over in the main hall Tank had just finished tearing down the last of the tall sets of curtains from their rails. Rich and Al had made a pile in the centre of the hall and were already pouring on the kerosene they had brought with them.

Tank dragged the curtains and threw them on to the edge of the pile.

Al took out his lighter and struck it alight. He paused, looked across at Tank and offered it to him, "It's your school Tank, do you want the honour?"

Tank laughed, "No mate, the pleasure is all yours."

Al bent down to the curtains and struck the lighter again, the flame bloomed and he put it to the damp material. The burst of flames blew him backwards and he landed heavily on his backside next to the other two who looked at each and laughed out loud.

Richie spoke first, "You idiot."

Tank added, "That was an eyebrow remover."

All three of them laughed.

Nathan and Scruffy had been in the neighbouring food hall when they had heard the whoosh of the curtains igniting. They looked at each other and smiled. Their intent was to set a fire in the main school kitchens and then head to the main entrance to support Brad's attack. Scruffy had already started some small fires using the small bottle of kerosene he had brought with him as Nat gestured him over to the side door to the main corridor.

The other small bottles of kero, taken from the local Wilkos only the day before were now on the floor above in the hands of Nelly and her team.

They had left one in each of the offices and the Inclusion Room with a slow burning fuse, something they had looked up on the internet during the week.

They were now heading along the Humanities corridor to the stairs at the far end where they would be able to come to support Brad's group, approaching the main entrance from the other side. Two small, soft explosions alerted them that their plans had worked but it also alerted others on that floor.

Two or three teachers appeared further up the corridor having heard the explosions and an alarm went off from the now burning Inclusion room.

At the main entrance, Brad smiled at the members of staff he saw through the huge panes of glass, recently installed after the last attack.

Whether or not the staff secure inside the building felt safe was hard to tell. John Reynolds and Katy Howard looked at each other, both realising this was it, the major attack they had both feared but been expecting. Euan Robshaw stood next to them looking perplexed, Ian Taylor too.

Joanne Tindell moved towards the windows daring her nemesis to try something. She glanced towards the security lock and Brad followed her gaze.

She smiled at him.

Alarmingly, he smiled back.

He walked towards it. The three grinning scouse lads stood behind him.

Realisation struck Joanne as Brad pulled a blue and white security card from his pocket. It was the same colour as Joanne's. He dangled it, waving it in front of Joanne. He saw the sheer look of terror on her face as she turned to head back to the main reception area.

Brad slid the card over the small panel. He watched closely as the red light changed to green and the main door made a popping sound. He assumed the locking mechanism was being released.

As he gleefully pulled the door open he first noticed the increasing volume of police sirens - with the door half open he glanced over his shoulder and saw two police cars pull into the entrance. His plan of totally incapacitating the mobility of the police had failed. He flung the door open and with Ozzy at his shoulder he entered those hallowed promises.

Inside reception, the few seconds warning Joanne had given her team was enough for them to lock and bar the main door into the school. Ian Taylor and the powerfully built Euan Robshaw now stood immediately behind the reception counter, hockey sticks in hand.

0816hrs

Unbeknown to any of the gang members who were all now inside the main school site, more police cars and Army vehicles had arrived. Some officers were despatched to the rear of the hall, others supported those at the main entrance, unsure of the location of the gang members.

It was there that Army personnel had turned up too. Two landrovers were parked on the opposite side of the road and troops, under the command of Sergeant Fuller, were deployed along the three-foot wall that separated the school grounds from the roadside pavement. They were armed with automatic rifles and wasted no time in selecting targets to follow through their sites.

Inspector Short looked startled as he saw the half dozen or so camouflage-clad soldiers taking up firing positions to his left. His eyes automatically drifted to the man stood behind, brandishing a pistol in one hand and a small hand held radio in the other. The man in authority. He vaguely recognised him and as he approached him he spied the three stripes on a rank slide in the centre of his chest.

His memory quickly caught up, "Sergeant Fuller isn't it?"

Surprised by the approach of the Police officer, Malcolm Fuller was stunned for a few seconds. He regained his composure as the officer waited for an answer.

"Yes Sir," Fuller paused not wanting to give too much away. "We were just on a routine patrol and heard the commotion."

The Inspector eyed him suspiciously before continuing. "Well the commotion is that while some youths petrol bombed our car park, the rest appear to have attacked the school."

"Is there anything we can do?" the Army man asked tentatively.

"At the moment, nothing. We are still assessing the situation." The officer glanced back over his shoulder up the street towards some people who were approaching, some carrying equipment. "The press are arriving," he turned back to the sergeant. "They must have been on routine patrol too!" He gave a knowing smile.

They both watched as various members of the press approached south along Esse Lane.

Gary Short turned to face the senior NCO, "Keep those weapons safety catches on sergeant. I don't want any accidents. I retain overall command of this situation, do you understand?"

"Yes Inspector, I understand, completely!"

Sergeant Fuller had his men lower their weapons.

Inside the main entrance Brad, Oz, Smooth and Bill were fighting a running battle with staff to try and gain entry to the rest of the school. Oz was slamming a chair off the large Perspex panels covering the reception hatch, to no avail. Brad seemed happy just taunting the staff, especially Joanne Tindell, whilst the other two tried to batter their way past the formidable Euan Robshaw using half pool cues they had brought with them from the YMCA. At the same time the three Liverpool lads held centre stage outside in the car park brandishing their imitation pistols and firing off the odd shot. They were in their element.

Nathan and Scruffy were slowly working their way to reception to help Brad and his group but behind them things had gone wrong in the main hall. The smoke from the age-old curtains had driven the rest of their group back into the opposite corner from the main doors. Two police officers burst in through the fire exit and quickly apprehended and handcuffed Rich and Al. The timely arrival of Phil Dawson and Alex Small from the kitchen entrance had helped to coral the two youngsters.

They quickly set about dragging the flaming and smouldering curtains to the fire exit and outside.

As the smoke cleared two more officers arrived to help drag the two young arsonists away, kicking and screaming as they went.

Several open doors now created the draughts required. The choking smoke quickly dissipated.

Tank stood motionless against the wall opposite the fire exit.

A police officer moved to block the kitchen exit and the two caretakers who had removed the curtains now stood, hesitantly, at the other set of doors. They looked to the officer who was at the other end of the long main hall. He held up his hand, silently asking them to stay in position thus blocking any possible escape.

This they did.

Tank looked in both directions and saw he had no means of escaping into the main part of the school. He eyed up the fire exit just as the two officers returned after having put his two friends in the police van.

The older of the two constables at the fire exit spoke up first, "Come on son, come quietly." With that he took out another set of handcuffs and slowly walked towards Tank.

As he approached him he realised what a formidable unit the young man was.

Tank, looking straight ahead past the advancing policeman saw bright sunshine and the green of the fields and the river beyond. Mind made up, he burst into a sprint. Like most people his size he wasn't built for endurance, but over ten or twenty yards his rugby coach had said he was unstoppable!

Tank hit the large framed window at full tilt. The result was shattering but with all momentum lost the young man staggered and stumbled sideways into the jagged glass still supported by the frame.

As the others in the hall ran to help him it quickly became apparent that he had severed a number of major arteries, mainly the jugular. Blood spurted from his neck as he pulled himself away from the window frame. He clumsily put a hand over the large gash to try to stem the flow. It still oozed through the gaps in his fingers, covering his top in an ever-growing pattern of dark red. As he collapsed to the floor the police officers and caretakers quickly crouched beside his convulsing frame.

It only took a few more seconds for the young man's body to give one more violent convulsion and then it slumped, lifeless in the ever-growing pool of its own lifeblood.

As Tank lost his very short battle for life, upstairs the meticulously prepared plans were going awry. Having set fires in the offices to the southern end of the first floor, Nelly and her four cohorts were now being forced back in that direction.

The sudden appearance of school staff from classrooms on the Humanities corridor had caught the group unawares. Smash and Bang were quite willing to fight their way through but curiously Nelly halted them.

The teachers advancing towards them were asking them to stop and hand themselves in to the police. All this achieved was to make the youngsters more agitated as they retreated past the Humanities office door towards the staircase and the four offices they had earlier set fires in. The only other doors in the Head Teacher's corridor were the two toilets opposite the office they had just passed. With Smash and Bang checking out the burning offices and Nelly looking down the staircase the two final members of their group, Josh and Macca, panicked and rushed into the toilets to hide.

0818hrs

Outside the main entrance and the pressure was building. Police officers were now advancing on the gang members there, forcing them into an ever-decreasing area. The three armed lads from Liverpool, so cocky earlier, were now frantic. They had noted the arrival of heavily armed soldiers. Now police officers were moving towards them, trying to get them to surrender.

One police officer was untying one of the security guards they had recently tied up, and another was tending to the one they had wounded in the leg. Terry looked down to the gun he held so tightly in his hand. He glanced into the main entrance where the rest of his group were still struggling to get in. They had to do something.

He pointed his weapon at the two nearest officers, a man and a woman. "Coppers, get away!" he shouted.

Dayna Thomas and Eddie Grey stopped dead in their tracks, the former holding out her hands, palms forward.

The sudden change in movement caught the eye of one of the soldiers, Jock Thomson. He reacted. "Sarge, weapon up!"

Malcolm Fuller spun around having just messaged his OC on the radio, "Where Jock?"

"Up by the entrance Sarge, can't make out if that's a fake pistol or not?"

Smudge Smith, kneeling next to Jock cut in, "Don't matter mate, they've already shot one of the security guards and at that range it would be classed as a threat to life."

Fuller, peering through a spare rifle sight suddenly gasped. He saw Dayna with the weapon pointing directly at her. "Make ready!" he shouted.

The surprise order caught a couple of the soldiers out but the rest reacted instinctively, left hand over the barrel, cocking handle brought back sharply to its extreme then released. The left hands now drove forward, ensuring the cocking handle was fully forward before returning to their grip below the barrel handguard. Each of the rifles now had a 5.56mm round in its chamber.

Remembering earlier he glanced right, quickly searching for the police inspector. He was 100 yards along the road with his back to him, speaking to the press.

In the car park in front of the school, Dayna advanced one step at a time, noting the hesitation in the young man's eyes.

Terry Oldfield suddenly felt trapped; his position of power diminishing rapidly. The ever-smiling police sergeant, unarmed, was walking step by step towards him, slowly but monotonously.

Fearful, he pointed the pistol skywards and pulled the trigger, firing into the relative safety of the air.

Unknowingly, it sounded his death knell.

Fuller reacted instantly, "Take aim, pick your targets carefully, single shots only," he paused as his men identified their targets. "Fire!"

The volley of shots that followed caused pandemonium both inside and outside the building.

Two of the three uniformed figures fell instantly. The third target, moving, had been missed. There were no other clearly defined targets but the two soldiers to the right had a clear sight of someone just inside the building. They both fired second and third shots into the mayhem.

Inspector Short was sprinting up the road, after hearing the shouted orders, too late to prevent the carnage.

Fuller, realising the danger to civilians stopped the shooting, "Cease fire!"

In the car park everyone had gone to ground.

Dayna and Eddie stared at each other across the tarmac. Lying as flat as they possibly could.

As the shooting ceased everyone took stock of the situation.

From where Eddie was lying he was looking into the lifeless eyes of one of the uniformed youngsters, lying not five metres away from him. A moments thought of sympathy quickly disappeared when he remembered the pain on the face of one of the school's security guards minutes earlier, who had been shot by these lads. Duty bound he got up on all fours, still fearful of more shooting, and quickly moved towards the lad. Once there he checked for a pulse, both brachial and carotid, nothing. He was dead. He quickly glanced across to see where his Sergeant and friend were.

Dayna Thomas had seen the actions of Eddie and had herself moved towards the prone figure of Phil Robinson. After a quick check and the obvious destruction to his head by at least one high powered round she knew he was gone.

More officers approached and this forced the third of the camouflage dressed youngsters to break cover and bolt. With little knowledge of the immediate area, Chazza headed south past the

Science block towards DT, the only open space that was free of police or Army.

Screams were heard from inside the main school building.

Smooth, knowing that this massive show of violent force had ended the impetus of the attack on the main entrance looked around for an alternative.

He grabbed Brad and dragged him back through the glass doors. Seeing the chaos outside and the approach of more police officers he suddenly remembered an old trick he used to use when late for school. As Brad stood there in shock at seeing the blood pooling around the head of his new friend, Phil the Scouser, Smooth pulled him to the left around the corner. Brad saw the panelled windows of the staff room. He glanced across at Smooth and smiled. As Smooth approached the strange looking glass door, ready to slip the lock, he heard a splintering smash.

As he slipped the latch to open the door he turned to look at a grinning Brad who had seconds earlier launched a large stone through one of the windows, successfully breaking the whole pane.

Smooth pulled back the door and gestured Brad to go in first.

Even in this most god awful of situations Brad barked out a laugh and jogged forward before climbing through the remnants of the large, broken window.

Smooth just shrugged as he stepped through the open door, gently pulling it closed behind him, it may be needed for a quick exit later.

After the shooting had stopped all those inside the building had recovered their positions. Some of the teachers watched as Brad and one of his cohort had gone back out of the main door and gone around the side of the building. With just two gang members now standing in the entranceway, unsure of what to do, Euan saw a chance to repel them. He turned round to the others, hockey stick in hand. Just as he was about to issue a rallying cry, he froze.

John Reynolds, already armed with a baseball bat turned to see what Euan was looking at.

Half slumped on one of the reception staff's chairs was Katy Howard, a dark crimson circle on her normally immaculate white PE department polo shirt.

John could not take it in.

Euan had, his hockey stick crashed off the floor. "Katy," was all he could muster in a quiet, croaky voice.

John, strangely having known poor Katy for a lot longer than Euan produced the opposite response.

He stooped, picked up the hockey stick, handing it to the now crouching Glaswegian and in a strong, resolute voice declared, "Let's get these bastards!"

Euan, shock imprinted on his face, wavered for a second or two, took another glance at the deceased Katy and grabbed the hockey stick so tight that his knuckles turned white.

The projectile that had penetrated the heart, thus ending the life of Katy Howard was a 5.56mm Army issue.

As the two of them, entirely enraged now, followed the final two gang members outside they spied the third uniformed figure who stood, out of breath, next to the main fence just outside DT. All thoughts of the two they had followed out now forgotten they pursued the one they thought to be the culprit.

At the same moment, Chazza saw them and the pure hatred in their eyes. The distance was about 30 yards; he had about five seconds before they would be on him. He raised his air pistol and fired a shot, missing. The weapon then jammed. After two more attempts at firing and failing he hurled it in the direction of the two members of staff who had now restarted their advance towards him. They were wielding weapons. Hate filled their faces. He used the DT storeroom to boost himself up and grabbed the roof. It was slippery and he fell back.

He looked again; they had covered half the ground between them. He placed his foot on the handle again and after two practise boosts he threw his weight up and grabbed the edge of the roof. This time his hands held and as he pulled his bodyweight up, he felt the door handle snap beneath his foot. His momentum was already taking him up and over the edge.

He quickly swung his legs up just as the younger of the two men made a grab for them.

With the handle smashed there was no leverage to get up on the roof even for someone as fit as Euan Robshaw. He and John watched as the youngster ran along the storeroom roof. They backed up to keep him in sight.

John let out a chuckle.

Euan looked at him perplexed.

John turned to his young friend still smiling, "He has nowhere to go." They both laughed now. "We blocked off the fire escape a few weeks ago."

They both turned to look at the forlorn figure as the young man had just realised this himself.

After a quick glance around there seemed to be nowhere to escape out of his current predicament. His assailants couldn't get to him but he couldn't get away and there would soon be ladders or the suchlike appearing.

He looked down seeing the two men, grinning, and he knew they both realised this too. He looked beyond the fence and could see no police or Army. The distance was only about five or six feet and the ground looked soft enough. He turned to the teachers, smiling, and gave them the middle-fingered salute. Backing up to the edge nearest them he lined up for his escape run.

John now realised that he might be able to escape. He quickly moved around the small storeroom and looked at the gap before he shouted to Euan, "He might make it!"

Chazza was steeling himself for the jump. It wasn't the five or so feet gap to the fence that worried him but the ten-foot drop once he cleared the spiked railings.

Euan took a few more steps backward, hockey stick now dragging on the floor.

Chazza said, "Go," to himself, more as a gee up than anything else.

John stepped back against the fence and looked up to where the youngster would jump from.

The youngster from the Wirral set off at a sprint, arms pumping.

In a total instinctive reaction, Euan took a step forward and launched the hockey stick.

It flew, cartwheeling, end over end.

Chazza was just a couple of strides away from launching himself across the abyss and hopefully to freedom. He never heard the object rapidly approaching but he felt the sudden pain as it caught his right shoulder.

John saw a hockey stick fall into the gap between building and fence, five metres to his left.

Chazza stumbled, lost momentum and took off from a crumpling left leg.

Euan saw the boy lose balance.

John looked on in horror as the next thing he saw was the lad's flailing arms.

Chazza's loss of momentum was not going to take him over the fence.

His body hit the railing with a sound so sickening John had to force his eyes closed. A strangled shout of anguish left his lips, "No!"

Euan ran quickly to where he had seen John move earlier. As he rounded the corner he saw John, motionless, blood dripping onto his smartly pressed white shirt, his face a mask of horror.

Euan's eyes naturally drifted upward to the hanging, near lifeless body impaled on the spikes of the fence a few feet above John's head. Spikes that were designed to deter any would-be climbers so harshly barbed, a foot apart, inwards pointing with external facing spikes in between.

The hatred drained along with the colour from Euan's face as he grabbed John by the arm and started retracing his steps, trying to look away from the horrific sight that he knew would haunt his future dreams.

0821hrs

Brad looked around him. So this was it. 'The sanctity of the staffroom' teachers used to say. 'Our safe haven.' He let out a short laugh and spying the massive set of pigeonholes, entirely filling the short wall of the room, he walked towards them.

Smooth was already at the door, looking through a slight gap in the glass pane. "Brad, come on." He looked back and watched in bemusement as Brad with a huge effort pulled the whole frame of the pigeonholes off the wall. It slammed to the floor, mail and personal belongings flying everywhere.

He couldn't see the point but Brad enjoyed it.

Suddenly he was knocked off balance as the staffroom door flung open.

Jenny Sayers stood there looking from one to the other, "You two, get out of here!" she screeched.

The two lads were taken aback for a second or two.

Smooth actually took a couple of steps back.

Brad gathered his senses and charged at the woman. Even in this situation he wouldn't raise a fist to a woman, something his Mother had taught him from an early age, but he gave Jenny Sayers a forceful shoulder charge. She flew back into the doorway, cracked her head on the doorframe and collapsed to the floor.

Smooth was a second or two taking it all in. The shock of her sudden appearance, her bravado and then the horror of Brad's charge.

Both lads turned left out of the door, approaching reception from the rear.

Neil Weston was halfway down the stairs when he saw Jenny's head appear, sticking out of the staffroom doorway, eyes closed. "What the fuck!"

Behind him on the stairs Jimmy Nelson was following, "What's up mate?"

They had been upstairs repelling the group there but came down with the intention of going up the stairs at the opposite end of the main corridor thus trapping the group upstairs and forcing them to surrender. The appearance of Jenny's head quickly followed by two gang members including their leader, Brad, changed those plans.

Jimmy recognised Brad instantly. He was one of the many members of staff that Brad had intimidated or threatened. He grabbed Neil's arm to stop him potentially giving away their presence. The lads hadn't noticed them yet so they had an element of surprise.

As Brad and Smooth peeked around the corner towards reception Brad recognised a few members of staff: Tindell and Cawthorne, whose offices were hopefully in flames by now; Taylor who was crouching over someone - oh shit he thought, that was the lovely Miss Howard from PE. Brad had fantasised about her. Judging by the amount of blood though, she was a goner or near enough anyway. Reynolds, baseball bat in hand was just coming back in to the building with a young bloke in PE kit. Oz and Bill had been restrained, the latter looked a bit worse for wear, blood trickling from a gash across his cheek.

Behind them Neil and Jimmy were approaching quietly but just as they were about to strike a shout of warning came from behind them.

"Brad, look out!" Nathan screamed as he ran towards the two caretakers.

Jimmy was now staring directly into Brad's eyes, feeling a little intimidated having forgot how powerfully built he was.

With his military training and reflexes, Neil turned to face the threat from behind just as Nathan reached him. He dropped low and brought his arm across his assailant's stomach, knocking the wind out of him. Nathan crumpled to the floor, gasping for air.

Scruff was two paces behind Nathan in his attack and as he quickly approached Neil from behind, Jimmy stepped into the diminishing gap. Scruff still held the knife he had used to help cut down the curtains. He collided heavily with Jimmy Nelson. As they drew apart they both instinctively looked down, the knife protruding from Jimmy's guts. He stumbled back a couple of paces and Neil caught him. All hell broke loose.

On the first floor things hadn't gone to plan for the Killingburn Road Posse.

Nelly retreated backwards from the stairs.

Phil Dawson and Alex Small were coming up the stairs slowly. Blackened from their fire-fighting exploits, they looked ethereal to Nelly.

Her attention was caught by Smash who gestured her towards the Head's office and beyond. There was a fire door at the end of that corridor leading onto the bridge to the Science block. A chance of escape.

At that moment four members of staff came around the corner. Pete Thornton whose dander was up, Orianna de Suza who was intrigued more than scared never having witnessed a situation like this in her native Spain. Although the group moved slowly trying not to show any aggression, Bob Dunleavy was an uncompromising figure as he strode confidently towards the three youngsters. By holding out his hands, palms facing them he was showing them he meant peace but his facial expression left them in no doubt of his intent.

Smash and Bang had been hammering at the door to no avail as Nelly arrived. They glanced at each other and a look of resignation slowly dawned on their faces. As an external door it was pretty much impregnable and in the securing of the school the staff had made it more so. As the situation seemed to be drifting to a peaceful conclusion the opening and slamming of one of the toilet doors stopped everyone present dead in their tracks. There was an eerie silence.

Josh and Macca ran out, dodging various swinging arms but stopped abruptly when they saw the look on their friend's faces, defeat. Macca shrugged and turned to face the members of staff who had renewed their approach.

The youngest member of the gang, Josh, a year eight student looked around nervously then made a bolt for the top of the stairs just as two staff members reached the top step. He thought of himself as a bit of an expert at parkour (or free running as he explained to those uneducated in the activity).

As Alex Small and Phil Dawson had now cleared the stairs, the undaunted thirteen year old saw an escape route. He flipped over the balcony rail, landing on the other side and looked down.

Tommy Johnson stepped across quickly and grabbed his arms.

Josh struggled but Tommy an ex-serviceman, had him in a vice-like grip. To counter this Josh sidled along the narrow ledge, two inches wide at most, taking a similar side stepping Tommy with him.

The drop below him grew with each sidestep they both took.

With six members of staff now in the corridor, the four remaining youngsters had given up hope of escape. All were transfixed by events on the balcony.

Stood facing each other either side of the rail with nowhere else to go, Josh took one more look behind himself. 'Opposite wall is less than ten feet away to spring off then same distance down to the bottom of the stairs, maybe more. I can do this', he thought to himself.

As he turned back Tommy seemed to catch his intentions. "Come on son, back over on this side now." Tommy glanced over the edge himself. "No need to be foolish is there?"

Josh pulled an arm free, "Let go of me old man!"

He tried to pull his other arm free but Tommy held on as tightly as he could. As Josh hung in the air Tommy reached forward to try and grab his shirt with his spare hand.

Josh kept wriggling.

Tommy lost his balance but refusing to let go his body weight took him over the rail and the two of them looked each other straight in the eye. What passed between them was a mixture of sorrow, anger, sympathy and shock.

Tommy spiralled as he fell, still holding on to the young man he had tried to save, landing heavily at the bottom of the stairs. Josh turning in the air bounced, spine side against the lower railing and then landed adjacent to his would be saviour.

The life had left Tommy on landing, multiple broken bones and head trauma.

Josh lasted a few more seconds, his spine severed. Long enough to see the life leave Tommy's still open eyes.

On the first floor landing the tragedy resounded as people slowly moved to the railing to look down. Nelly felt nausea grip her at the sound that the two bodies had made on landing but she sensed an opportunity. Still controlling her emotions she casually walked past the sombre group and then danced down the stairs.

0825hrs

Brad quickly realised that facing off to Euan Robshaw, with his obvious martial arts training, was more than a match for him. He took a step back and looked around. Police and Army were coming through the main entrance facing him. Over his left shoulder he saw two police officers emerging from the food hall. As he looked along the corridor he saw hope in the form of Nelly, not just hope but deeper feelings. More, much more than any of his gang meant.

Nelly waved him toward her.

He didn't hesitate. He side-stepped the new PE teacher's next attack and barged into the tussling couple of Will Cawthorne and Scruff. The couple stumbled and knocked over the recently arrived Jenny Sayers who still appeared very groggy.

Brad had made a gap and he bolted through it.

Halfway along the corridor he saw that no one was following him. He let out a muffled laugh but he couldn't read the strange expression on Nelly's face as she too had noticed that he wasn't being pursued. As he reached her he turned to look back and his feelings of jubilation crumpled to dust. He saw Nathan being pinned to the wall by two burly coppers.

Their eyes met. One's wracked with guilt. The other's disgust.

He was brought back to reality at the sound of footsteps on the stairs directly behind them.

Nelly dragged him over towards the DT storeroom where he chanced one more look at Nathan as he is was wheeled away by an officer in handcuffs.

"Come on Brad, this way." Nelly led him to the storeroom.

Brad responded, "I'm not going to hide in there like a rat in a trap!" He glanced through the open doors at the end of the main hall and saw the remnants of the ashes from the fires, and then he stopped dead in his tracks. An open window. He could only imagine how that had happened given the size of the massive glass panes.

He looked up and saw old Bob Dunleavy slowly coming down the stairs with Mr Thornton. Two bodies lay at the foot of the stairs: one belonging to Tommy Johnson, the other he knew was one of his gang but the name escaped him.

A quick peek up the corridor and he saw another two coppers with the Head (Bitch) and Cawthorne advancing towards them. Finally he looked at Nelly, her eyes seemed tearful.

"It's over," she said, grabbing hold of his hand and giving it a gentle squeeze.

Brad raised one eyebrow and smiled, "Ha, you think so?"

Still holding her hand he dragged her past the stairs and through the double doors of the main hall. After a quick look around to see there were no police Brad moved towards the smashed window releasing Nelly's hand.

"Let's go." He looked back at her as she stood motionless. "We're free Nel, come on!"

Brad stepped through the shattered window pane. He noticed that there was a lot of blood around. In fact it was splattered everywhere. Again he wondered what had happened there, hoping it was copper's blood.

This time when he looked back he saw Nelly running towards him and two officers, a male and female, coming through the doorway.

He turned and ran across the grass, seeing the river in the distance.

After a few seconds his legs were taken away from beneath him.

He had little time to get his hands up for protection as his face planted the ground, the wind knocked completely out of his lungs.

Before he had any chance to recover he felt direct pressure on his back, weight forcing him down. One hand and then the other was taken behind his back and he heard the sound of handcuffs closing around his wrists.

After a few seconds, hands grabbed his belt and shoulder, rolling him over.

He saw Nelly crouching next to him and two out of breath uniformed officers, hands on knees, stood to the side.

"Brad Jones, you do not have to say anything but it may harm your defence."

Brad spluttered, "What?"

Nelly continued, "If you do not mention when questioned."

Brad's head was spinning, "You're filth?"

"Something which you later rely on in court."

"Get the fuck off me!" Brad screamed as he struggled to get up.

"Anything you do say may be given in evidence. Do you understand your rights as I have given them to you?"

"What?"

"Brad, do you understand your rights as I have told them to you?" Nelly repeated forcefully.

"Yes," Brad cried, then spat in her face.

Dayna and Eddie were quick to move in and each grabbed an arm, hoisting Brad to his feet and marching back towards the fire exit where a crowd had now gathered, smiles on some of their faces.

Brad tried to make a lunge towards Joanne Tindell but Eddie brought him back into line.

Brad tried again.

With a quick nod from Dayna, she and Eddie grabbed higher up the back of Brad's shirt and straightened their arms. With the handcuffs secured behind his back he was forced to stoop forward making him walk with his body at ninety degrees to his legs.

Outside, Nelly was squatting on the grass looking out towards the river and the castle beyond. She placed her head in her hands and whispered gently to herself, "I fucking hate undercover work!"

Epilogue

The month of July began quietly enough in the town of Ashton. After the turmoil of the previous month, much of the place had started to settle back into as normal a routine as possible. The sun still rose and the sun still set. What had happened in this town, more so than any others, would never change that.

The same could not be said for the lives of many of the residents of Ashton and the surrounding areas, or those visiting who in one way or another had been part of the dramatic events. Local residents who had left to escape those final events slowly returned. Businesses re-opened and started to claw back some of their lost profits.

Buildings and properties lost or damaged were being rebuilt. The school was a shining example of this as it had opened its doors less than a week after the final battle. Exams were completed in a variety of locations and those who had come to help stayed on to aid with the rebuild. The Army had chipped in too, although an air of guilt still hung over them as they worked side by side with the school staff who were friends with Katy Howard, shot and killed by an Army bullet.

The initial report had shown that six men had fired a total of fourteen rounds and it couldn't be proven who had fired the actual round that smashed its way through poor Katy's rib cage and tore through her heart. An accident, a fluke, bad luck had all been bartered around by the press but it didn't help her family or friends make any real sense of her loss. There were plaques put up near the school entrance to all the staff who had lost their lives and every morning Joanne Tindell stopped and stared at them before she entered the school. Some days she had tears in her eyes, some days not.

The loss of life on that final day had seen many funerals during the following week and longer. Some were less attended than others, but maybe each family found some kind of peace.

Many awards were handed out, mainly to the police officers involved although some civilians, members of school staff, received them too. Their heroics during that final phase made a dramatic difference to the final outcome. As a lot of people said afterwards, 'It could have been far worse'.

Throughout the country other police forces took immediate action on the lawlessness that was creeping into their territories. This managed to nip a lot of potential trouble areas in the bud and many arrests were carried out which subdued the remainder of the troublemakers. These acts pretty much exonerated DC Billy Phillips and his actions of leading the police raid on the Miner's Tavern.

There were still many unanswered questions.

Who would take responsibility for the shooting of Katy Howard?

Why did the countries police force as a whole adopt a policy of non-interference and allow the situation to reach such an advance stage?

Rumours were rife that the police had an undercover officer involved with the gang but no information about them was forthcoming. Why was more warning not given about the final assault?

These were questions that were best left for another time. For now, things were being put back together and for most involved, that was enough. Normality.

Acknowledgements

Family

To my Mam and Dad who over the course of my formative years instilled in me a deep sense of family values and respect, two things I still hold very dear.

The British Army

They took me on as a sixteen year old and until the age of 41 they instilled in me the need for discipline and honesty, which will never leave my body or mind.

To all the friends, comrades and colleagues, many who have passed, who have had a profound effect on my adultness and made me the man I am today!

The British Educational System

Namely one year served at St Mary's in Longbenton, also Burnside College in Wallsend, sandwiching eleven years at my hometown school of Ashington High.

To all the staff, students and other professionals who instilled in me the work ethic and patience which came in very useful, and still do today.

Individually

I would thank my younger brother, Sid, and his family whose regular contact kept me sane towards the end of production. Sid, after scaling the heights of Kilimajaro with you in June, writing and typing the last 8 chapters thereafter was a breeze.

From Ash High: Sarah, Helen, Lee, Claire, Emma, Ray, Tracey, Trish and the others who kept me focussed on the goal at the times when I lapsed.

Inspiration comes in many forms and I wish I could have put some of our stories into this thing but they remain in my heed, maybe for future use?

To Linda who was the first to read my scribblings and offered valuable feedback and encouragement.
Linda, I will keep the flow of NZ Sauv Blanc going if I need more novel assistance in the future.

To Ian at Diadem Books for having the faith and considerable intelligence to print and publish the monster.

Finally, to my beasts both past and present: Hamish, Jenny, Sheena, Snowy, Jinky, Jamie, Alba, Jimmy and Bolt. My constant companions in life and witnesses to all I have endured and enjoyed in the process of producing the scribblings that is 'Kidz'.

Ciao M

About the Author

Mark Barrass - I left school at sixteen to join the Army. After completing over 24 years of service and the loss of my Father I returned to my hometown of Ashington in Northumberland and spent the next fourteen years working in the local high school, and another as a Cover Supervisor and Cover Manager. After the loss of my mother, I left full time employment and worked as a minibus driver, still in education before reaching a point where I wanted to semi-retire somewhere quiet.

Over the year 2019, and the period which has seen this novel completed, I have lived in the beautiful Eskdale valley whilst working part time in a café.

This is my debut novel, but be warned, there will be more to come. Planning is already underway.

Printed by Amazon Italia Logistica S.r.l.
Torrazza Piemonte (TO), Italy